CHOICES

LARRY
CUNNINGHAM

Cover Design – Jaycee DeLorenzo
Publishing Coordinator – Sharon Kizziah-Holmes

Paperback-Press
an imprint of A & S Publishing
A & S Holmes, Inc.

ISBN -13: 978-1-951772-17-8

I KNEW

I always knew you were there,
Not the color of your eyes or hair,
But I knew. I have always known.
I have watched and waited for you.
I have saved a place for you.
The link has always been there,
A cosmic bridge between our souls.
The span exists for us alone.
Meet me in the middle.

...Author

Chapter One

OLDE CONCEPTIONS

Amy Roman radiates classic Mediterranean beauty. She is tall and slender with enormous flashing dark eyes, luxuriant black hair and a flawless olive complexion that most fashion models would kill for. She has it all: brains, musical talent, social position, money and splendid friends. Amy appears to have everything. Almost. Something is missing. She seldom seems truly happy.

At the moment, she is standing at the window in her office watching a sailboat streak down the white-capped Charles River basin in North Boston. She is not jealous that they play while she works, regarding the magnificent scene as just another of the many benefits of her job at *OLDE CONCEPTIONS*, one of Boston's fine art galleries. Routine events have swirled about her all day. Nothing remarkable has materialized to moderate her sense of contentment, nor has there been a mysterious whisper of warning to forecast the looming, life-defining event that will soon surface and change her life forever.

OLDE CONCEPTIONS occupies a renovated red brick

waterfront warehouse, once part of Boston's flourishing maritime shipping district during the days of sailing ships. The ancient building holds an illustrious place in the ranks of American art galleries. The wealthiest and most discriminating patrons frequent *OLDE CONCEPTIONS,* browsing through rooms of antique furniture, intricate ivory carvings, marble statues and columns, Asian porcelain– mostly antique–and the paintings. The paintings. The walls are filled with paintings, some contemporary, but mostly dated, age-oxidized images by the old European masters. Paintings of gloomy people who lived hundreds of years ago, and those paintings are flanked by landscapes and a few pricy etchings of various disciplines. Amy often wondered if the somber people in so many of the old paintings ever laughed or experienced joy.

The intercom buzzed, snapping her attention from the sailboat to the desk where she keyed the flashing button while automatically reaching for her dictation tablet. "Yes, Miss Hopkins?"

Leitha Hopkins' stern voice pierced the room. "I need you, Amy. Now!" The summons conveyed the unmistakable sound of authority–Leitha's customary tone.

"On my way, Miss Hopkins." Amy sighed, delayed at the window for a brief, longing look at the peaceful world outside, and then dashed down the hall to Leitha's opulent office.

Leitha pointed to the door as Amy entered and snapped, "Close it!" She disguised the curt command with a thin smile, although news had just arrived that could reverse months of demanding work. Her bland smile failed to camouflage the specter of calamity foremost in her mind.

Amy assumed her customary place in the uncomfortable upright wooden chair beside her employer's desk, pen and paper in hand, prepared to take orders. Her thoughts had centered on Leitha all that day, and not in a complimentary manner. Leitha Hopkins had managed the art gallery and boutique for sixteen years, yet remained an enigma to her staff. No one knew much, if anything, about her private life. She presented a veneer of mystery, sequestered in the privacy of her plush office suite on the mezzanine. Though she rarely emerged to conduct business, the employees knew she watched their every move from behind the enormous one-way window overlooking the gallery's main showroom, and from a row of monitors above her desk connected to cameras throughout the store. Leitha seldom displayed the slightest trace of emotion, even to the few select clients she handled personally, but certainly never to a subordinate. She considered civility to inferiors an unproductive waste of time and disdained even the wooden manners too many upper-class people employ to keep subordinates outside of their comfort zone.

Amy estimated her superior to be near fifty, but thought Miss Hopkins added years by wearing her hair pulled back harshly. Leitha used almost no cosmetics or jewelry, other than the ever-present pair of monster defensive sunglasses that she wore indoors and out regardless of light conditions. New employees whisper and bow respectfully in her presence. The gallery's more seasoned workers embellish Leitha's acerbic peculiarities to the ever-changing flock of intimidated apprentices. Her disapproving glare and sharp tongue do not inspire loyalty, and few, usually the older, hardened employees, remain for long.

"Better not let her catch you standing around, friend. She's up there right now watching every move you make."

The target of such taunts usually sneak a cautious glance at the mezzanine, then whisper, "I'm doing my job."

"Sure, that's what the last guy said. Look, kid, find something to do. Always look busy. Don't lean on anything, and never but never sit down. Find something to dust."

Leitha remains insulated behind an impenetrable wall of haughtiness. None of the underpaid staff regard her as mortal, with exception of Amy. Amy Roman, however, has the advantage of serving as assistant manager. She has access to the inner sanctum of Leitha's office, and only she, after three years of experience, understands Leitha. She knows how much effort Miss Hopkins squanders pursuing her image as a tyrant, and she alone knows why Leitha needs the insulation of mystery, and why she treats employees so indifferently. Amy has long recognized Miss Hopkin's major weakness: Leitha simply does not have the business acumen or experience to function competently as an art gallery director, or director of anything for that matter. She is intelligent enough to hide her shortcomings and shrewd enough to conduct most gallery business indirectly through Amy and two experienced salesmen that she cannot afford to alienate. Amy began shielding her employer's mysteriousness after recognizing Leitha as an impostor; a terrified pretender dealing with severe experience deficiencies. Leitha's greatest asset resides in her taste for great art, and a rare ability to buy it for the right price. Leitha is a buyer, not a manager.

Amy understands much more, having recently discovered that her unknowable boss is even more mystifying than anyone imagines. She learned, quite by accident only the night before, that Leitha Hopkins leads two lives.

*****

She shared the startling discovery with her best friend for life, Celia, while seated at Celia's kitchen table sipping coffee. Her friend reacted predictably, theatrical, as always, mouth open, hands pressed to cheeks, eyes wide, every aspect of her expression, as usual, overstated.

"You actually saw Leitha Hopkins with her hair down? Wearing a slutty dress? No way! Oh, come on, Amy! You have got to be kidding." Celia had known about Leitha for three years and regarded her as some fictitious Victorian character, or, on occasion, a comic book witch.

"Never been more serious," Amy countered.

Celia reclaimed some semblance of normalcy, as much as her animated nature permitted, and studied Amy skeptically. "Really, Amy?" She examined Amy's eyes. "Nope. I'm not buying it. No way. Just too hard to believe, but do go on." She propped her elbows on the table, cupped her chin in her hands, fluttered her eyebrows and smiled gleefully, impatient for Amy to elaborate.

Amy sipped the coffee, deliberately prolonging her friend's torment, and then leaned forward to whisper, "Just listen to this. I drove back to the gallery last night about nine-thirty to finish the monthly books. I didn't turn on the lights, just slipped in quietly so I wouldn't bother her." She leaned closer, spurring Celia's fondness for gossip, and whispered, "All right, now try to picture this: There I was, creeping along half way up the stairs when Leitha backed out of her office and locked the door. I started to say something–you know, to announce my presence–but for some reason I just didn't. Instead, I shrank back into the darkness, up there on the half-way landing." She motioned upward with the coffee cup. "You know, behind that life size bronze statue of Apollo she stores there. Anyway, for some reason that I simply cannot explain at the moment, I just froze and held my breath."

Celia sat up, placed a shielding hand over her breasts, recoiling theatrically. "You sneak! Why would you do something like that? Honest to God, Amy! That is so unlike you. Honestly." She smiled mischievously, rolled her hand for more, and said, "And...?"

Amy shook her head and shrugged. "I don't know. It's hard to explain." She held up a finger to check Celia interference. "Just wait. Oh, you should have been there, Celia. It was sooo, so strange. I was embarrassed for her. She was wearing the most slutty clothes."

"Wait! Leitha Hopkins?" Celia's facial contortions conveyed growing skepticism. "Are you sure?"

"Yes, absolutely. And she was wearing the most vulgar smear of cosmetics you can imagine. Oh, she looked positively garish!"

Celia's disbelief intensified. She sat back, folded her arms and regarded Amy suspiciously. "No. Now c'mon. I don't believe this for a moment."

"I'm trying to be serious here, Celia! Leitha was, as usual, wearing those gaudy, oversized sun glasses like always, but the dress! You should have seen that dress, Celia! Thin black leather. Short and tight, the neckline plunging nearly to her navel. Absolutely unbelievable. Oh, and!" She paused and raised a finger again for emphasis. "I bet you will definitely find this little tidbit interesting: she really has a nice figure. Yes! That's right. You wouldn't believe it. Very feminine, leaving nothing to imagine."

"Leitha Hopkins?"

"Yes. No kidding. There is more to her than we imagined." She concentrated a moment before continuing. "Anyway, she ran down the stairs–right by me–out of the gallery and into a chauffeur driven black limousine with dark tinted windows."

Celia blinked incredulously, then placed the heel of her palm on her chin and pretended to force her mouth closed. "Leitha Hopkins? Good heavens!"

Amy nodded conclusively. "Yes. As I live and breathe. Honestly, she looked like a cheap hooker."

*****

Thoughts of the previous night faded as Amy settled into place beside Leitha's massive antique mahogany desk. She waited a moment before looking up to see the perpetual mask of self-control slowly evaporate from her supervisor's face. The facade of composure faded in phases until Leitha's features twisted with rage.

She exploded. "That insufferable, irritating little worm! I suppose he was so damned busy consorting with one of those skinny little things he keeps in that dump he calls a studio that he lost track of time." She closed her eyes, took a deep, slow breath, opened her eyes again and gave Amy her best fake smile. "Anyway, he just called and told me he probably won't have the paintings here on time."

"I presume we are talking about Anton P. Simon?" Amy ventured.

"Who else?" Leitha shrieked. She grimaced, rebuking herself for losing poise, flopped back into the folds of the leather executive chair and stared at the ceiling. Her flared nostrils returned to normal only after a concentrated effort. She smoothed her face, leaned forward, hands folded on the desk, smiled pleasantly and began speaking quietly, once again the picture of composure.

"Amy, now listen carefully. I want you at Anton's place before five." She checked her watch. "And you are going to need to hurry. Get out there and hold the little jerk's hand until he gets those paintings loaded into your car. Bring them directly to the gallery, Amy. I need them here so we can be arranged before tomorrow's show. Stay on top of him every second." Her features hardened. "Do whatever you have to, but get those damned paintings here!" She forced the words through clenched teeth, scowling viciously, growing more enraged by the moment, unable to suppress the anger. Finally, slapping her hand on the desk, she said, "And I mean tonight! Just as soon as you can get back here. The viewing opens tomorrow, Amy, with or without him. And I promised." The scowl softened as she discarded the momentary tantrum, mentally preparing for her next strategy. Persuasion. She inclined forward with the most condescending smile and said, "You didn't have anything planned tonight, did you, love?"

Amy did exactly as Leitha expected: smiled cheerfully, swallowed the disappointment of yet another ruined evening, and departed without delay directly into an encounter with death and the turning point of her life.

Moments after leaving *Olde Conceptions*, Amy's sleek Italian sports car screeched around the sharp curve of a northbound on-ramp, accelerating quickly to join the commotion on the expressway below. The Friday afternoon crush of rush-hour traffic on I-90 in suburban Boston was, as usual, a snake dance of chaos. She powered the expensive automobile into traffic on the eight-lane expressway, steering the streaking machine into a way too-tiny space in front of an unsuspecting but reasonably cautious motorist. Once established in the flow of traffic, she turned to flash a radiant smile to her victim as compensation for the encroachment, waving appreciatively, implying that the offended party had surrendered position by choice. She had deliberately selected the unsuspecting pigeon half way down the on-ramp, correctly assuming that anyone driving a shiny BMW would abdicate the space she needed to preserve the paint on his precious car. The suit-and-tie man in her mirror didn't seem to care that the source of his irritation appeared to be a dark-haired beauty, nor was he soothed by her generous smile or the wave of thanks. She only added to his vexation by smiling even more brightly and waving again after he favored her with a rigid middle finger.

The car she maneuvered with such reckless abandon cost more than two-hundred-thousand dollars. Her supporting stepfather had always served as a fountain of instant capital. She exhibited a casual contempt for money, like most of her affluent, overindulged friends. Money meant nothing to Amy Roman. She had the best of everything: riches, clothes, a palatial apartment, a year at a snooty aristocratic European finishing school followed by four years at Yale. However, in her favor, she supplied the industry and intellect to graduate with honors with a degree in Mid-Eastern antiquities that prepared her for being prosperous while living among other people from privileged circumstances.

Amy lived far beyond the fiscal compensation financed by her gallery position. The source and legitimacy of her good fortune had begun to weigh heavily on her conscience of late. She willfully ignored the fact that, one way or another, with or without her knowledge and consent, her stepfather had always and still did furnish the financial means for her expensive tastes. She knew but would not admit that he provided practically everything she owned. He did it openly when possible, clandestinely when necessary, and she never objected. He was responsible for the Italian sport car, her fashionable downtown apartment, select yacht and country club memberships, clothes, jewelry–practically everything. Amy had been trained from birth to accept without question his generosity, never doubting her birthright. Until recently. She didn't ask for anything from her stepfather, not anymore, but neither did she object to his benevolence. She simply wasn't conditioned to worry about money, not after a lifetime of affluence. Amy understood, however, deep down inside, where the money came from. Of course she knew, yet blithely chose to think of herself as an independent person, having been, in her estimation, self-reliant for several years. She almost believed it, until of late.

Celia once remarked, "With your connections, you have it made in the shade. Why even bother pretending to work. What's the point?"

Amy protested, "I love my job, and I pay my own way. I got the job at the gallery by myself and worked my way up to assistant manager on my own, too. I have worked hard to get where I am, Celia. Three years of dedication and sacrifice to get where I am. How dare you!"

As usual, Celia apologized and the crisis passed. To Amy's credit, her stepfather's paternal altruism didn't have anything to do with the Second Violin chair she occupied with the Boston Pops Orchestra. That honor came deservedly after twenty years of lessons and practice. But now, nearing thirty, she assented to her stepfather's extravagant gratuities with second thoughts. She often frowned at her reflection in the mirror as troublesome traces of conscience jabbed at her lifestyle.

*****

The traffic congestion seemed worse than usual, even for a late summer Friday afternoon. Amy followed too closely, switched lanes impatiently, and then dashed to close on the next car. Mile after anxious mile passed as she accelerated and braked, swerved and jerked, exposing more anxiety by the minute. She finally breathed a sigh of relief as the traffic snarl began to unravel. After glancing at the clock on the dashboard, her tensions returned. She would never make it to Simon's by five. Amy directed the car into the far left lane and zoomed to eighty-five-miles-an-hour just in time to notice the sign announcing her intended off-ramp on the far right, four lanes over.

"Oh, dammit!" she muttered and started plowing back through traffic, all the way over to the right hand lane in order to make the turnoff. None of the determined motorists obstructing her intended path paid the slightest attention to the pleading blink of her turn signal. She repeatedly feinted toward the wall of traffic on her right until a break materialized, if only in her imagination, and then navigated quickly through the invented opening amid the inevitable tumult of screeching brakes and honking horns. She was still short of the right hand lane when the off-ramp entrance loomed ahead. Amy glanced over her right shoulder, allowing the car to drift toward the off-ramp entrance and the dim likelihood that someone would let her in. She soon found herself pressed into a rapidly developing situation with little left to do but surrender to the obvious and join the stream of traffic on the freeway and miss her turn. She reluctantly decided to concede defeat and returned her attention to the front.

Too late.

She swerved and slammed on the brakes in an effort to miss the wedge of yellow plastic barrels placed at the intersection to protect motorists from the hidden steel guard rail of the off ramp. Amy handled the maneuver skillfully and might have escaped unscathed except someone slammed into the rear of her car. Everything happened in slow motion after the collision. The "V" of yellow barrels received her car tenderly, like a baseball into a catcher's mitt. She distinctly heard the popping, crackling noises of bending metal as the car compressed and folded around her, followed by splintering sounds of breaking glass. Air exploded from her lungs as the air bag burst open. Afterward, after all sound and motion ceased, she sat motionless for a moment, amazed that she felt so composed. She didn't look left or right, just sat there staring straight ahead, clutching the steering wheel with all her might, and then lost consciousness. Her first lucid thoughts after that were focused on the taste of blood–blood and a desperate requirement for oxygen.

I can't breathe!

She couldn't focus, but felt the steering wheel crushing into her chest. She couldn't move away from the pressure and couldn't stop coughing, though the effort created severe pain. At least the exertion cleared her thoughts. The steering wheel wasn't the problem. The seat had slipped forward pinning her against the steering wheel, that was the problem. She struggled to reach the seat control and trigger the mechanism to relieve the pressure. Her arm wouldn't move.

Doesn't anything work?

She heard pounding at the door and turned to see several men just outside pulling at the door.

Thank God!

The sounds of excited voices penetrated the swelling roar in her ears. She tried unsuccessfully to twist around to look through the back window. The unyielding firmness of the side window was pressed harshly against her face. She couldn't see them clearly, but she could hear voices of men on the other side of the glass. Their voices sounded so close. Amy experienced a rush of relief and began to relax though still smashed tightly between the window, the crushed roof, the seat and steering wheel. The pressure against her chest blocked her power to breathe. She could only breathe by taking short, painful, shallow breaths, but help seemed near.

Why are they running?

The men *were* running, running while pointing toward something behind her. Amy could think well enough by then to understand that whatever the something was, it had frightened the men. Prompted by a mounting sensation of heat, she twisted away from the window to look back over the seat. Flames were raging over the rear of the car and through the broken back window. She could hear voices clearly.

"It's going to blow!" a voice in the distance shouted. "Clear out! The whole thing is going to blow!"

A terrifying hysteria flooded her thoughts. She began clawing and fighting against the forces holding her captive, totally panicked, and then began vomiting.

I can't get anything to move.

"Help me!" she whimpered. "Please help me!" The strange, plaintive voice sounded so pitiful. Her voice. Amy Roman, typically, would have been mortified to display such primitive instincts as fright. The trapped Amy, the wounded Amy, the frightened Amy didn't have time to ponder how pathetic or vulnerable she sounded and began screaming and crying at the same time. She couldn't move, not even to take a deep breath. Terror and exertion depleted her remaining strength. Her mouth pressed against the window, gasping for air. The acrid smell of rubber and electrical smoke began searing her throat. Flames singed the back of her neck. She vomited again in her lap while looking through the window at the crowd of men. The men were now standing in a huddle, way off in the distance.

Are they just going to watch me die?

"Help me!" she screamed, tears clouding her vision.

No one moved. One of the men bowed his head sadly and turned away. She could read his thoughts.

He is giving up. They are going to let me die.

Consciousness began fading. Amy sensed life ebbing, now

too weary and drained to breathe, too exhausted to move and too spent to care. Nothing seemed important. Dying suddenly seemed so easy. D*ie? No!* She gasped and began screaming again. "I don't want to die! Please! Somebody help me!"

The window next to her face exploded. Amy forced her stinging eyes open in time to see a giant hand plunge through the jagged shards of broken glass. She watched the hand pull and rip the glass away like bathroom tissue. The hand turned into a pair of hands working together, tearing the entire window out piece by piece. Her wavering perception centered on those hands.

Amy may have been semi-conscious, but she fully understood the circumstances. Her life depended on those hands. She could barely see through the searing smoke as her eyes followed the hands, now gripping the window frame, and now bending the entire upper half of the door outward. The door popped open with a grating noise. A wave of cool air washed over her. She still could not move and continued to stare at the hands, completely mesmerized as they gripped and bent the steering wheel away from her chest. The spectacle before her seemed surreal, unlike any movie, unlike any dream. It might have been a dream except the smoke, the heat and pain all combined to confirm reality. The hands didn't appear to be attached to a human form. They were just there, floating in the smoke, separate from anything material. The heat was intolerable, and now the passenger side seat was ablaze.

"Hurry," she begged. "Please hurry!"

A man's body emerged from behind the hands. He didn't speak, working silently, attempting to remove her from the car after releasing the seat belt latch, but the instant she screamed his efforts ceased. Her legs were pinned between the dash and the seat. He was able to move the seat back but drifted off into the smoke, coughing and gagging. He soon returned, pounding the crushed roof with the heel of his hand, attempting to bend it upward and away from her head. He disappeared again–more coughing–then returned and began forcing his way over her and farther into the car. The pressure of his body was unbearable and she screamed repeatedly.

What is he doing?

She heard him grunt from exertion and then the roof of the car began to pop and crack as it bent upward and away from the top of the seat. Even in such desperate straits, she knew what was happening and that his strength was extraordinary. She could hear the metal roof pop and yield as he labored. The buckling metal lifted an inch at a time. He paused for a moment and lay still, his chest heaving against hers as he gasped for air, his breath coming in great, tortured spasms. The smoke and heat returned and Amy once again floated on the edge of consciousness, scarcely aware of his actions.

She felt additional pressure and whimpered as he gathered his strength and began straining upward again against the wreckage. Then silence. Then darkness. Then nothing.

Chapter Two

HIM

Amy regained consciousness in a careening, vibrating world with the whistling sounds of wind rushing by and a shrieking siren overhead. She could not recognize anything through the pool of tears in her eyes, at least not clearly. Movement of blurred images suspended over her head gradually materialized into a uniformed man pressing an oxygen mask to her face.

"Just take it easy," he said, forcing her back down, easily countering her feeble efforts to rise. Amy lay back, eyes wide with panic. He reduced pressure and permitted her to tug the mask away. After attempting repeatedly to sit up against the gentle pressure of his hands, his strength slackened and she sat up. Pooled reservoirs of tears spilled down her face. Amy blinked to clear her vision, bringing the attendant into focus.

"You're okay," he said with a reassuring smile. "You have been in an accident, but there is nothing seriously wrong with you physically. You're going to be just fine. You need to lay back now and try to relax."

"Where am I?" Her voice trailed away as she studied the

surroundings.

"In an ambulance. You're on the way to a hospital. We'll be there in a jiffy. Try to relax. I know this is all confusing, but really, you are going to be just fine."

She eased back, more from dizziness than his soothing words. Her vision became more focused by the moment. Images of the crash and fire swept through her mind like a nightmare. She panicked again, remembering the fire. The possibility of being disfigured pounded into her thoughts. "Am I burned?" she demanded in a voice clear and strong, dreading the probable answer.

He shrugged. "Meh. Maybe a little bit. Nothing to worry about. Don't worry."

"Be honest with me. Please."

"I am serious. You are okay. Probably nothing worse than mild sunburn. You may have a few cuts and bruises, but I am being honest. There is nothing serious." He seemed to understand her anxiety and smiled. "Come on. You can trust me."

She had learned never to trust anyone who said trust me.

He patted her cheek and spoke earnestly. "Listen to me. You are absolutely not going to have any permanent damage. I am not kidding. Now, try to relax. We won't be long."

Amy could not relax until noticing the absence of tubes protruding from her arm, correctly assuming that he was not just appeasing her and the injuries were probably not too serious. Her legs hurt, but at least she could move them. *But people sometimes imagine they can feel a missing limb.* "Are my...?" She reached to touch her legs.

He laughed. "I would never lie to you, Miss. You are all in one piece. No missing parts. Come on. You're okay." He laughed to reassure her.

She took heart and breathed a sigh of relief as the initial panic subsided, but objected as he attempted again to place the oxygen mask over her face. Amy felt well enough to sit up and talk well before her mother rushed into the emergency room an hour later.

*****

Her mother looked exactly like movie stereotypes of middle-aged Italian mothers, which, in fact, she was. Maria Lambertino had immigrated to America twenty-eight years before at seventeen, the mother of an illegitimate infant daughter, packaged as part of an inter-family marriage arrangement.

"She's a comely woman, Alberto," the prospective husband's brother reported to the soon-to-be groom while waiting for the soon-to-be bride at the dock.

Alberto Romano stopped pacing and implored, "I won't be disappointed?"

"No. It's a good arrangement, Brother. You have a proper woman from the old country. She will be a grateful wife and you have gained a fair bed partner in the bargain." He winked suggestively.

Alberto wasn't convinced. "Is she stupid?"

"She don't say much, but I think she may be clever enough. Who cares? She's a very suitable woman. You are a lucky man. She is pretty, Alberto."

They were married an hour after Alberto laid eyes on her.

Maria Lambertino-Romano was, indeed, a very attractive woman. For reasons Amy never understood, her mother deliberately sought to hide her good looks, and succeeded. She always looked older than her age, maturing early in life. Amy couldn't remember when her mother didn't look matronly. A tall, olive-skinned woman, usually slightly overweight, with luxurious long salt-and-pepper hair pulled back strictly and wrapped in a bun at the nape of her neck. She never learned to speak better than halting English, typically adding unnecessary o's and a's to the unfamiliar language. Maria didn't need to learn to speak the new language well, though. Throughout the years, her close

17

friends were all immigrants from the old country. They banded together, speaking Italian to each other, scornfully condemning the strange American customs.

Amy thought her mother wore distressingly unattractive clothes, usually hand sewn at home from dark, unadorned fabrics from the old country. Maria typically embellished the finished product with a lace shawl, nothing more. Amy never saw her mother wear anything but everyday clothing.

*****

Maria burst into the emergency room, stood for a moment studying her daughter, then fell to her knees praying and weeping uncontrollably, thanking God and Jesus for the miracle. She, as always, had imagined the worst. An orderly appeared and wheeled Amy from the emergency ward to a permanent room.

"Does Father know what happened, Mother?"

Maria shrugged indifferently and threw her hands up theatrically. "What can I tell you? I called. He will come soon enough." She didn't appear to be the least concerned.

"Did you call Celia, Mother?" Amy always thought of her best friend in an emergency.

*****

Celia Wright, her friend from the first grade. Blood sisters who wore matching scars on the back of their hands to prove it. The two girls had formally mixed their blood on a cold winter day beneath Amy's front porch. The ritual union happened after school during the third grade, but only after several squeamish false starts.

Amy sliced her own hand with a razor blade, much too deeply as the scar revealed later. She pretended no pain. "Come on, fraidy-cat. Your turn."

Celia turned away and gagged. "No. I can't do it."

Amy bristled. "You promised! You can't chicken out now!" Amy thought she would bleed to death before Celia finally summoned the courage to make the necessary incision. They kept the wounds open for a full week, allowing their blood to mingle each day until the ceremonial bonding ended with a solemn vow: "Our souls are joined forever," or some such juvenile incantation. The twosome still cherished the scars, proof of their attachment.

*****

"Well? Did you call her, Mother?"

Maria didn't answer, deliberately procrastinating by puttering around the stark hospital room, inspecting every nook and cranny.

"Mother!"

Maria stopped surveying the room and faced Amy, hands on hips, then snapped, "Family first, remember. Family first! She is not family."

Maria resented Celia's favored status in Amy's life, and in keeping with her matriarchal nature, she never suppressed an opinion.

"Mother, please, either you make the call or move the phone here so I can."

"Move the phone. Oh, sure, strangers first," Maria replied bitterly. She didn't move.

Amy persisted. "Mother, I have to tell her. Celia will never forgive me."

"Oh, all right!" Maria turned away to conceal her displeasure, but soon turned back, smiling grimly. "I will as soon as you get settled."

Amy fell back and noticed warmth for the first time since regaining consciousness. *Finally, the shivering is letting up. I'm going to be all right.* She sighed and smiled, then sobered as her thoughts returned to the wreck. *I'm so lucky to be alive. Who was he?*

The ward nurse marched into the room and notified Amy's mother of the doctor's decision: "Doctor Pinkley left orders for our patient to remain overnight. He wants to keep her for observation. Don't worry. There is no emergency." She turned attention to Amy, checking vital signs, making notes. "Well, I am told that you are a very lucky young woman. The other driver wasn't so fortunate." She smiled blandly.

Amy's feeling of well-being faded as the announcement sank in. "Oh? What about the other driver?" She closed her eyes and prayed silently to protect herself from the answer. The possibility of another person being hurt or killed hadn't occurred to her while occupied celebrating her own good fortune. Guilt swept away the initial euphoria and Amy murmured an already doomed prayer: "Please. Please don't let anyone die."

The nurse had seen it all before, too many times, and callously declared, "Sorry, honey, but these things happen. You might as well know that the other driver didn't make it." She brightened. "But you made it, and that's the important thing. You can thank the Good Lord for that. You are very lucky."

Amy didn't feel favored. "It was my fault."

"That is certainly not what I heard, honey," the nurse proclaimed with the decisive conviction of a judge. "Nope. Not your fault." She squeezed Amy's hand and said, "Listen to me. I've got years of experience with this sort of thing, and the first thing all survivors think in cases like this is that the accident was their fault. Well, it was not your fault." She squeezed again and then released Amy's hand. "Honey, the ambulance attendant is a friend of mine. He told me what happened. The other driver hit you from behind, driving too fast and drunk. Very drunk apparently. And! And, to top everything off, he was driving with open cans of gas on his truck. So, you see, it was not your fault at all."

Amy remembered forcing her car through traffic and realized that the sense of guilt would probably never diminish. "But he didn't have to die." She turned to the window and wept.

The hard-boiled nurse prattled on, fluffing pillows, arranging bedding, adjusting fluid dispensers. "Now don't you go getting all emotional. It's over. Never a good idea to worry about what you can't control. Okay, now I'm going to give you a sedative so you can sleep. You'll feel better after a good rest." She held a vial up to the light to prepare a hypodermic.

"No!" Amy snapped, then closed her eyes and apologized. "Sorry. Please, I really don't want a shot. I do need some information, though. What about the man who saved me? Is he hurt?" She hadn't spoken to anyone about him until then, though he had been foremost in her thoughts. The questions whirled through her mind, *Who was he? Is he okay? Where is he? How could anyone be that strong?*

On one hand she wanted to know everything about him, on the other she wanted to keep the memory of what he did separate from the possibility of any disagreeable truth. *Maybe I wouldn't even like him. Maybe he's coarse and dumb. Maybe it's best not to know too much.*

She owed her life to a stranger, a memory too precious to ruin with what might be the ugly truth of reality. Amy's inquisitive nature had to know. "Nurse, please, did the attendant happen to say anything about the man who saved me? Anything at all?"

The nurse studied the paperwork at the foot of Amy's bed a moment before replying. "You'll just have to ask the police about that when they come, and they are for sure going to come. And they will ask you a million questions." She cocked an eyebrow. "You know how they are. Lay back and rest now. Just ring if you need anything, honey."

Amy's mother settled into a chair beside the bed and took her hand.

"What were you doing way out there, Anna?"

No one in her immediate family ever called her Amy, only

her friends. Her family rarely agreed on any subject, but remained united when it came to her Christian name–Anna.

"I was on my way to pick up some paintings for tomorrow's exhibition at the gallery." She suddenly sat upright. "Oh, my God! You have to call Miss Hopkins for me, Mother. She will have to make other arrangements."

Maria placed the call at once and returned to her post at bedside.

"Oh, Mother, this is all so awful. Someone died. Why did someone have to die?" Tears streaked her cheeks. Maria dabbed her daughter's face with a tissue and clucked sympathetically.

*****

The police arrived and took her statement. Before they left, Amy said, "I want to know about the man who saved me. I would be dead if he hadn't been there."

The two officers exchanged doubtful glances and shrugged. "We didn't get to the accident scene until after the ambulance left, Miss Roman. The witnesses all had quite a bit to say about him, though, but nobody had the presence of mind to get his name." He looked at his partner and shrugged. "Sorry, we don't have any idea who he is. May never know."

Amy's hopes collapsed. "Oh." She despaired momentarily, but determination returned with a rush. "I have to find out, don't you see? It's important. I have to find him!" The emotion in her voice took everyone in the room by surprise. She brushed the tears away and glared at the officers. "I have to know."

Puzzled looks passed around the room. Everyone present seemed to need guidance. The older officer finally said, "Well, I guess we could ask around, but he sure left in a hurry. All we know is that he stopped in the median and ran across the highway to pull you out of the wreck." He nodded solemnly. "Good thing he did. The truck that ran you over burned and exploded right after he pulled you out. You had a close call, Miss Roman. What that guy did was amazing. We interviewed some of the people watching. He stayed with it until he got you out. Amazing."

The other officer added, "Witnesses said he waited with you until the ambulance came, then ran across the highway, jumped into an old truck and drove off. Oh, yeah, that! He's driving an old brown Ford pickup. That's all we know about him. I have to be honest with you, Miss Roman. You may never know who the guy is unless he decides to come forward. But we'll ask around and let you know, okay? Guess that's all we need here."

*****

Amy's stepfather stepped into the room thirty minutes later. He didn't bother to take off the black fedora or remove his black overcoat, nor did he even acknowledge her mother's presence with a nod. He walked directly to the bedside and bestowed upon Amy his customary, superficial peck on the forehead and made a few banal comments about how lucky she was. He seemed nervous and anxious to leave. It didn't surprise or upset Amy that he had not spoken to her mother; that's the way things had always been between her parents. She wished he hadn't bothered to come. He left a few moments later, apologizing unconvincingly about an unavoidable business meeting. He paused and turned at the door. "Don't worry about the car, Anna. Insurance covers it."

"Thank you, Father. Please don't bother about the car. I want to buy my own this time."

He didn't protest, just shook his head sadly and clucked to himself much the same way her mother had earlier. He started to say something, raised an arm, let it drop, and then spoke to Maria, banishing Amy to third person. "Well, well. She's all grown up now, isn't she? Too grown up to take anything from her father." He turned to Amy, smiled indifferently and said,

"We will talk about the car later. Ciao." He bowed his head deferentially and departed with two associates in expensive suits trailing along. Amy knew the men were standing in the hallway during his visit, just as they were always there, attempting to look nonchalant, blending into the scene. Such men had attended her stepfather for as long as Amy could remember. Not always the same men, but two or three watchful young men served her stepfather at all times; tough looking young men who struck her as being much too serious for their age. Her stepfather never went anywhere without an entourage of "associates."

As a girl, the entire world revolved about her mother's husband, and even though she tried to dismiss his importance as she matured, her life still revolved around him more than she desired. He didn't dominate her life by physical presence, not anymore, but everything she did, everything she had, her entire life still seemed attached to her stepfather. He had been nothing more than a transitory figure during her childhood–an unpredictable presence. She had many friends more loving and constant than her stepfather. He was tall and thin, a dignified man who commanded an inordinate amount of respect from the escort of men perpetually at his command. He spoke quietly, smiled infrequently, and seldom slept at home.

"He is nothing to me," she once told Celia. "I don't know him. I don't care about him. He is nothing to me."

"Yeah, right. Nothing more than God." Celia knew, and the girls were only fourteen.

Amy cried for her stepfather's attention as a child, begging for notice, learning the piano, the violin, taking dance lessons–anything to please him. He never once attended a recital and remained a shadowy figure in the background; someone to thank for a steady stream of gifts, gifts always delivered unwrapped, usually with price tag still attached never given personally. She grew unconcerned and detached after years of his lack of interest and now only felt uncomfortable in his presence. He was an enigma, circulating mysteriously on the periphery of her life–never actually a part of it. Even approaching thirty, she still vacillated between feelings of scorn or a childlike reverence, though she knew both emotions were wasted.

*****

Amy spent a restless night at the hospital, waking often with her mother still at bedside.

"It's okay, dear, just another bad dream. I'm here."

A cool, damp cloth invariably followed the assurances. She woke each time gasping for air, on the verge of panic, perspiring and trembling, visions of smoke and fire still fresh.

Celia dropped by early that morning and stayed until mid-afternoon. Their conversation seldom strayed from the subject foremost in Amy's thoughts.

Who was he?

She received an examination and the doctor released her that afternoon. She went home with her mother and a head full of plans. *I have to find him. How could any man possibly be that strong? Why did he take such chances? Is he hurt?*

Her mother brought newspapers and helped scour the accident reports for information. The media didn't know any more than the police–nothing.

"Why are you so concerned about him, Anna? He must not have been hurt."

"Did you check the hospitals, Mother?"

"Yes. Just as you asked. You shouldn't worry so much about him. He must be all right."

"Mother! He saved my life for God's sake!" She sighed and smiled apologetically. "Sorry. I would be dead if not for that man, Mother. Finding him is important to me."

"No swearing in my house! You know that. Now, I think you should probably just let it be, child. Maybe he doesn't want to be known. Perhaps you would be meddling? Let it go."

Amy remained in bed two days as the doctor ordered, but more to appease her mother's maternal anxieties. She departed for work on Thursday, despite Maria's whimpered protests.

"I'm fine, Mother. Please stop worrying. Life goes on. Work goes on."

"I'm fine," Maria mimicked. "Fine? Look at you! You can't even walk! You have to hold on to something to walk. I know you hurt, Anna. I can see it on your face. What's so important about work, eh? You should rest. Stay with me another day."

"Please, Mother. I will hurt just the same here as at work. Please stop worrying." *God, only three days and I already feel smothered.* "I'll call you after work, okay? Thanks for everything. I don't know what I would do without you. Now stop worrying."

*****

Amy took a cab to *OLDE CONCEPTIONS* but only to ask for the remainder of the week off. After leaving, she headed for police headquarters. The crusty precinct desk sergeant didn't know much about the accident, but loved to talk and chattered freely about the subject of her investigation.

"I don't know who he was, Miss Roman, but he must be one hell of a man. Our reports are full of witness accounts about what he did. Unbelievable. Yes sir. One hell of a man."

"*I know* what he did, Sergeant. I need to locate him."

"Well, I'm afraid you're on your own there. We don't have his license number or much of anything else to go on." He leaned over the counter and spoke confidentially. "You know, there must be at least hundreds of guys driving brown Ford pickups in the Boston area. I sure wish we could help you, but there's just no way."

"Will you let me know if you learn anything?" She handed

him a calling card.

"Oh, sure thing." He smiled sincerely and dropped the card into the waste basket the instant she walked out.

Amy called to set up the weekend at Celia's home in the suburbs and felt much better after that. At least she would escape her mother's constant chatter and fidgeting.

"I need to talk, Celia. You are my sanctuary."

"Okay, I'll fresh up your room, kiddo. See ya."

Celia provided a predictable and tranquil haven from the glitter and pressures of Amy's chosen lifestyle. Amy loved her work and the glitzy people involved in her everyday life, but her best friend's controlled domestic world furnished a sense of order and normalcy. Celia had a home, a family, and a refreshing regard for all things practical. Amy counted on Celia for logic and reason, but most of all the pleasant perception of a possible family life, if and when she ever decided to settle down.

She needed Celia. Amy's mother would go to any length to avoid encountering the world outside her simple life. Her mother's entire world centered about common things: the next meal and grocery shopping and the weather, but most unbearable and embarrassing of all, her wearisome, uncompromising obsession with babies.

"Mother, please! You know I hate being asked when I plan to start a family. I hate constant reminders about my advanced age for child bearing. How could I *ever* forget how many of your friends already have grandchildren? I–am–not–ready, Mother!"

Amy didn't feel comfortable around her mother, not any more, in fact not since she was twelve. She loathed the parochial commonness of her mother's life, her old-fashioned, old-country philosophies and practices. She couldn't talk to her mother about anything important as their conversations seemed always to gravitate to food and babies.

*****

"I am absolutely desperate, Celia. She's driving me nuts!"

"Bring it. I'll be here."

Amy not only used her friend as a window to the conventions of normalcy, but savored the homey surroundings that she occasionally thought she wanted. Celia also served as a sounding board of logic. Celia Wright, unlike Amy, had dropped out of college to support her new husband until he finished law school. Celia was in every way Amy's antithesis: short versus tall, pleasantly plump opposed to borderline thin, ordinary looking and unconcerned about it as opposed to Amy's classic beauty. Celia had blonde hair. Amy's hair was darker than black. Celia was happy and comfortable. Amy was sometimes moody and restless. One was a housewife, the other a working woman, and so on. The only thing about Celia that truly corresponded with Amy's lifestyle, other than their friendship, was the violin located in her hall closet. They were members of the Boston Pops Orchestra. Both women played violins and were gifted musicians, playing from the first grade.

*****

Amy left the police station and took a cab directly to her friend's home, there to collapse into her customary chair in the kitchen. They talked all afternoon about Amy's accident, but mostly about the mysterious man responsible for saving her life. Amy relived the scene over and over, agonizing over him.

Him

Bud Wright, Celia's handsome husband, immaculate in an expensive suit, sporting a pencil thin mustache and slick dark hair, arrived late that evening from his partnership job at a brokerage firm and joined their conversation. Amy had known Bud from the time he and Celia first began dating. She knew more about him than she would ever reveal to anyone, let alone Celia. Bud Wright was a scoundrel, notorious for his vices. He routinely attempted to seduce every attractive woman he met, including Amy, once trapping her in the kitchen during a party early in his marriage. She scorched his ears with a resounding rebuke. Bud absorbed the scolding graciously and they became good friends. He had treated her like a sister since, much to Amy's relief.

Bud, a brilliant attorney, had a lawyer's penchant for orderliness. "Let's make a composite of the mystery man," he announced, seizing upon the subject of their conversation. "Tell me everything you can remember, and I do mean everything." He produced a notebook and prepared to write.

Amy closed her eyes and concentrated. "Okay. He had a beard, I think, or maybe just a heavy growth of whiskers. I simply can't remember."

Bud scribbled and Amy continued, "He was big. Like, enormous. Brawny. I mean he was *really* huge, Bud, and unbelievably strong. He literally tore the car apart. And with his hands. Big? Large? I am running out of words here."

Bud made another note, raised his eyebrow without looking up and said, "By large? Fat? Tall? What?"

"No. Not fat, Bud. He was just big. Oh, and dark hair."

He motioned for her to go on. "And? And? Come on, Amy. I need more. Think."

She frowned. "This is tough, Bud. I couldn't see through the smoke. I really didn't see him very well." Bud's assertiveness irritated her.

He didn't react defensively, nor did he relent. "Anything, Amy. Concentrate."

She closed her eyes, rested her head on the back of the chair and groaned. "Ohhh! You are frustrating me! So damned practical, Bud!" She took a deep breath and concentrated. "I really don't remember that much about him. I'm sorry." Her eyes popped open. "Oh, maybe there is one thing. Yes, his hands. His hands were enormous. He had huge hands."

Bud nodded and recorded the comment. "Any rings? Anything on his hands? His wrist? A bracelet?"

"No, just bandages and blood." Amy sat up and exclaimed, "Bud! His hands were already bandaged! Isn't that odd?"

"It certainly is to me. Okay, bandages. Describe."

Amy's brow furrowed deeply as she thought. "Little bandages on all of his fingers. Not completely covered. Just the joints I think. Not really sure." She studied her hands. "Isn't that odd? His fingers were partially bandaged before the accident. What do you suppose?"

They discussed the revelation at length, debating reasons for the bandages until running out of ideas. Bud finally called a halt to the analysis, stood and stretched. "Okay, guys, let's sleep on what we have, but I'm going to need more than this, Amy." He snapped the notebook closed. "This isn't much."

The next morning, Sunday, Bud interrupted the two women at breakfast, entering the room smiling, waving the Sunday sports page triumphantly. "I broke the code," he declared smugly. "I know who your mystery man is."

Chapter Three

THE CRASH

The blast didn't hurt too much, not that Ed would have noticed under the extreme circumstances. The concussion felt more like a sudden blast of wind, a force boosting him away from the burning car. He staggered, tried to catch his balance, failed and sprawled awkwardly onto the highway. It all took place so fast that he barely managing to roll to the side at the moment of contact, only just sparing the unconscious woman in his arms. He struck the concrete on the point of his elbow–the elbow chronically scabbed over from recent injuries. That hurt. Routinely, he would have rolled and bounced up no worse for wear. Not this time. This time his concern for the woman, that his weight might bring about even more damage, prevented a graceful tumble. He scrambled to his feet, the woman dangling in his arms, vomit dripping from his shirt, and ran an additional thirty paces before pausing to look back. A raging inferno had completely engulfed the smashed vehicles, black smoke now boiling aloft. The spectacle of the flaming wreck and the mounting sensation of heat provided incentive to keep moving. He crossed over the westbound lanes in front of the already backed-up traffic jam and placed her gently on the grass in the median.

A crowd of curious onlookers materialized from growing rows of vehicles stalled by fragments of debris from the fiery wreckage. A swelling crowd gathered on the median, forming a whispering, murmuring circle around Ed and the unconscious woman.

It required several moments of gasping for air to catch his breath before kneeling to check her pulse and breathing–both steady–then removed his shirt and covered her. He stood for a few seconds to survey the scene, then knelt up-sun with her in the shade of his body. She had not moved.

An older man stepped close and said, "Ambulance is on the way, bud. I can hear it. You done real good."

The growing ring of spectators gawked and babbled until two aggressive ambulance attendants shoved them aside and assumed control. Ed merged into the crowd and filtered through unnoticed on the way to the truck. He thought about lingering to talk with the police, but decided against it. *No reason to stick around. I didn't see the accident happen so I can't tell the cops anything. I sure don't want the attention that will go with this. It's time to do something about my back.*

The stinging pain on his back and shoulders furnished abundant reason to seek immediate medical attention. Ed drove to the first exit, crossed over the highway and sped back westward. He thought about driving to his apartment for a shower. *I smell like smoke and vomit.* The pain on his back intensified, delivering plenty of incentive to drive directly back to the team clinic at the stadium.

He stopped in the team's empty locker room to rest for a moment, sitting on a scarred wooden bench. The locker immediately behind bore his name, CONKLIN. A blue and red number "98" stood out beneath the name. A few moments later, an assistant coach noticed him and after a brief but concerned discussion ran to notify the team's head trainer. The trainer, a bald hulk of a man in baggy sweats, bringing to mind nothing more than an aging weight lifter, arrived at a trot. He inspected Ed's back for only a couple of seconds before exclaiming, "Jesus H Christ, Ed! What the hell happened to you? This is serious, man! How did this happen?"

Ed looked up and smiled. "Hi, Abe. I had to help some gal out of a car wreck. Turned into a huge fire." He pointed to his back. "I expect I'm going to need your help to get this shirt off so you can take a peek at it. I'm afraid to look. Really starting to hurt."

Abe Goins filled an added, if less important, place in Ed's life other than his capacity as team trainer. He also functioned as Ed's only challenging chess opponent on the team.

Abe departed and ran to his desk to return with a medical kit and placed wire-rimmed Ben Franklin glasses on his warped nose. After tilting Ed's head forward, he moved in for a closer look. "Carney said you had a wreck or something. That true? But this...this looks like.... Oh, man! I sure as hell don't like the looks of this." His voice trailed off as the damage to Ed's back became apparent. "Hells bells, man. This is a damned mess."

Ed started to remove his shirt, but cringed and stopped before complaining, "It stings like fire, Abe. Feels like the shirt is stuck to me. How bad is it?"

"Bad enough. Here, let me give you a hand with that. Jesus, Ed, you smell like a rancid garbage can. Did someone puke on you?" He tried to peel the shirt away gingerly, eventually changing his mind as Ed sucked air through his teeth. "Jiminy, Christmas! What in the hell have you done, here?" The stocky trainer fumbled in his medical box for scissors and began cutting the shirt away from the mass of seeping blisters on Ed's shoulders. Afterward, he stood back, frowning, surveying the injuries. "These are some real bad burns. You really got yourself toasted, Ed! This is a mess.

How the hell did you get burned like this? This is really serious, Ed!" He stepped in front and said, "This is way out of my league. Let's get you to the training room and then I gotta call the team physician in on this."

Later, the head coach paced back and forth near the edge of the crowd of hushed medics and trainers treating Ed's wounds. "Well, you sure won't be putting any pads on that for a while, Conklin," he announced woefully. "Damn, you're going to miss at least the first two regular season game, that's for sure. What a hell of a deal." He shook his head and continued, "Well, when you finish here, come on up to the office and tell me what happened." He left mumbling to himself. "Dammit all anyway."

*****

That evening, following the team doctor's advice, the coach announced to reporters the decision to place Ed on the disabled list for two weeks. The sports page headlines trumpeted the news the next morning, the same headline Celia's husband had noticed.

ALL PRO DEFENSIVE END ED CONKLIN OUT FOR TWO WEEKS

The short article following the headline reported a few sketchy facts about an automobile accident without elaborating on Ed's heroics, ending by stating: Conklin, the Harpoon's fifth year, six-five, 270 pound defensive end is now projected to play against San Francisco the second week of the regular season. The Harpoon front office refused to give details about Conklin's injuries, reporting only that the injuries were not sports related. Conklin could not be reached for comment.

Ed asked the coach for a week's leave of absence from training camp before leaving the stadium that evening.

"Sure, Ed. Go on home. You damned sure ain't gonna do no good around here. Anyway, I know you have family problems to see about. Be back here a week come Monday.

We'll have another look then. I really hate this for you, but from what I hear you did the right thing." He tipped his baseball cap back and added, "And while you're home, you might take some time to see if you can scout up some quail, but only if you have time." The two men usually hunted together each year in the farming valleys near Ed's home town. "You might also try get some jogging in if you can, but don't press too hard and do even more damage."

The following morning found Ed sitting beside his father's bed in a Wilkes-Barre, Pennsylvania hospital. The old man, breathing fast and shallow, slept on unaware of his son's presence, separated from worldly events by an oxygen tent and the deadening veil of morphine. Intravenous tubes and monitors protruded from his body. Ed remained in the room well into the afternoon waiting for the opportunity to speak with his father's doctor. Doctor Donovan Presley arrived at four.

"Does he sleep all the time now, Doc? He hasn't opened his eyes all day."

"I'm afraid so. He is in a persistent coma, Ed. I'm sorry to say, but your father will probably never regain consciousness. Heavy doses of morphine do that. That and his brain cannot get enough oxygen."

Ed frowned, gazing down at his father. "No hope at all, Doc?"

"I'm not going to shade his condition, Ed. So no, there is little reason to believe he will ever be better or even regain consciousness. I'm sorry, but you know how Black Lung disease is. It's a terrible price to pay for such a meager.... Well, you know the deal." He shook his head sadly, tapped Ed on the elbow and steered him from the room. "Wish I could say something positive."

Conklin accepted the verdict, sighed heavily and said, "Thanks anyway, Doc. I appreciate honesty. I'm going to be around a few days. I expect I'd better check in at home."

They left the room walking slowly, heads down, both

wearing somber expressions. The doctor ventured, "If you get a few moments sometime, I wonder if you would mind stopping by the rehab ward. We don't get celebrity visits often and I know the kids down there would sure appreciate it if you could stop by."

"Sure, Doc. I'll look in on them every day. Looks like I'll be around for a while."

Doctor Presley paused at the nurse's station. "Thanks, Ed. Oh, and by the way there is a high school kid up on the second floor with a football injury. Broken neck. Partial paralysis. Maybe you could...?"

Ed nodded. "You bet. I'll get down there today before I leave."

"Things look pretty bleak to him right now, Ed. He could use some encouragement."

Ed was sincerely concerned and extended the conversation. "Is he going to be okay? What's the deal?"

"Too early to tell. Lot depends on his attitude. He isn't responding to us right now. Doesn't seem to care. He has given up, I'm afraid. Pretty tragic. We could use some help with him, that's for sure." The two men, at one time high school football teammates, patted each other on the back and bumped chests like old times. Donovan Presley had been a senior during Ed's sophomore year and a great high school quarterback, but chose medical school over offers to play college ball.

Ed spent the next hour with the injured high school player. The boy's spirits soared long before the conversation ended, after Ed promised to see him each day and pledged a game jersey.

The boy, a brawny, clean-cut youth of seventeen, grinned and said, "This is really great! I never thought I'd get to meet you, Sir. Ed Conklin. Wow. This is really something. You're the best. You've been my hero for as long as I can remember. I want...." He looked down despondently. "Well, I wanted to be just like you." He brightened again. "Don't let anyone clean that jersey after the game, Mister Conklin."

Ed laughed. "Okay, hoss, but I have to warn you, it's going to smell worse than you can imagine. I'll look in on you tomorrow. You pay attention to the nurses. Now, I mean that. They only want to help you. Listen to them, you hear me? You can beat this if you try. Just do it!"

He moved from bed to bed in the ward, shaking hands and joking with the kids. Those who didn't recognize him were fascinated by his enormous size and friendliness. He signed autographs and only then, an hour and a half later, drove to his parent's home in Milsap. Ed smiled as he passed the city limit sign, recognizing his hometown for what it was: a typical back country, down-and-out coal mining company town. The entire population of five-thousand lived on the slopes of a steep valley. Ed noticed most of the stores on Main Street were closed and boarded, a stark reminder of bad times in the mining industry. Milsap had crashed years ago. All that remained were old or crippled people who didn't have any place else to go, and poor families on government relief programs.

His mother, Greta, tall and wrinkled, a spare woman wearing a permanent worried expression, like she expected nothing but trouble, met him at the door. She had seen far too many of life's trials. No one remembered his mother as a happy person. She didn't smile as he entered the house, not even after he hugged and kissed her. She looked tired and worried. Ed sat down to an enormous meal. She had prepared the feast after he called to say he would be home; prepared it exclusively for his taste; everything he liked. Greta hovered over him during the meal, serving and fretting, attending every request before he asked, just like old times.

"How did you find your father, today, Eddie?"

"He looked fine, Ma. Slept all the time, though."

"Yes, I know," she sighed. "He does sleep all the time now." Her haggard appearance intensified "I worry about him, Eddy. I don't think he is ever going to...." She shrugged and Ed let it go. They didn't talk about Willard Conklin or his illness that evening, preferring to ignore the obvious. They had both seen Black Lung deaths before. Greta Swartz had immigrated to America from Germany as a child. Hard times were her only times. She married Willard before finishing high school and knew nothing of life except coal mining and Milsap. Her father and brother both died of Black Lung, and now her husband. The only luxuries Greta ever knew came after her son signed to play professional football. Ed provided money to pay off, repair and refurbish the meager home she refused to leave, though she knew he could and would provide much better.

"Don't fret, Eddie. I don't want to live anywhere else. I would be lost without the things I know. My friends all live here. I won't live anywhere else. This is home."

He once bought new appliances and she grumbled, preferring to cook over wood heat. He gave her a car that she resisted learning to drive. Her next door neighbor, another Black Lung widow, served as chauffeur.

"What do you hear from John, Ma?"

"Oh, you know John. Your little brother doesn't write." She smiled. "He does call once a month though. His grades are good." Greta frowned. "You know, I think Johnny is too involved with that little Evans girl." She clucked disapproval while stirring her coffee with a fork. After shaking her head, she added, "Such a spoiled girl. Do you remember her?"

Ed didn't look up. "Oh, yeah. Debby Evans. Did she go on to Penn State, too?"

"Yes. You know Debby. She can talk her daddy into just about anything. I wouldn't be at all surprised if Johnny isn't spending too much time with her. You know how young people do now. It's scandalous."

"Ma!" Ed feigned shock. He knew John and Debby had been living together for at least two years. Everyone but Greta seemed to know. His mother's puritan scruples wouldn't allow her to admit that she also knew.

"I swear, Eddy, Johnny looks more like you every day. You two boys could be twins."

"Really? Has he been gaining weight?"

She looked up and smiled for the first time. "Big as a house." She sighed and shook her head. "Wouldn't you know it? So skinny in high school and wanting to play ball so bad. But he's nearly as big as you are now."

Greta hustled Ed away when he offered to help with the dishes after the meal. He roamed around the house gazing at the relics of his past. She had saved everything: pictures, news articles, high school and college trophies–everything. Images of his career hung indiscriminately all over the living room walls. Three thick photo albums lay on the coffee table, all dedicated to the preservation of his football fame. The house looked like an exhibition hall–a memorial to Ed Conklin.

Ed thought, Poor, John. No wonder he feels ignored.

His brother had been in trouble with the law from the time he was big enough to throw a rock. Ed understood why John felt neglected, growing up in the shadow of a famous brother. Ed had served as president of the student body, played the sax in a pretty good garage band, sang in the school glee club. Mister Everything in high school: honor student, All State football and basketball, and then three time All American football player at Penn State, and, all too evident to John, first in the heart of his mother.

Ed had taken a paternal interest in his little brother after the boy's mischief became too much for his mother. Surprisingly, John responded, finished high school and began working in the mines to save money for college, maturing into a responsible young man. Ed pitched in and helped with money for John's education to keep him out to of the mines.

John thanked him effusively. "I'll pay it all back, Ed. I swear it."

Ed locked his brother's neck in a wrestling hold and said, "Just get the damned degree, you jerk. That will be payment enough." They became better friends than brothers, they were best friends.

Greta traveled with Ed to the hospital that week, arriving early each morning until Ed returned to Boston and the football wars the following Monday. The injured high school football player, with Ed's encouragement and assistance, took his first steps before he left. Some of the nurses cried. They all clapped and cheered. Ed exchanged addresses and phone numbers with the boy.

"You can't let this injury beat you, hoss. You can get back in the game if you don't give up. Never give up. Never."

"I won't quit, Mister Conklin. I'm going to play again. You just watch."

"That's what I like to hear. I'm going to hold you to that promise, and I'll be there watching when you do. Keep in touch. Let me know." He gave him a card with his numbers.

Ed began practice with the team on Tuesday, running through a light workout without pads. The burn lesions oozed through his shirt. His greatest difficulty came at the end of each practice. The trainer had to provide assistance to separate his shirt from the gummy, festering mass of sores and scabs. The Harpoons lost their first game of the season to the Redskins with Ed watching from the sidelines. He was determined not to miss the San Francisco game, the team's home opener.

Chapter Four

THE COLOR OF HAIR AND EYES

A my returned to the gallery a week after the crash and promptly begged Miss Hopkins for the day off. She then exploited her friendship with a wealthy banker who produced a courtesy pass to the Harpoon's practice sessions. Her banker friend apparently also owned a sizable share of the team. She arrived at the stadium that afternoon and took a seat near a grizzled, avuncular man sunning alone in the stands. She opened conversation with, "Excuse me, Sir. Would you happen to know a player named Ed Conklin?"

"Yeah. Sure. I'm a big fan of his. Hell, everyone is." He patted crutches propped on the seat next to him. "Being a fan is about all I can do any more." He turned his attention to her. "So, you want to know about Ed Conklin, do you? Well, I can tell you that he ain't here today, Miss. I know that much. Supposed to be back tomorrow, though. You a friend of his?"

He isn't here?

She forced a smile to hide the disappointment. "No, not really. Do you know anything about his injuries? Are they serious?"

"Some burns on his shoulders, I think. Not good, that's for sure, but from what I hear they ain't all that bad. Least that's what is running through the grapevine. We sure could have used him Sunday, though. The Redskins ran right through his slot all day." He shook his head sadly. "They sure know how to pick on a weak spot." His eyes squinted to add emphasis to the next statement. "I'll tell you something, though, They wouldn't have rolled over us with Conklin in there. I'll guarandamntee you that." He waved an unlit cigar in her face. "And I'll tell you something else. If he isn't back in time to play against the Niners, we gonna likely get our butts kicked again."

"Do you know him personally?"

"I do know him. He stops to talk with me sometimes. Now, let me tell you about that. I have been here for years, Miss, and I can tell you that he is the only player who will ever take the time to talk to people in the stands."

"Do you mind if I ask you what he is like?"

"Be glad to tell you what I think. Ed Conklin is about the nicest guy I ever met. That's what I think. Yup, he's a friendly guy. I'd gladly give any of my daughters to him."

She laughed. "Really?"

He grinned and said, "I don't have daughters, but if I did…."

She discovered much about Number 98 that day.

*****

Amy left the stadium feeling frustrated, and then thought about Ed Conklin all night. She called in the next morning to beg another day off and drove to the stadium again, quickly located the friendly old man and took the seat next to him.

He looked up from a crumpled sports page and smiled. "Well, I see you're back. Still lookin' for Conklin?"

"Yes. Is he…?" She pressed her hands together in mock prayer.

He took the cigar from his mouth with one hand, patted her arm with the other and directed her attention to the field with the ever-present cigar. "Yep. That's him, right over there. Number 98. The only player without a helmet and pads."

Her gaze followed the aim of the cigar toward a group of sweating players, settling on the only player without a helmet. He appeared to be taller than the others. "The tall man?" she asked and pointed. "You mean the guy wearing shorts?" His trim physique surprised her. He appeared to be out of place compared to the group of behemoths surrounding him.

"Yeah, that's him. Number ninety-eight."

Amy sat back and concentrated. From a distance, the player wearing number ninety-eight could have been an ordinary man on the street. He wasn't dressed in a football uniform, just athletic shorts and a light cotton shirt with his number and the team logo of a muscular man throwing a harpoon. Conklin's body looked almost ordinary–not the big stomach and bulging muscles she envisioned. Measured alongside the other players, his body seemed, much to her surprise, quite normal.

"He's the best there is, Miss. His motor never stops running." The old man then added, "If you're interested in watching a real man play football, you won't find a better example than Ed Conklin." He squinted at her suspiciously. "You a reporter?"

Amy gathered her purse, the daily newspaper and the Harpoons publicity pamphlet. She had all the information she needed. Now she wanted to find an isolated place and observe without her talkative friend's constant interruptions. She smiled and said, "No, just a fan like yourself." She shook his hand. "Thanks for your help. I'm going to move down next to the field. Do you think he would talk to me?"

"I expect he will. Just get someone's attention and ask for him at the end of the practice session. He will be easy to find after the other guys leave. He's always the last player to leave the field."

She descended to a secluded seat in the shade almost at field level, as close to the men on the field as possible, and watched, eyes locked on Conklin. Everything about him intrigued her. The team lined up for calisthenics, a dull performance she found boring, until, to her horror, she observed bloodstains spreading across the shoulders of Conklin's shirt. He apparently didn't notice, or else he didn't care. She grimaced, forced her eyes from the sickening sight and read his autobiography in the team's public relations pamphlet. *Nothing exceptional here. Just another typical jock.* She laid the pamphlet aside, located him again and murmured, "Or is he? Ed Conklin. Hmmm."

Her eyes followed him as the practice intensified. He didn't look at all like the man at the wreck, at least not the way she remembered, and he was clean shaven. He certainly didn't fit her preconceived stereotype of a football player. He seemed much taller than she imagined and his dark, short hair remained in place throughout the workout. Some of the players groaned and complained, but the rigorous exercises didn't seem to bother Conklin. He grinned and bantered, leading by example.

Amy's attention centered on his facial features. His face revealed permanent wrinkles around the eyes and mouth. Smile marks, she thought. That's a good sign. She enjoyed watching him, admiring his boyish enthusiasm and caught herself smiling.

He is contagious. He never stops smiling. He looks and acts like a mischievous little boy, she thought. He is easy to look at, she conceded. Not at all the way I imagined a football player would look. He's different than I imagined. Very different.

Despite Conklin, the monotonous practice brought back her biased attitude about sports in general. She harbored nothing but aversion to sports and a loathing for violence of any kind. Amy didn't pretend to understand why a grown man would waste time playing football, and by choice had never associated with anyone connected to sports, particularly professional sports.

Conklin ran through the drills enthusiastically, smiling and laughing all the time. He clearly enjoyed joking around with the men around him. The other players obviously liked him, and so did the coaches. The longer she watched the more he intrigued her. When the practice ended an hour later, Amy had almost forgotten her mission and waved down a passing player.

*****

"Yo, Conklin! You got a visitor asking for you." One of the assistant coaches yelled the message and pointed to the stands as Ed continued running laps after the other players left the field. He motioned for Ed to come over. "You Better watch your butt, man." He nodded toward Amy. "This one don't look like no football groupie to me. Probably a reporter." They both looked toward her position in the seats near the end zone. "You know her, Ed? I don't think I ever saw this one hanging around."

Ed recognized her instantly, even from a distance. *Amy Roman*. He had seen her name in the newspaper the morning after the accident. He had been intrigued and googled her. He knew where she worked and where she went to school. He waved at her. She waved hesitantly, seeming to be unsure of herself. Ed held up a forefinger signaling that he would be there in a minute and turned away to think. *I'll be damned. Wonder how she found me? And I wonder why*? He jogged around the running track, slowing to a walk with thirty yards remaining to give more time to think before facing her. He thought he probably knew what she wanted and started programming how to withdraw from what he anticipated would probably be a gushy scene. He looked up just as a gentle breeze blew her hair aside.

Wow! She is more than a little attractive. Keep your head, Conklin.

He was close enough to see the long, flowing black hair complemented her olive complexion. She had a straight, refined patrician nose, much like he remembered seeing in renaissance paintings, and yet everything about her seemed secondary to the enormous, dark eyes. *Oh, this could be interesting. This might be different.* He blinked to break from what had turned into a stare. *Those eyes.* He couldn't tell much about her otherwise, hidden as she was beneath a loose-fitting dress that effectively barred anything more than vague speculation about her body. *Well, if nothing else, she has a beautiful face.*

He noticed that she had taken a seat behind the first row of seats, assuming she chose the location deliberately–not too close but near enough to permit conversation. She smiled uncertainly as he approached, either embarrassed or losing her nerve, he wasn't sure. Ed positioned his forearms on the stadium rail, smiled and spoke first, "I'm told you might be here to see me?"

She leaned back, unconsciously pulling away, clearly embarrassed. "Yes. I am if you are Ed Conklin."

He looked away and smiled, aware of her discomfort. When he looked at her again, he said, "That's me, and you are Amy Roman."

She looked away, failing miserably to conceal her surprise. A moment later she faced him and said, "How? How could you possibly know that?"

"Easy. The newspaper," he said, grinning broadly. "And we do go back, you know. I have seen you before."

"Oh, of course." She looked away again, flustered.

He didn't want the uncomfortableness to build any further and said, "I read about you in the news the morning after the accident." When she looked at him again, he smiled and said, "I needed to know you survived. That was quite a crash. From what I can see, you don't seem much worse for the experience."

"I am okay. Yes, I am doing well. Thank you so much."

She stood and moved slowly to the rail to be nearer, still not comfortable, taking time to consider what to say next. "I needed to know how you are. I also read the paper. I saw the report that said you were burned. I'm sorry."

She looked genuinely concerned. Ed straightened. "A little blister or two. I'm fine now, thank you. Really, I am okay."

"I don't believe you." When he looked surprised she added, "And I don't believe for a moment that you have blood on the back of your shirt from playing football."

A glance over his shoulder confirmed her observation. He grimaced at the sight. Ed hadn't noticed the condition until she mentioned it. Blood and blister fluids had mixed and seeped through his shirt. He pushed away from the rail and turned aside to conceal the sight from her. "Sorry. Really, it's nothing, though. I expect to play this Sunday."

Her eyebrows elevated skeptically. "Now it's my turn to say, Really? That's not what the newspapers say."

"Oh?" His interest kindled. The innocent comment betrayed just how much she knew about him and furnished added significance to her presence. Apparently she had also done some homework. "And what do the papers say?" he asked.

She looked down for a moment, running her fingers over the rail near his arm. "That you are questionable Sunday–whatever that means."

She appeared to lose composure and became uneasy again. The signs were clear: averted eyes, the hint of a crimson flush creeping up her neck. He suspected the performance was probably not typical. "Oh, that. Well, sports reporters are traditionally alarmists," he countered. "I *will* be in the lineup Sunday. Absolutely." Ed thought he knew the reason for her visit, and it was not to pass the time of day. *Quit playing her along.* "Look, Miss Roman, you don't need to say anything about last week. I only did what anyone would do." Much to his surprise, she laughed. He said, "Now what? Something I said?"

"Forgive me, but no one knows what happened better than I do, and what you did is not what anyone could or would do, Mister Conklin." She tossed her head, flicking strands of long hair from her eyes and continued, "I was there, remember. I saw what happened. I know, because I watched an entire crowd of your anyone men run away from the fire before you arrived. You risked your life for me, a complete stranger, and I can never thank you enough. So, yes, that is why I am here." Her eyes were intent upon his now; unwavering; tears running freely.

Ed looked away, taken aback by her openness. "Really, no thanks required, Miss Roman."

"Wrong again. I would have died if you hadn't–"

He held up his hand. "Please stop. Look, I'm relieved to know that you're okay. I'm glad I could help. You went out of your way to come by to say thanks. That's good enough."

Her eyes remained locked on his. "Nevertheless, Mister Conklin, I am indebted to you and needed to express my gratitude." She smiled warmly and added, "And I will not leave until I have. So, thank you now and forever from the bottom of my heart." She offered her hand and he took it. They held firmly for a moment. She apparently contemplated something more, then squeezed his hand and said, "What you did for me will be a lasting memory. I will never forget you." With that she let go, stepped back and smiled. "I'm sorry you were injured. I hope you heal quickly." She turned abruptly and walked up the steps, pausing at the tunnel entrance before turning back to see him still watching. She smiled and waved.

He thought the smile seemed troubled, perhaps wistful. There seemed to be something sad about her. After she disappeared into the passageway he breathed what could only be regarded as a disappointed sigh of relief before returning to the track, thoughts firmly locked on Amy Roman. The next time around, he glanced up to the tunnel and spotted her standing in the shadows. He didn't want to embarrass her and jogged on, pretending not to notice.

After he passed, Amy left the stadium and drove directly to her friend's home.

*****

Celia opened the door, started to say something before noticing the expression on Amy's face. She frowned and stepped back to study her pal. "Amy? What is it? Are you okay? You look flushed." She held Amy by the shoulders, searching her eyes, then said, "Ah ha! Something *is* wrong. I can tell. I know you. Okay, out with it. What?"

"Let's sit first, Celia." They took their favorite conversation places at the kitchen table before Amy began. "I met him today, Celia."

Celia's eyebrows lifted. "Him? Well, that's good I guess. Soooo, who is him?"

"You know, the guy who pulled me out of the wreck. I met him today."

"Really? Did he come to the gallery?"

Amy related the past two days' events to her astonished friend. When the story concluded, Celia said, "I just can't believe that you, of all people, went to all that trouble. Good heavens, girl! Why didn't you just pick up the damned phone?"

Amy rolled her eyes. "Sometimes you really are insensitive, Celia. Why? How about because the man saved my life! How about that? That, to me, would seem important enough to thank him personally. That's why."

Celia nodded. "Well?"

"Well what?"

"Amy! It's me, remember. I know you. You didn't take two days off and drive all over hell just to tell me you met him. So, what about him? Tell me!"

Amy smiled at her friend's infallible intuition. Celia could always see through any pretense and straight to the heart of Amy's thoughts. She flipped her wrist nonchalantly. "Oh, I just went to thank him, that's all. I wanted to thank him face to face. That's all there is to it."

Celia sat back, arms folded, eyes narrowed suspiciously. "Amy, honestly. Do I have to drag it out of you? I know there is more. I've seen that little 'I've-got-a-secret smile' of yours before, you know. You came here to tell me something and you are not leaving until I hear it. Now, out with it!"

Amy smiled. "I can never hide anything from you. You've always been able to read my thoughts."

Amy didn't have many male friends, and none steady. She had never made it a practice to exhibit anything close to transparent excitement over a man. From Celia's viewpoint, if Amy Roman ever even suggested overt curiosity about a man, that behavior would have been completely out of character.

"I said thanks. That's all." She could tell by Celia's expression that she wasn't buying. "No, really. That's all there is to it."

"Yeah, right. Bullshit. Okay, Amy, I can wait." She tapped her fingers, started a whispered whistle and studied the ceiling. "Anytime you're ready. I know and you know that you came here to tell me something. Come on. Let's get on with it. Tell me."

Amy sat back and exhaled. "Oh, I might as well." She closed her eyes, took a deep breath, smiled blissfully, and then said, "Oh, Celia! He is the most drop dead gorgeous man I have ever seen!" She covered her face with both hands.

Celia's mouth fell open. "Oh–My–God! Did I hear you right? Gorgeous? Amy, he's a football player for God's sake! Gorgeous? Have you lost your mind?"

Amy peeked through her fingers and said, "No. No, Celia, he is *not* just another football player. A Greek god could not be more perfect. You should see him."

Celia stripped Amy's hands away. "For heaven's sake! Do you hear yourself?"

Amy didn't retreat. "I don't know exactly what it is, but there is something so, so different about this guy. I know that sounds crazy, but I now wonder if the accident really was an accident. Do you believe in fate? Destiny?"

Celia slipped down until her head rested on the chair back, eyes rolling, fingertips on her temples. "Good grief, Amy. I cannot believe this." She stood suddenly and patted Amy's shoulder. "You poor baby. Don't you dare move. Just sit there and try to be calm. I'm going to pour a nice strong drink for both of us, and then we are going to start all over. Do not move!" She backed away, palm out, holding Amy in place.

*****

Later that week, Ed mailed two tickets for the Forty-Niner game to the gallery. She wasn't in the booth at the start of the game. Much to his surprise and delight, he looked up at the beginning of the second half and spotted her in the booth, alone. He would have been disappointed if she hadn't come, and even more disappointed if she came with another man. He knew where she lived by then, having paid a few bucks on-line to get the address and phone numbers. He also knew she wasn't wearing a wedding ring. Her presence in the booth furnished inspiration and he played the game of his life during the second half. The Harpoons won. Ed received a brief, bland thank you note in the mail the following Tuesday. Thanks for the tickets–that's all.

Okay, that leaves the ball in my court. Here goes nothing. He called her at work.

*****

Celia couldn't believe it. "He called and asked you out? And you.... Wait a minute. I thought you only went to say thanks, and now he wants a date? What is going on?" She pointed an accusing finger. "Look at you! Amy? You are thrilled he asked, aren't you? You little sneak! All right, what did you tell him? You aren't seriously thinking about letting this go on? Are you actually thinking about going out with him?"

Amy fiddled with her coffee cup, resisting the urge to confront her friend. "Of course not. It was all just a lark. I came to my senses, okay? I told him that I would think about it, and then sent a candid little note that should resolve the matter for all times. I'm sure he will get the idea. I don't know what you were thinking, Celia, but you should give me more credit. I certainly don't need a relationship right now, and particularly not with a sweaty football player."

Strangely, Celia didn't seem delighted with the answer. "And why not?" She held Amy's face in her hands, gazing into her eyes. "Look at me, dammit! Please tell me you are not planning to go back to Carlo." She scowled. "Amy, don't you dare even think about that!" She became intensely concerned. "You promised, Amy! Carlo is no good for you, or any other woman on this planet. Please tell me that you haven't changed your mind."

"Relax. I meant what I said about Carlo."

Celia looked relieved and sat back. "Well, at least that's good. Now, about this football player?"

Amy waved her friend's inquisitiveness away. "I just don't see any future there, Celia. What more could there be other than a purely physical relationship?" She looked up from the coffee cup. "A football player? Really? How could he possibly be anything to me?"

"How? Well, hell, I don't know. But more to the point, how will you know if you don't come out of your defensive shell? And how can you make any sound judgment without knowing more than you do about him? Maybe there is more this guy than you know."

"You know better than that. I thanked him, Celia. That's enough. I went out of my way to thank him. Do I owe him more than that?"

"Of course not, but it just seems to me–"

"That's enough! Let's just chalk the whole thing off as a momentary indiscretion, okay? I was curious, that's all."

Celia lost hope. "Okay, it's your life. I just thought.... Oh, what the hell." She raised the glass. "To us."

To Celia, Amy seemed determined not to venture out of the controlled environment of work and a few close, politically correct friends; no man romantically challenging; no man challenging in any way at all. The conversation returned to topics usually discussed over the kitchen table: the orchestra, Celia's two children and Amy's recent apartment redecorating venture.

*****

The rejection stung at first. Ed shrugged it off, accepting his disappointment as nothing more than busted ego. *I assumed too much. Should have known better*. He condemned himself for taking advantage of her good manners. *A woman should be able to say thanks to me without worrying about me taking it as open season. Well, no matter. Forget her.*

Her brusque note read: "Thanks for the offer. Football is not my favorite sport. Good-bye and good luck." Guess that's it, he thought. I think what the woman just said is she doesn't like football players. Fine. I have more than enough to do without a woman in my life right now. His disappointment slowly receded. *She's history. Get on with your life, Conklin.*

*****

After that, Amy's daily routine altered somewhat, subliminally at first, and then she made a conscious and premeditated shift by beginning to read the sports page and watching sportscasts each evening. She stayed home on Sundays and secretly watched the Harpoon's games on television, feeling a jab of shame for taking interest in something so brutal and primitive as professional football. She tracked Ed Conklin's progress as the season wore on, taking great pride in his successes and agonizing over defeats.

She read every available report and story about him and rescheduled weekends to watch football in the privacy of her apartment. She became a football junky. Amy cringed at the sight of blood on the back of his jersey during the first game. After that, the weekly team injury report always listed him as "doubtful," but he played in every game. She was certain his "doubtful" status stemmed directly from burns on his back.

Those are my burns. He risked his life for me.

✱✱✱✱✱

On a brisk winter Saturday afternoon while shopping with Celia at an exclusive Boston mall, Amy suddenly stopped, frozen in place, braced against the milling throng. Scanning. Listening. Disorganized.

Celia had walked on ahead, unaware of her friend's absence. She stopped the moment she noticed Amy missing and hastened back to find her friend lodged in the jostling crowd, white-faced and visibly shaken.

"What is it? Are you okay?" Celia's concern increased as she noticed Amy's bewildered expression–a faraway look, seemingly listening or seeing something. Celia followed Amy's eyes but didn't see anything significant. "What happened?" She placed her hands on Amy's shoulders and shook. "Amy, look at me. What's wrong?"

Amy pushed Celia's hands away and motioned ahead. "It's him, Celia." She pointed. "That's him."

Celia's eyes followed Amy's directions to a makeshift booth in front of a sporting goods store where three men wearing football jerseys were busily signing autographs. A line of autograph seekers extended around the corner and out of sight.

Amy appeared to be in a trance. The man in the middle suddenly stopped signing and hesitated. He looked puzzled, struggling to detect something. He suddenly stood and looked directly into her eyes. He stared for a moment, then smiled pleasantly and waved, verifying recognition. She didn't respond. She couldn't move. Frozen in place. Bewildered.

"Is *that* your football player?"

Amy blinked and turned away, still disoriented. "That's him, Celia. Yes, that's him." She whispered, more to herself. "That's him."

Celia became more interested in the man than her friend's condition. "Wow, were you ever right. He *is* gorgeous. As you said, drop dead." After a low whistle, Celia's interest returned to Amy, still disorganized, eyes still oddly vacant. "Amy?" Celia shook her by the shoulders again and waved a hand in front of her eyes. "Amy?" she whispered. "For God's sake, snap out of it!" Her eyes traced Amy's stare back to the booth.

Ed's smile faded after she failed to acknowledge his greeting. He frowned, hesitated, and then after repeated glances her direction, sat down and turned back to the business of attending to the endless line of eager fans.

Celia's exasperated voice broke through Amy's trance. "Get a grip! I have never seen you act this way. Come on! You're scaring me."

Amy turned and hurried toward the exit, her baffled friend trailing along. Celia surged ahead, stopped in front of her and snapped, "Amy, dammit, will you please talk to me!" She stamped her foot. "Right, damned, now!"

Amy hesitated, eyes closed, breathing deeply, head bowed, eyes closed, smiling.

Celia blocked the way and growled, "What in the hell is wrong with you? What's going on here? You look like you've seen a ghost."

Amy suddenly hugged her friend and said, "I don't know, but something very strange happened back there. It almost worries me. So odd, Celia. Scary."

"Scary? What?"

"Celia, I know you won't believe this, but it's like I knew he was there before I saw him. Honestly. Maybe I heard his voice before I looked, but I really don't think so. It seems to me that I felt his presence before I saw him. Isn't that odd?" She smiled and brushed the tears from her face.

"You need to get a grip, kiddo, or a stiff drink, or get the hell out of here. Come on."

After that, Amy began, by chance, to see or read about Ed Conklin every day, sometimes several times a day. His face popped up everywhere she looked: billboard advertisements, on the side and backs of public busses, taxis, in the newspaper, on television. She saw him on TV with groups of children and while performing duties as the National Football League player representative for United Way commercials, and while winning Boston's Young Man of the Year award for voluntary public service. He appeared with senior citizens and children during funding campaigns for the underprivileged and homeless, and, much to her amazement, the newspaper listed Ed Conklin as one of Boston's ten most eligible bachelors. He became a refreshing new part of her secret daily routine.

Then, unexpectedly, Ed Conklin entered her life again at the spring celebrity pops concert, listed as one of three guest local celebrities. The Boston Pops featured local personalities once a year–all proceeds to charity. She encountered him early the first morning of rehearsals as the conductor introduced the luminary performers to the orchestra before practice. Their eyes met and he winked. No one noticed the familiarity. Conklin's presence so distracted Amy that she didn't play a note during the first number.

"I told you, smarty," Celia accused during a break. "Just a common football player, huh? Well, I'll bet that even you have to admit there is more to him than you thought. He's not a bad musician, either. Maybe not in the classical sense, but you must admit, he has talent. That is no ordinary man." She tweaked Amy's cheek and said, "If you don't want him, can I have him?"

He played an old baritone saxophone during his short solo

segment of the concert, not quite well enough to be considered professional, but the crowd loved the performance and awarded a standing ovation.

Amy summoned the courage to approach him after the concert. "I am impressed, Mister Conklin. Where did you learn to play?"

"Ah, Miss Roman." He imitated her formal greeting and bowed deferentially. "This is my grandfather's instrument. I learned to play sitting on his lap. He also taught me to play the piano a little bit."

"I am impressed."

"Thank you. I consider that high praise coming from a member of this orchestra." He smiled politely and added, "My friends call me Ed. I wish you would."

His nearness and awesome size was disturbing. He hadn't looked so large standing beneath her at the stadium rail, or when compared to the other players. Now, on level ground, he towered over her and everyone else nearby.

He would make two of me.

She said something inarticulate about the uniqueness of a football player with musical talent and regretted the remark at once; in fact she felt sick.

Clearly resenting being typecast, he sighed and said, "Yeah, you're probably right. I sometimes delude myself with the notion that I might actually have musical talent. Some critic usually brings me back to earth."

She wilted under the weight of self-censure and began edging away, believing a quick exit her only hope to salvage the moment. She desperately needed to go someplace dark and isolated. Celia rescued her from more embarrassment by diverting Conklin's attention with polite conversation. A striking blonde invaded the tense little group at that juncture, ending Amy's tactless social disaster by affixing herself to his elbow.

"Well, Ed, I see you found some new friends." She smiled long-sufferingly at the two interlopers. "I just can't leave him alone for a second."

Ed introduced her as Gloria something-or-other. Amy wasn't listening. After another synthetic smile, Gloria said "Bye now." and steered him away with an air of authority that, to Amy, smacked of ownership.

Chapter Five

TOGETHER

A my relaxed in Celia's kitchen the following Monday after work, two days after the concert and two hours after a hand-written note from Ed Conklin arrived at the gallery– an apology for his behavior at the symphony.

"He apologized to you? Why? Why in the hell would he do that after you acted like such a complete ass after the concert? And what about that perky little blonde who led him off by the nose? Hmmm?" Celia raised an eyebrow to underscore the remark. "Sure looked to me like she had a pretty short leash on Good Ol' Ed."

Celia's acerbic comments didn't bother Amy; nothing so trivial could interfere with their life-long friendship and years of BFF harassment.

"Before you go too far, jerk, that's not all he said," Amy declared smugly, steering the conversation away from the blonde and back to the setting of her choice.

Celia's eyebrow lifted again. "Oh? And now I suppose you expect me to believe that he wasn't offended at all, and to express his regard he has nominated you for Miss

Congeniality."

Amy started to lash back but caught herself, sighed instead and said, "I really could stand a little more empathy here, Celia. He apologized! Let's take it from there."

Celia sat back, ready to listen. "Now don't get huffy on me. I just don't get it, Amy. The first decent man to come along in what–years? and you charge through him like an enraged rhino that just ate some spare Jeep parts. Fine, I'll keep my big mouth shut for a moment. Please, do go on." Celia had never approved of Amy's male friends, most of whom were gay guys associated with art and music, or the moneyed, indolent country club types who acquired their fortunes and names through inheritance. She rarely squandered an opportunity to chide Amy about her guy friends.

Amy regained control of the conversation. "All right. Enough. I am overly familiar with your opinions about my gentleman friends. Now, let me direct your attention back to Ed Conklin." She waited for Celia to nod. "You appear to be more upset about my absence of social skills Saturday than Mister Conklin was, or apparently is. And for your information, smartass." She unfolded the note, held it up and tapped it with the back of her fingers. "Ta Da!" Holding it at arm's length, she read, "Mister Conklin sends regrets for the formality of this note and hopes Miss Roman will not be offended if he calls."

Celia held her traffic cop palm out. "Whoa! Now you just hold it right there. Like, he's going to ask you out?" She sat back. "Phhhtt! Anyway, so what? What in the hell difference does his maybe way-too-polite little note make to you? You won't take a chance. You never do."

Amy's calculating smile indicated pleasure at something secret or amusing. "Give me a moment here, Celia. I'm thinking. I'm thinking."

"Really? Well, miracles never.... No. Wait. Please tell me you aren't thinking about some of your past performances that always seem to end with rejection." She leaned closer, slapped her hand on the table and almost screamed, "So, tell me, dammit! What are you thinking?"

Amy closed her eyes and feigned concentration. "I don't know, Celia. There is so much to think about. Anyway, perhaps he won't ask. He didn't exactly say he *would* ask, did he? Maybe he's just testing the water. Maybe he just plans to repay me for my rude comment and has no intention of calling. Who knows?"

"Yeah, right. Who knows." Celia rolled her eyes and gestured helplessly to the ceiling god. "Who knows? Would you, just for one fricking moment wake the hell up!" She shuddered theatrically and returned her attention to Amy. "Who knows? Well, I know! That's who knows. Every junior high school girl on the damned planet knows. That's who knows. I swear, sometimes you are almost too dense to...." She flopped back in the chair. "Oh, I give up."

Earlier, Amy had rejoiced when the note arrived, smiling and happy, excited. Excited until the predictable questions and doubts surfaced to temper her enthusiasm. *He won't call. I have done just about everything conceivable to frustrate his interest. So, what does he really want?* Even so, she couldn't stop smiling.

"Okay, that's it!" Celia declared, standing suddenly, marching across the kitchen to the door. "You go home! Right this minute! I mean it!"

Celia's sudden, determined termination of their conversation surprised Amy. "What? Why? What did I say?"

"Go home!" Celia said while holding the door open. "It is making me extremely nervous just to have you sitting here in my kitchen at a time like this." Her charade ended at that point and she could no longer suppress the delighted grin. "Because, right now, Amy, if I were in your place, I would be at home waiting like a fourteen-year-old, all alone, by myself, holding the phone to my heart waiting for him to call. I would. I wouldn't want to be with anyone." She hugged Amy and then pushed her through the door. "And you better call me the instant he hangs up. I'm serious, Amy. Go straight home. Do not stop. Go."

Amy hesitated on the porch, not defiantly, but still reluctant to take Celia seriously. "Do you really think he–"

Celia stamped her foot. "Yes, you Dodo. Of *course* he will. Now go. Shoo."

*****

He called not ten minutes after Amy returned to the apartment. She held the phone tentatively before answering, barely able to control her excitement. *Wait. Not too quick. One more ring.*

He didn't give his name before asking, "Did you get my note?"

"I di...." Her voice broke and she had to clear her throat. "Sorry. Yes, I did." To salvage the moment she quickly added, "You certainly didn't need to apologize for anything."

"Maybe. Maybe not. I shouldn't have taken offense."

Amy's paralyzed ability to think began to revive in a race to catch up with her emotions. "Well, I didn't notice that you took offense. Let me say this first. I'm so sorry for what I said. It was rude and thoughtless. I had no reason to treat you the way I did, Mister Conklin. Please accept my apology."

"Accepted. Now, are we finished making amends?"

She cuddled into the corner of the sofa, eyes clamped tightly closed, living in the moment. "Yes, please. Thank you."

"All right, then. First, I much prefer you call me Ed. And second, I wonder if you might consider having dinner with me sometime?"

Bang! No small talk; no preparation; nothing delicate or sophisticated about his approach. Amy's eyes popped open wide. She took a deep breath, permitting a satisfied smile to underscore her delight. She couldn't remember feeling so happy.

"Are you still there?" he asked.

She laughed, more at her own nervous reaction than his apparent concern over the prolonged silence.

"Miss Roman? Did I say something funny?"

His voice snapped Amy back to attention. "Oh, I'm sorry. No, it's not you." She took another deep, broken breath and said, "Yes. Yes, I would like that very much. And please call me Amy."

There. It's done.

After an exaggerated sigh of relief, he exclaimed, "Whew! I thought there for a moment.... Never mind. Okay, that's great. Would tomorrow be too soon?"

"Tomorrow? Let's see. Noooo. I suppose tomorrow would be fine." She laughed again. She couldn't help laughing. It had been such a long time since a male of any significance held her interest for more than a day, and an entire lifetime since any man had ever affected her this way. She felt giddy.

"About eight? I will pick you up."

Amy didn't pause to consider the defenses she planned to employ in case he called and threw discretion to the wind. "Yes. Yes, that will be fine."

"Dinner, then? Someplace proper and quiet where we can talk without screaming?"

"Yes, that sounds pleasant. Now, if you have something to write with, I'll give directions to my apartment."

"Three blocks north of the interstate on Berkeley–Back Bay Apartments–Three B. Is that about right?"

The fact that he had taken the effort to find out for himself didn't upset her. She was pleased. "You *have* been busy. Very well, I'll brief the doorman to let you in. Eight then?"

"Eight is good. I will see you tomorrow."

Amy tapped the phone off and collapsed into the confines of the plush sofa, eyes clenched tightly, whispering, "Yes! Yes!"

Miles away, Ed patted the phone and said, "Bingo!" He

laid out clothes for the date, realizing everything had to be ready in order to make it to her apartment on time after practice the next day.

*****

Amy greeted him at the door but didn't invite him in. She stepped through and locked the door before turning to him. "It's nice to see you again, Mister Conklin." She didn't feel comfortable making small talk. Her smile was thin and set. She felt more nervous than for any date in her life.

He grimaced theatrically. "Mister Conklin? Please, if you will, call me Ed." He rarely regarded another person's choice of clothing as crucial, but he noticed everything about Amy Roman. She was wearing a medium length plain brown silk dress with long sleeves and a high collar, revealing nothing provocative to draw attention. He suspected that she had picked the dress to make a statement and assumed the garment probably conveyed her thoughts: *"This dress is deliberate. This dress is bullet proof. Don't get any ideas."*

In spite of the dress, everything about her glistened: her long black hair, her eyes and the unpretentious but still obvious diamond earrings and broach. She would have been just as stunning to Ed without the jewelry. He had concluded by then that, without a doubt, Amy Roman was easily the most beautiful woman he had ever seen. Taller than he remembered. Graceful spike heeled shoes elevated her an additional four inches. He barely controlled an irresistible desire to stare.

Ed had worn his best party clothes: an expensive summer sport jacket and dress trousers, but felt completely underdressed in her presence. Everything about her revealed class with a capital C. Class and money. He felt self-conscious, unrefined, out-of-place and fumbled with strained conversation after they drove away in the rental car. He was thankful that he had not succumbed to the idea of driving his ratty old truck.

"Let me say this ahead of time," he managed to say without stammering. "I have wanted the opportunity to know you from the first time I saw you. I mean after the wreck, of course."

"Really?" She seemed genuinely surprised, and then down-played his seriousness with an easy smile, trying to lead him into being at ease. "Well, what took you so long, Ed?"

"Oh, one thing or another. Football. Road trips. School. My life is too busy right now. That and I didn't think…." He stopped short of confessing that he didn't think she would accept.

He is more nervous than I am. She settled back into the seat and changed the subject. "I'm sorry your team lost the playoff game."

"Thanks. We played poorly and probably should have lost."

"Possibly, but I thought *you* played well."

His eyebrows lifted and he looked over. "Oh? Were you at the game?"

"No. I watched from home."

"Home was a good idea. It was freezing assed…." He grimaced. "Ahhh! Sorry. Locker room talk. Do you follow the Harpoons?"

"Not that much until recently."

"I didn't think you liked football." He watched her frown as she obviously recalled the tactless note.

"Let's just say, I have recently developed an interest."

He pondered the answer for a moment, wondering if she might be implying something, and then asked the obvious: "So, I take it you found something interesting about football?"

Amy usually enjoyed playing word games, but his pointed response effectively ended the contest. "Yes, I have, and that would be you." She immediately regretted the impulsive answer. *Oh, that was way too fast. What must he think?* She amended the response slightly. "I must confess, the game of football eludes me, but I am cultivating interest because I have become somewhat familiar with one of the players." She looked directly into his eyes. "You're the only football player I have ever known, Ed. I really didn't have a good reason to watch until now."

Ed turned his attention back to the road but still felt her eyes on him. His concentration wavered. She didn't look away when he glanced her direction again. He noticed the trace of a smile playing at the corner of her mouth. *Easy, big fellow. Keep your head. She's teasing.* He replied, "Well, that's a nice compliment, I hope." Her smile and gaze lingered. *Uh, oh. I wonder where this is going.* He almost shivered, but managed to relax after that and their conversation flowed easily.

She asked, "Why do you play football?"

He laughed. "Oh, there are a couple of good reasons. Let's see. The money is good, that's for sure. And the game suits me. I have always loved playing."

"I know you love it." She closed her eyes, leaned back on the headrest and said, "Let me see if I can quote: 'Ed Conklin, selected All-Pro for the fourth straight year. He is projected to become the highest paid lineman in football,' She paused and looked over at him. '*And* the most valuable player in the league. *And* Conklin's agent is asking for a three year, no-trade sixty million dollar no-cut contract negotiation. *And* Conklin will become the highest paid defensive lineman in football history, ever.' She looked over and said, "How am I doing?"

He smiled and nodded appreciatively. "I'm impressed. Do I have any secrets?"

Amy leaned closer and whispered, "Just one. Who was the smashing little blonde at the concert?" She smiled playfully to temper his reaction.

He didn't mind and laughed good-naturedly. "Who? Oh, yeah. That was Gloria. She is a good friend from back home.

I have known her since first grade. Gloria lives and works here in Boston now." He looked over and smiled. "You sure upset her entire day. I can tell you that without a doubt."

Amy straightened, momentarily unsettled by the reveal. "Oh? That's an odd thing to say. Did I do something to upset her?"

"No. Well, nothing other than being who you are and what you look like." He glanced over and grinned. "I'm pretty sure Gloria has you marked down as a complication."

Amy protested, "What! Why would you say that? I don't even know her! Ed, did she actually say that?"

He laughed again. "No, she didn't have to. I know Gloria pretty well. We have been friends forever. She also knows me well enough to be a good judge of how I react to other women."

"Meaning?"

"Meaning? Well, I suspect she knew right then that I would want something like this to happen with you."

"Really? Are you two...? Is she...?" She motioned with a rolling gesture of her hand for him to complete the statement.

"No. Well, sort of, sometimes. Depends on.... As I said, Gloria and I go back a ways. Hometown, school, always have been and still are good friends. All that."

Not exactly the answer Amy hoped for; not quite candid; not altogether secretive.

What did I expect, a monk? He could probably have any available woman in Boston. But sort of sometimes?

She asked, "Do you have anyone special?" She couldn't help it. The question seemed reasonable.

"No, but I am sure going to start working on it." He glanced at her and smiled.

Amy understood that he had slyly skirted the question, leading her to ponder what he meant.

Working on it?

She didn't know him well enough to decipher the message, if any. At least her questions about his personal life hadn't bothered him. He seemed to enjoy the exchange. She was well aware that he hadn't asked about her personal life. They ate at a posh restaurant near the Commons. Amy managed to suspend her curiosity about his private life during the remainder of the evening and they exchanged the usual questions of a normal first date throughout the meal. "How did you know where I live?" she asked.

"I might have googled you. Does that bother you?"

Another answer-a-question-with-a-question answer. "No, but humor me. How?"

"You know a lot about me. I didn't ask how you found out." He had used the internet and paid fifteen dollars to get her phone number and address.

Amy considered the answer as yet another non-answer. She decided to change the subject before he asked about her life. "I know you went to Penn State, Ed. What was your major subject?"

"Engineering. Just plain old basic engineering."

"That must have been demanding, what with football."

"It was. I loved it, though. Stayed busy."

"Are you planning to use engineering after football?"

"Maybe. Not sure of that."

"Any interesting minors?"

"Math, of course. Ah, and you may find this somewhat interesting. I also have a minor in creative writing. Took all my electives there."

"Creative writing? That is interesting. Why?"

"Goes along with interest in books, I guess. I have always loved to read, and I occasionally write."

"Write what?"

"Essays. Some short stories. I have a few poems."

"Please don't take this wrong, but I don't associate poetry and football. I find that very interesting."

"Of course you're right. Not too many players involved with poetry. I dabble."

"I would love to hear…. Sorry. That may be a wee bit

premature."

"I hope we will have time to discuss it some more."

"Great. Now, tell me, what are you planning to do now that the football season is finished?"

"I'm going to complete a Masters degree this winter and spend some time at home with my mother."

"Oh? What degree?"

"Business Administration and Accounting." He held up a finger. "Ah! And you just might be interested in this: I was on the way to class the evening of your accident."

His reference to the wreck provided additional meaning to the evening for Amy. "So, then I guess you can now say that you and I *also* go back a ways, Ed. What do you plan to do after football? I mean after you quit playing."

"I have a couple of options. I could coach. The general manager has asked me to stay on as a line coach, and I have my heart set on a construction company back home. That's the reason for the business Masters. Well, that and it looks like I should probably learn how to handle money as I am in the market to make quite a bit. Anyway, I'll probably go back home and forget about football."

"Oh." The surprising feeling of impending loss almost startled Amy. Her brow furrowed. "When do you plan to stop playing?"

"Well, if I get the contract the team is promising, I plan to stay three years. I have always planned to retire from football at thirty-one, if I'm lucky enough to last. Three more years, maybe. If I don't get the contract, I might quit at the end of this season."

"Thirty-one? That's seems awfully young."

He chuckled. "Not in Pro ball. Most football players past thirty are ancient, believe me. Too many injuries."

Her concern deepened. "Have you been hurt?"

"Sure. Nothing permanent. Just the normal aches and pains. I'm still healthy enough."

She found his nonchalance disturbing and frowned. "Why

would you take a chance with your health? Oh, never mind. I know. Money."

"I know it's a risk," he said. "But football has been good to me. So it's a gamble I am willing to take."

She turned away. "I don't understand why anyone would risk disability." She didn't attempt to hide disapproval.

"Okay, let me explain. My dad is in a hospital as we speak, dying from Black Lung disease. My uncle and grandfather were also miners, and they both died from the disease. Without football, I would probably be working in the mines and be just another Black Lung candidate. So you see, football has been good to me and I am grateful."

"I'm sorry to hear about your father. Is football the reason you are involved with so many voluntary civic functions?" She quickly explained, "It's hard to miss you on television, Ed. You are on every channel promoting some community event. Your picture is on taxis and busses. You are on billboards. You are everywhere. I see you on something every day."

"You do know everything don't you. Yes, and that is also because I owe football so much. I enjoy the opportunity to help and I like being involved in community affairs. Keeps me busy."

She didn't invite him in when they arrived at her apartment and he didn't try to kiss her. Ed stepped back and said, "I enjoyed the evening with you, Amy. I want to call again. Soon."

She smiled and nodded. "I would like that. Call me."

*****

They both parted feeling good about the evening. He called before practice the next day and arranged dinner at another quiet restaurant in two days. Amy wore a red dress, a variant of Audrey Hepburn's little black dress in *BREAKFAST AT TIFFANYS,* and a matching jacket for the date. The ensemble changed not only Ed's first impression of her, but also improved the scenery and elevated his expectations. He whistled appreciatively. Amy's smile revealed satisfaction that he noticed. She expected him to notice and would have been disappointed if he hadn't.

Ed couldn't help surveying the view as he removed her jacket at the restaurant. The dress was sleeveless with thin straps straining over her shoulders, laboring to support a plunging neckline that did very little to conceal what, much to his satisfaction, appeared to be considerably more to cover up than he imagined. She had worn nothing in his presence up to that time to emphasize feminine attributes.

She is stunning!

Ed suffered through the evening, trying not to make a fool of himself by staring.

Amy laughed and smiled easily, much more at ease than their first date, touching his hand occasionally. The contact conveyed encouragement, but her smile furnished all the information Ed needed. The revealing dress, her easy openness, everything combined to create an aura of assurance. She had been more than interesting to him before, perhaps even fascinating, but the woman Ed encountered now completely captivated him. She did nothing that led him to imagine she was eminently available, but sensuality literally oozed from her eyes and mouth, and her body language added to the perception. Ed didn't think she was pretending or teasing. She seemed natural and genuinely at ease. Amy didn't say or do anything flagrantly suggestive, but her appearance and behavior affected him erotically: she savored food with murmurs of delight, closed her eyes and relished the wine's fragrance. She literally radiated sexuality.

Ed felt wonderfully energized, but above all, happier than he could remember. Amy smiled and laughed throughout the evening, at least until he asked if she had seen him that day at the mall.

She stopped smiling and sat back, her face the picture of

concern, suddenly wary. "Why do you ask?"

He felt as though their relationship was suddenly at risk, hanging in the balance, that he could spoil everything with one bad move. "Amy, I hope you don't misinterpret what I am about to say–I don't intend it as a come-on line–but something happened to me the day I saw you at the mall. It's.... I really can't explain it." He gestured helplessly.

Amy's hand betrayed her feelings by moving to cover the exposed sweep of her neckline–not as a defense against something unwelcome, rather the instinctive act of a woman surprised. She dropped her hand and said, "Really? What do you think happened?" She regained composure and gazed directly into his eyes.

He thought she might be teasing and measured his answer carefully. "I'm not deliberately being mysterious, Amy, I'm just inept. It's hard to...." He cleared his throat and tried again. "Okay, let me give you a.... I won't be able to explain it that well, Amy, but something compelled me to look up just before I saw you at the mall. I know this may sound fanciful, but I somehow sensed that you were there before I looked up. I did." He cringed, thinking she would surely ridicule the confession. "Okay, I know that sounds ridiculous." He held his hands up, looking sheepish. "It happened though. I'm not kidding. I knew you were there before I saw you."

"Good heavens! You can't be...." She covered her mouth and turned away.

He sat back, distressed. "Well, I thought it would probably sound ridiculous. I shouldn't have mentioned it." He dropped his gaze, wondering if anything at all happened at the mall, if it might have been nothing more than a coincidence or his imagination. He felt foolish.

Her eyes were waiting when he looked up again, wide with delight and excitement. She recognized his embarrassment. "No, Ed. Oh, no! That's not what I meant. I meant the same thing happened to me! And that's not all. I cannot tell you how many times I open the newspaper and see your picture or your name, or turn the television on just in time to see you at an interview, or hear someone talking about you on the radio. A week ago you were no part of my life, and now...."

Her positive response couldn't have surprised him more. "Are you making fun of me?"

"No! No, Ed! It happens all the time. I am not imagining. I suppose I could be willing it to happen and I have thought perhaps I'm just having fanciful notions. But, no, Ed, I'm sure that's what happened to me at the mall as well. It was real. I don't know how or why, but it happened. Her eyes were gleaming.

He covered her hand with his, still not quite sure.

She said, "Isn't this all so strange?" Her brow furrowed in a puzzled frown. "Do you suppose something.... Am I just being silly, Ed?"

He pulled her hand to his lips and said, "I don't know what to think, but I will tell you this much: It sure has my attention. It's like we are on an exclusive frequency. I can also tell you that this is all very pleasant to think about. Makes me happy."

"I hope you aren't joking, Ed."

"Nope. Do you believe in ESP?" He was still surprised that she hadn't laughed at him.

"No, and that makes what happens so extraordinary. Anyway it is to me."

His eyes held her captive. He kissed her hand again and said, "Well, something has definitely happened to me, Amy, and I hope it isn't just wishful thinking. I hope there really is such a thing as a special frequency between two people." He hesitated and then added, "And I also hope you don't think I am out of my mind."

Her smile erased his doubts. "No, not in the least. This is all so fascinating to me, Ed."

He breathed a sigh of relief. "In that case, I want to say something pretty personal. Shall I?"

She leaned forward eagerly. "By all means."

"You are the most beautiful woman I have ever seen, and

that is an absolute fact."

All previous tensions between them dissolved.

"And you, sir, are a most agreeable companion. Thank you." She smiled openly, no longer secretly pleased.

"I mean it, Amy. I can't stop looking at you. Does that annoy you?"

They leaned across the table to hold hands, gazing intently into each other's eyes, searching for answers more meaningful than words. The message in her eyes suggested more than he hoped for. "Let's get out of here," he said, holding her fingertips to his lips.

She pretended to pout. "Ed? I'm not ready for this to end."

"Me either, but let's go someplace more private."

"My place?" she asked.

He looked surprised. He had been thinking about a park, or sitting in the car. "Well, sure, if you.... Sure. That sounds good to me. My place is usually trashed."

She sat quietly next to him on the way, occupied with thoughts of what might happen next.

He turned the ignition off in front of her apartment and sat perfectly still before facing her, searching her eyes, discovering a vulnerability that disengaged his intent to pursue what he had taken as encouragement on her part. She seemed to be thinking, then smiled and the moment of indecision, if that's what it was, passed. The invitation of her mouth, the lure of her smile, would not have escaped the most naive adolescent.

He pulled her close. "Are you going to be terribly upset if I kiss you?"

She whispered, "Probably. But I won't sleep one way or the other. Please do."

Ed kissed her lightly on the mouth. Her lips didn't part. He separated, somewhat uneasy. "Amy, I–"

"Ed, just hold me for a few moments."

They embraced comfortably, remaining close until Amy leaned back in his arms to look into his eyes. She initiated the next kiss, this time without indifference, this time consciously sending a clear and compelling signal. Her lips parted and melted beneath his as he pressed for more. They both took deep breaths after he pushed away to look for distinct signals of her emotions. She leaned away, her head resting on the seat-back, eyes closed, savoring the moment. "Mercy!" she exclaimed, fanning her face with both hands. "My heart is running away."

"Mine too. Let's go for a walk."

"A very good idea."

They walked slowly, lost in private thoughts. Several moments later she stopped and looked into his eyes with a questioning look, and then said, "Play it again, Ed."

He took her in his arms and kissed her, a lengthy, intense kiss.

She cuddled to him. "Again. More please."

He complied willingly. They broke apart and walked slowly around the block, his arm around her waist, bodies brushing together, gently at first and then with more familiarity. They walked until the yearning to touch demanded satisfaction and stopped in the shadows to embrace. Ed slipped his hands beneath her jacket to get closer. He was content with the familiarity.

Amy wasn't.

She wanted to explore the pleasant softness of his mouth again, to savor every sensation of the new relationship. She initiated the next kiss. Ed soon took control and she eagerly surrendered to his rising aggressiveness. His mouth was deliciously warm and their lips fit together perfectly. She hadn't enjoyed kissing so much in–ever. The hungry inquiry progressed by stages to demanding, exploring kisses. The urgency to possess consumed her. She locked her arms around his neck and elevated on her toes to get closer. "Let's go back, Ed." She was breathless again, heart pounding, too stimulated to think clearly.

They stopped again on the way to her apartment to enjoy

the wonderful new intimacy. The yearning for familiarity didn't diminish once inside. Ed kissed and caressed until Amy pulled away, bowed her head, covered her face with both hands, and whispered huskily, "Let's stop Ed. This is too fast. I'm sorry."

"I don't want to let you go. Not now."

Without a sign of modesty, she began inspecting him from head to foot. Ed didn't hesitate. He stepped forward, removed her jacket and dropped it on the couch without permitting his eyes to drift from her body.

"What are you thinking, Ed?"

He smiled mischievously. "I think you are perfect, and I think.... I think this is a poor time to think."

She edged back, unconsciously sheltering her neckline with a hand. "Ed, I wouldn't stop this for anything, but I need some time to think."

After studying her face, Ed detected more doubt than he wanted to deal with. *Time to think with your brain, Conklin. She isn't ready.* "You don't need to say anything, Amy. I am pretty sure we are going to have plenty of time. I will happily take a raincheck." He watched the tension drain from her face.

"Thank you. There is so much I need to.... Can you understand?" She hoped he wouldn't think she had been teasing. She felt like a teenager for letting things get out of control.

"I do understand. Please don't worry about it."

Her heart ached when she looked at him. She groaned miserably and then stepped right back into his arms, crushing against him. She felt the pressure of his fingers unfastening the buttons on the back of her dress, and then his hand slide down the naked small of her back. His mouth held her captive. She couldn't resist. The feeling of his hands on her hips heightened the need to press against him. As his fingers moved up her waist toward her breasts, Amy's breath caught and she stopped breathing. Her heart accelerated wildly. She did nothing to stop him. Ed hesitated after his lips traced the contour of her neck downward to encounter the preliminary rise of her breasts. He kissed both sides of the exposed cleavage and then retraced the path up the curve of her neck to kiss her lightly on the moth, and then separated and stepped back.

"I'm going to get out of here," he announced. "When can I see you again?"

She was completely bewildered, holding the unfastened dress over her breasts. "Ed? What are.... I don't...." She couldn't think.

"Amy, I'm not strong enough to go on like this. And you were right–this is too fast. So I'm going home to take a long cold shower. I expect we both should take some time to think."

"I can't see you tomorrow," she said, eyes closed, concentrating on what needed to be said before he walked out.

He stopped at the door. "Thursday then?"

"Yes, please." They kissed briefly, without hands.

He gazed at her intently. "I don't want anything to go wrong, Amy. Just so you know, there is nothing I would rather do than...." He gestured helplessly. "Well, you know. I don't want to spoil anything. Thursday?"

"Yes, Thursday." She closed the door slowly, let her dress slip over her shoulders and fall to the floor, then hugged herself and whirled across the floor smiling happily.

Amy visited two people before she went to work the next day. First, a scheduled visit to Doctor Hendrick's office ended her medical appointments following the wreck.

After a complete physical examination, the doctor said, "You are very lucky, Miss Roman. There are no signs of after-effects. You are extremely fortunate."

She walked from the doctor's office to the Medical office of Phineas Sprague III, a debonair, tall, thin man balding beneath a brave toupee that looked exactly like a toupee.

Phineas was a dapper, fastidious man with impeccable manners, and an old and trusted friend.

After a short conversation, she handed her medical papers to him and asked for a favor. His questions quickly drifted to Amy's personal life.

"Now Phineas, you can speculate all you like, but I will not share my private life with you."

He asked about the about the possibility of a new man in her life. "I haven't seen much of you lately, Amy. Are you slipping around on me?"

She smiled wryly, considering the comments Phineas would undoubtedly make if he knew that she was, in fact, considering the possibility of a romantic relationship with a professional football player. Phineas was a good friend, a country club acquaintance who had periodically tested the waters himself, asking for dates, flirting, and always openly available.

"I see," he said, somewhat miffed by her coyness. "Well, I will have the nurse insert the IUD and have the paperwork you asked for in ten minutes. I am jealous Amy, but I wish you good luck." Later, papers in hand, he touched her elbow as she turned to leave and said, "I don't suppose I need to tell you to be careful."

"I can handle this, Phineas. Thank you."

Amy felt wonderful. She strolled slowly back to the gallery, noticing little things she normally wouldn't have seen; a crippled man feeding a crippled pigeon; the intensely blue sky, and how wonderful the autumn air felt. Afterward, she couldn't remember walking the entire distance. She stopped at the flower shop across the street from her office.

*****

"Yo, Conklin! Hey, look, guys! Sweet little Eddy here has flowers. Aw, ain't that nice?" The assistant coach skipped through the locker room with a bouquet of flowers held high.

The players jeered and teased Ed mercilessly. He removed the envelope from the flowers and crammed it into his jock before anyone could snatch it away, then retreated to the practice field. Outside the tunnel on the sunlit field and safe from prying eyes, he removed the envelope. It wasn't some sappy greeting card from a groupie as he expected. The envelope contained a doctor's certificate describing Amy Roman's physical condition in the usual medical terms. Ed smiled joyfully as the entry at the bottom, conspicuously outlined in yellow magic marker, arrested his attention: NO CONTAGIOUS DISEASES.

Chapter Six

SURRENDER

E d's blood test results arrived in Amy's mail two days later, along with a humorous card. The playfulness of their relationship ended the moment he arrived at her door that evening. At first they were reserved and apprehensive, clearly conscious of the implied agreement their impulsive exchange of tests now seemed to suggest. The whimsical exchange practically sanctioned a sexual free-for-all, and they both knew it.

Amy had deliberated about canceling the dinner date, but didn't, and prepared the meal in a daze. Upon greeting him at the door, she sensed that the whole arrangement was sophomoric madness. She served a light dinner with the same wine he had ordered on their previous engagements. An air of suppressed tension suffocated their pathetic attempts at polite conversation and they floundered through the evening, picking at the food, thoughts and misgivings so deafening that they could barely hear each other. Amy gave up pretending to be composed, placed her knife and fork on the plate and admitted, "I'm not very hungry, Ed. Don't let me spoil dinner for you."

"I'm not hungry, either, and I should be starved." He folded his napkin and gazed at her sympathetically. "I think I know how you feel. This tension needs to stop. Okay, how do we get beyond it?"

"I don't know. I do know that I am sorry I started it. All my fault, Ed. And now I'm too nervous to think." She smiled wistfully. "I hope you won't think too poorly of me for the way things are going. I have never been so jittery in my life. You can help by taking the lead, Ed. I'm talking too much."

"No chance I will ever think unkindly of you, Amy." He pushed back from the table.

"I really am sorry for the way this turned out," she said, unable to look at him.

"Okay. Let's start over by trusting that what we feel is nothing to worry about, just normal dating stress."

His understanding smile helped, but Amy needed more reassurance. "Then why am I so nervous?"

"I don't think it has much to do with sending flowers or unusual greeting cards, Amy. I expect we would feel the same way tonight with or without the funny paperwork. It sure seemed humorous at the time, though, didn't it? As it turns out, it might not have been such a good idea."

"I so regret sending that stupid piece of paper, Ed. That was impulsive."

"Okay, sure, maybe we did place some unnecessary pressure on ourselves, but I think we are probably just suffering the usual tensions of a new relationship. I am anxious because you are already very important to me and I don't want to spoil anything. We don't know enough about each other to predict how things will go, but I am confident that what we have started is going to last for a long time. I hope so. I expect what is happening and all the uncertainty is probably fairly typical for people as involved as we are. I believe we feel about the same way, so let's just try to move on. I wish.... I wish...."

She waited several seconds, and then said, "Please don't stop, Ed. What do you wish?"

"I know this is hopeful thinking, but I wish we could just drive up to Maine for some comfortable time away. Alone time. Time to discover each other. Some time and a private place to burn off the tension. If you can't sleep, or eat, or think clearly, then you need to know that I feel exactly the same. I don't know why this relationship seems so important so swiftly, but it is. I have known other women, even thought I was in love once, but no one has ever affected me the way you do, Amy. Never. I am going to explode if this tension doesn't diminish, and I am scared to death of doing something wrong."

"I'm sorry, Ed. I feel responsible."

He smiled. "You are, you know. I don't think there is a cure for what is happening to me, other than time with you. We need time together, and I mean right now. Being alone and without you is torment. I try to deaden the symptoms by running until I'm numb. That doesn't work. Nothing works, Amy. No matter how stressful this is, though, I don't want to miss a moment of it. If it's all the same to you, I would like to pick up where we were before things heated up the last time we were together and take it from there."

"You are sweet. Oh, I do wish we could go back and start all over. This is so awkward."

"We can," he announced, rising from the table to hold her chair. "Let me help with the dishes and then let's get out of here. A little air will be good for both of us. Some diversion."

They finished and abandoned the apartment. Several minutes later, after conversation became comfortable again, they settled on a park bench and skirted additional tension by discussing mundane topics. The colorless conversation eventually ebbed into silence and Amy unintentionally altered the mood by asking, "What are you thinking?"

Ed sighed, leaned back on the bench and said, "God, Amy, I don't know where to start. It's hard to know what to tell you. My thoughts wander constantly from what I should be thinking about, to worrying about what you are thinking. I can't get you out of my mind, but I'm really not trying very hard."

"I feel sorry for you, and responsible."

"No. Don't be." He turned to face her. "I know what I'm going to say to you now is too soon, Amy, and I realize that saying it probably won't ease the strain, but I need to say it. You ready?"

She took a deep breath, closed her eyes said, "Oh, Ed, I don't know. I am so nervous."

He touched her face and said, "Well, this should let the air out. Here goes everything." He cleared his throat and said, "Amy Roman, I thought you were just a dream that I have been waiting for all my life. This is what I know for sure: I am already desperately in love with you. I didn't think you would ever happen. Just a dream. I've never had the nerve to even hope for someone like you."

She covered his fingers with her hand and pressed them to her lips. "Oh, Ed, I am so relieved. I feel exactly the same and I have the same thoughts. I can't believe you are finally here and with me. It's wonderful to hear your words, but don't expect too much. I'm far from perfect."

After that exchange, their anxieties began to fade. Amy searched his eyes, looking for the source of excitement she had envisioned every moment during the past two sleepless nights. *Is this feeling really something special? Am I creating a castle in the sky? Do I want him this much? Can this be real?*

He didn't say anything but his eyes also searched hers for answers. Their eyes found comfort first, then their hands. Within moments they were kissing and the excitement and thrill Amy remembered clicked back into place. "Ed," she whispered, after pushing away to catch her breath. "I can't go on like this much longer."

"Me either.' He moved away. "So, now what?"

"Let's go back."

After the bolt lock snapped closed, she turned to face him, eyes wide, emotions exposed. His smile, his nearness, the smoldering look in his eyes, and the likelihood of what would probably happen next all sank in and she shuddered. *What am I doing?*

She leaned against the door for support, and then after a moment of confused thoughts, untied the ribbon and let her hair fall. More than her hair tumbled at that instant. Uncertainty, doubt and anxiety all fell away. Words would have been meaningless. Verbal communication was unnecessary. Everything happened instinctively after that–no dialogue required. Ed lifted the sweater over her head; Amy took his jacket; he unfastened her blouse; she removed his tie; he unbuttoned her skirt; she removed his shirt. In a matter of seconds they were standing before each other in nothing but underwear. Their previous smothering tensions disappeared along with the clothes.

Amy turned away so he could unsnap the brassiere. He didn't require prompting. Her skin chilled and tightened as the garment slipped away. He pulled her close and their bodies blended in warmth. Ed's fingers explored gently until she held his hands in place as they covered her breasts. She sighed and nestled her head into the hollow of his neck. Ed nuzzled beneath her ears until she could no longer endure the stimulation. She turned in his arms, pressing her breasts lightly against his chest and the preliminaries effectively ended. He picked her up effortlessly and a lingering kiss determined the course of succeeding events. Amy murmured something muted and pointed toward the bedroom, all without taking her mouth from his. Ed carried her to the bedroom.

"Put me down, Ed. Please."

He released her next to the bed. She stepped back deliberately to appraise his body. They had been so close, up to that moment, that she hadn't been able to see all of him. "I want to know if what I have imagined is real," she said, deliberately surveying his body. Her breathing caught and stopped. He wasn't fat and his muscles were not repulsive as she had feared. She breathed again after a sigh of relief. He was enormous, but his body was more refined than she imagined. He looked almost normal.

"Incredible," she whispered, unaware of having uttered the comment. Amy's previous encounters with men failed to prepare her for the immense man facing her. None of the boys in her youth compared, certainly not Carlo.

Poor Carlo.

Ed didn't move during her inspection, also exploring her. Amy's breathing faltered, then stopped as her eyes drifted lower. Some apprehensions about size had entered her thoughts, but she had disregarded the uneasiness as nothing more than adolescent imagination. But now, now with the towering man confronting her, and the reason for her previous concerns flagrantly obvious, she had reason for pause. The carefree spirit responsible for her daring during the preceding moments faltered. Never before had Amy suffered from juvenile indecision about anything, but this, this was different. He weighed two-hundred-and-seventy pounds, well over twice her size. *Oh, My God! This may be more than I....*

Ed sensed her misgivings and smiled reassuringly, beckoning with open arms. She stepped into the embrace without hesitation and the moment of doubt passed. His size and warmth enveloped her. She could feel his heart beating.

"You're trembling," he murmured.

"Am I?"

"I won't hurt you, Amy. I promise. Everything at your speed."

"I'm not afraid of you."

He threw the covers back, lifted and gently placed her on the bed.

"Let's don't hurry, Ed."

They lay quietly, holding hands, thinking, waiting for the

excitement to subside. An eternity seemed to pass before Ed propped himself on an elbow and began tracing the contours of her neck with his lips. Amy's apprehensions receded until he began caressing her waist and hips with his fingers. She tensed then, perceptibly, and Ed felt it. He didn't press for more familiarity until she quieted, and then began caressing again. Amy instinctively encouraged his developing aggressiveness by yielding without a sign of disapproval, then joined in the adventure by slipping her arms around his neck to draw him closer.

Her eyes were filled with excitement and her thoughts with anticipation. His soothing caresses thrilled her. Everything he did provoked even more stimulation and heightened her perception of pleasure and desire. Amy didn't try to control the parade of longings and hungers. She offered no resistance and couldn't have even if she wanted to. She didn't want to, spinning out of control in a racing whirlpool of excitement. She followed his hand with her eyes as it moved toward her breast. Her heart quickened and every sensory receptor in her body stirred. She didn't utter a sound, nor did she resist.

The dim light exaggerated the differences between them: her slender, olive-skinned complexion in contrast to his brawny fairness. He pulled the cover completely away. The clothes she had worn during their preceding meetings had done a remarkably effective job of hiding her figure, he thought. A silky-soft tone of Mediterranean tan heightened the beauty of her body, creating a blend of shadows accentuating each curve.

He stopped caressing and gazed. "You are perfect, Amy Roman. Perfect." Her breasts were not a complete departure from his expectations. He had imagined they would be pleasant to behold. They were unusually firm–rigid enough to retain their shape regardless of the position of her body. As his fingers drifted lightly over the delicate, satin softness of her skin, her breath drew in and held. He slowly traced the soft contours with his fingertips, allowing his touch to linger until she accepted the intimacy and began breathing naturally.

Her eyes looked like deep, crystalline pools, either spellbound or frightened. He brushed her lips softly with his. She responded eagerly enough to dismiss his worries. He touched her face and neck with his lips, and then her mouth. Amy murmured as the intensity of her hunger escalated toward abandon. She pressed into him and let the unquenchable longing route any pretense of reserve. Her hips stirred beneath him, instinctively straining to blend.

When he touched her breast with his mouth, Amy stopped breathing and closed her eyes. Her head rolled from side to side as he took the nipple. She pressed his head down to encourage more pressure. Musical whimpering appeals escaped as his hand drifted down. His fingers slipped beneath the elastic band. Her hand on his sanctioned the exploration. He hesitated.

"Do we need protection, Amy?"

"I took care of it. Please don't stop."

She sighed brokenly as his fingers continued slowly downward, then arched up to assist as he pushed the final obstruction away. She abandoned all control as Ed moved above and made no attempt to stop or delay consummation. Nothing mattered except to answer the craving. Afterward, content in his arms, she said, "I suppose that makes it official."

"What's that?"

"That was, to me, the initiation we needed. Now maybe all the tension and anxieties can unwind. Maybe."

He reacted by rolling on his side to assess her facial expression. "What? Was it that bad?"

She laughed and replied, "No, I can't imagine that anything on Earth could be more delightful. I didn't mean it that way. What I meant is, do you suppose we can behave normally now that the sense of urgency is past? No, Ed, it was perfect. I plan to keep you around."

"Great. I hope this can go on and on, Amy. I hope nothing

ever changes."

"Anyway, I think we may have managed to get by the suspense and nervousness."

"Agreed. If what is happening to me is as real as I think it is, I don't ever want to be without you, Amy. Not ever." He drove back to the stadium the next morning after more lovemaking and endless hours of intimate conversation. Ed knew enough about Amy Roman by then to know for certain that their relationship held the promise he had always dreamed of. The brisk pace of their developing affection pleased and surprised him. After three dates, a few brief meetings, and they were lovers. He cared more for her than he imagined he would ever care for anyone.

"Amy Roman," he said to himself, then shouted her name over and over: "Amy Roman! Amy Roman!" He believed that she could be the essential addition to his life that he had always dreamed of, but wouldn't allow thoughts to extend to something permanent.

A knock at his door early the next morning woke him. Sunday. Ed planned to sleep in, resting for the late afternoon All Star game.

"Well, hi, Amy. Come in. I didn't think I would see you until after the game." He noticed the overnight bag in her hand. "What's this? Is something wrong?"

"Yes. Yes there is. I cannot bear being away from you. Not for one moment."

They made love. Amy attended the game and rushed to him afterward to express her sorrow over his team's loss.

"It's not important. An All Star game is not serious football."

Her concern helped Ed overcome his usual inclination to brood after any defeat. He was always dispirited after a loss. They went to her apartment where he recovered nicely after making love until they couldn't.

"Poetry, Ed. I want to hear some of your poetry."

"I don't memorize much of it. I can give part of one I

wrote for you years ago."

She sat up and looked at him with a puzzled expression. "You didn't know me years ago."

"Yes, I did. I have known since high school that you would come into my life. I have been waiting for you. I have always known we would meet."

"I want to hear it."

"All right."

He seemed hesitant. She nodded and said, "Go ahead, Ed."

"Okay. Happiness."

"Is that the title?"

"Yes.

Happiness is loving a woman.
Nothing makes me happier,
disposed as I am biologically,
exposed as I am emotionally,
assembled as I am physically,
than the company of a woman."

He touched her face and said, "You make me happy Amy. You are happiness."

His father died the next morning.

Chapter Seven

CARLO

E d called Amy at work immediately after being notified of his father's death.

"I'm terribly sorry, Ed. How long will you be gone?"

"I don't know exactly, and probably won't know until things are stabilized at home. I'm going to miss you so much." He didn't ask her to attend the funeral.

That evening, Amy told Celia about Ed's father and expressed frustration. "I want to be there for him. I need to be there."

"I'm sure you do, and maybe it would make you feel good, but don't you think that is expecting too much of a brand-new relationship? You don't know him that well, and you don't know his family at all. Just think what it would look like if he shows up with a strange woman, Amy. They would wonder if your Eddy is just off on a holiday? Optics would be bad."

Celia, as always, placed the proper emphasis on common sense. Even so, Amy felt left out, desperately wanting–needing to be near him. Her memories were unforgettable and fresh.

Ed had packed and left town without delay. She hadn't heard from him for two days.

"I'm so frustrated, Celia. Why did this have to happen just when things were going so perfectly?"

Amy had not shared that much information about her new relationship. Celia's brow lifted alertly. "So perfectly? Amy, are you hiding something from me? What, and please be precise, in the hell is going on? What are you keeping secret?"

Amy looked away. "Nothing. I miss him. That's all."

Celia screwed her face into a clear declaration of disbelief. "You miss Him? You miss someone you hardly know? Really?"

Amy's chin lifted defiantly. "How well do you have to know someone to miss them?"

"Hmmmm. How very interesting." Celia studied Amy's face until she detected the hint of a tell-tale smile that revealed too much, a secretive little smirk, almost private, just not quite. "Well I'll be damned," she exclaimed. "You *are* hiding something! You little sneak!" Celia had noticed enough by then to support more snooping. "Okay, I know that look." She folded her arms and announced, "And I'm not moving until you tell me. So, out with it!" She tried to look hurt, tapping her fingers, stubbornly waiting for Amy to let go.

Amy had never been able to hide anything from Celia, not that she tried. "Oh, Celia. Three dates. Three dates with him and I am so far past anything I ever imagined. I have no defense against him. Truth is, I don't care. I would be embarrassed to tell you what has…. Well, never mind."

Celia didn't try to conceal her amazement. "My, God! I knew it the moment you walked in the door. I could read it on your face! Okay, what happened? Come on, Amy. You know you're going to tell me, and I want to know exactly what you are way more than hinting at. Have you gone off the deep end?"

Amy nodded gravely. " Perhaps. Maybe way too deep and way too fast, but…." After clearing her throat and patting her face briskly, she gathered nerve and said, "Don't you dare say anything, Celia. Just let me tell at my own speed. No interruption. No anything. Okay?" Celia nodded. "Now, I know this is going to sound premature to you." She sighed deeply and said, "But here it goes. Brace yourself. The fact is, I am so desperately in love with this guy." Celia's mouth fell open and she started to say something. Amy held up a cautioning hand. "No! You just sit there and listen! And, before you say something snotty, I am being entirely sincere here, Celia, so be gentle. Now, you see? So, yes, I miss him. Okay, your turn.""

Celia couldn't close her mouth. "My, God! How long has this…."

"Oh, Celia, not that long. Everything happened so fast, and I know that, so please don't scold." She clapped and smiled gleefully as the layer of moisture developing over her eyes threatened to overflow. "I can hardly tolerate a moment away from him. Everything in my life is on hold until I can be with him again. Isn't that crazy?"

Celia's normally expressive face still hadn't recovered from the shock. "You must be joking! What in the world has happened to you?"

Amy merrily admitted, "Ed Conklin happened. I think about him day and night, every waking moment. Just thinking about him makes me happy, Celia. Being with him makes me feel wonderful. I have never in my life been so happy. He is better than any dream I ever had."

Celia's mouth dropped open again and she collapsed into the chair. "Good grief. And a football player?" She frowned and stared at nothing for a moment. When her gaze shifted slowly back to Amy, her voice conveyed an ominous tone. "Have you told him about Carlo?"

Amy closed her eyes and grimaced, shaking her head

slowly. "Not yet. I will, and soon. Just let me have this moment, Celia." She bounced up and down in the chair like a little girl overcome by excitement. "Only three dates, Celia. Can you imagine? I haven't had time to think because nothing like this ever happened to me." Her smile faded. "And now I am going to lose him for a while. His father died yesterday and he went home to be with his mother."

Celia's dramatic powers of facial expression slowly returned. "Good heavens, girl! When are you ever going to come to your senses? I *am* happy for you, I guess. But I worry. Now you listen to me, Amy, and think hard about what I say. Carlo and a professional football player? That is a toxic mix that simply does not and cannot mix. Have you thought of that?" She stood and began pacing, fuming and mumbling to herself.

Amy suddenly brightened. "Last Wednesday. I came to my senses last Wednesday and called Carlo. I told him not to plan on me for anything when he gets out. I did, Celia!"

Celia slipped back into her chair immediately and smiled for the first time in minutes. "Well, all right! Now I'm beginning to appreciate this Conklin fellow. Good for you, girl. It's about time. How did Carlo take it?"

"How do you think? He had a Carlo fit, but that's nothing new, is it? I threatened to give an attorney the hospital records if he bothered me. Carlo understands the problems with that. He said he would forget about the agreement. And remember, Celia, I never once promised to marry him. That was all Carlo's idea–just something we talked about as kids."

Celia's mouth pursed sarcastically. "Yeah, right, like Carlo understands and is okay with it. Right. Did you by any chance tell Carlo about the football player?"

Amy's eyes narrowed. "His name is Ed Conklin, Celia! And no, I didn't mention Ed. Carlo is suspicious, though. You know how he is. Said he knows everything that goes on in my life. Again, what's new."

Celia covered her heart with both hands and pretended to

pout. "Oh, golly gee whiz, damn. Did the poor baby get a Dear John in prison?" She scowled. "Serves him right. You should have done it years ago." She reached across the table and patted Amy's hand. "I'm proud of you. It's about time you got on with your life. Carlo was never going to be good for you."

Amy sighed wistfully. "I think everyone knew a marriage with Carlo was never going to happen, not after he went to prison."

"I know, honey. I know." Celia patted Amy's hand. "Anyway, I'm glad it's over. You would have wasted your life on him. I'm proud of you." Her eyes narrowed. "You still have a problem though. You have to tell this Conklin guy about Carlo."

Amy moaned, "I know. Just not now. Not while he's away."

"Well, it better be soon and clean and fast. Your family name mixed with professional football is about as…. I swear, sometimes you are so clueless."

Amy stared. "I honestly didn't think anything serious would come of the relationship, let alone so fast. How could I possibly know?" She glared at Celia. "If you are going to be bitchy, I'm going home."

"Oh, no you're not! I'm not nearly through with you yet, old buddy, old long-time-I-have-no-secrets-from-you pal, old-Best-Friend-Forever."

Amy ignored her friend's phony wrath. "Oh, Celia. I hope this connection with Ed is as perfect as I think it is. You simply have to meet him."

"Thanks. I'll just watch well off shore through heavy lenses until you know he's for real."

"What do you mean by that?"

"Well, you said it first. Only three dates. Is he going to call again, Amy? Did you give the whole farm away after just three dates? Could it be possible that you were just a one-night-stand? Come on, Amy, face facts. You really *don't* know him that well. For all you know, he might never call again."

Amy straightened proudly. "It wasn't an overnight fling, Celia. I know him better than that. I do," she declared, not at all convinced. "You just wait and see."

*****

He called that evening.

"Hi, Beautiful. I hate to tell you this, but I'm going to be here longer than I thought. Ma isn't doing well. She has gone completely to pieces." His mother called in the background and he rang off quickly.

Ed called again two days later, hours after his mother tried to commit suicide. Amy experienced a crushing sense of disappointment. She felt the budding relationship slipping away. After stifling her frustration, she said, "I'm sorry, Ed. Is there anything I can do to help?"

"Thanks, but no there isn't. I want to see you in the worst way, Amy. I just can't leave her alone. Not now."

"I know. Family first. I can understand, Ed. If I can do anything...."

"Oh, yeah. There is one thing. I hate to ask, but everyone on the team has already left town after the season."

"What? I'll do anything I can to help."

"Thanks. You may reconsider if you like. I left a dog penned in my back yard."

"A dog? I didn't know you had a dog."

"I don't. Well, not really. Just a mutt someone dumped at the stadium. I've been feeding him. I only left enough food and water to last a few days."

"What do you want me to do?"

"When you have time, drive out to my place and turn him out. He knows how to make it on his own. Do you mind?"

"Just turn him out? That sounds so heartless. That's not like you, Ed."

"He's just a mongrel, Amy. Being free is better than starving to death locked up in my yard. Maybe his owner will find him."

She found the dog the next day, an ugly, deliriously happy mutt that groveled pathetically while peeing all over her shoes. She opened the gate and breathed a sigh of relief as he sped down the street. The dog returned before she could get in the car. An hour later, after trying everything she could think of to discourage the excited animal's frantic attentions, she sat on the curb, frustrated beyond endurance, and begged, "Please, you jerk, just go away and leave me alone. Get! Go!" The dog sat at her feet, smiling, wagging his tail furiously. Amy was absolutely certain he could understand her words and that he really was smiling.

He rode in the right hand seat all the way to her apartment, head hanging out the window, tongue flapping in the wind, slobbering a torrent down the side of her car. Amy didn't tell Ed about the dog, other than to say, "I took care of him." Less than a week later, she eagerly looked forward to the drooling affections of the dog at the end of each day. She named him Harpy, after the team–The Harpoons.

*****

Ed's mother's condition deteriorated and he didn't return to Boston that month. Before he finally returned, Amy's business life surfaced to interfere with the dormant relationship. Leitha assigned the gallery's annual buying trip to Europe to her. Three weeks in Europe and a week coming and going. Everything she ever dreamed of.

Just not now!

Leitha had promised the trip for two years. Amy knew the opportunity was too important to miss. She had to go and needed to go for the professional experience. Such momentous responsibility and trust would solidify her status in the art community, and she *had* been looking forward to it for so long. Before Ed. Now she felt trapped, desperately needing to go on the buying trip for the sake of her career, but detesting the idea of being that far away from Ed. He encouraged her to go and Leitha made some wry comments about taking care of business before pleasure to add pressure to the predicament. She decided to go.

*****

Celia objected vigorously before finally assenting to Amy's pleading requests to care for Harpy while she traveled for a month, or at least until Ed returned.

"What in God's name am I going to do with a dog for a month? Why don't you put him in a kennel?"

"I just can't do that, Celia. He's such a good dog. He won't be any trouble. Please?"

"Honestly!"

Amy detected the opening in Celia's defense and quickly forged an arrangement. She told Ed about the trip to Europe the next time he called.

"A month?" He sounded sincerely disheartened. "Damn! I didn't know it would be that long. That means I won't see you until…. A month?"

"I know. How is your mother?"

"Not good. We are going to place her in a home Sunday. The doctors aren't pleased with her progress. Amy, I think I could make it to Boston early next week for a day or two. Is there any chance you…." His voice sounded so intense, imploring, almost begging.

She nearly burst into tears. "Sorry. I have to leave the day after tomorrow, Ed. I'm going to miss you so much. This is terrible." She took a deep breath and prepared for the inevitable moment of truth. "Ed, I have something to tell you; something that I should have told you before; something I dread to mention."

"Sounds sinister."

"I haven't been completely open with you, Ed. Please don't hang up until I finish. I have so much to say. Please don't hang up, okay? I'm begging you."

A long silence followed. "Okay, I guess. So, whatever it is, let me have it."

"I didn't want to tell you this over the phone, but so many things have happened–your father and mother, and now this buying trip."

"Are you going to tell me or not?"

She took a deep breath and whispered, "I have, in a way, been involved with another man for the past several years. Actually since I was thirteen."

He didn't say anything. She could hear him breathing softly, but he didn't say anything. "Ed?"

"Yeah, I heard you. This is a joke, right? Since thirteen?" He laughed nervously. "Hey, I know. This is one of those Italian family marriage deals, right?" He laughed again.

"I wish this was a joke. I didn't know things between us would happen so fast, Ed. I know I should have mentioned him before. I'm so sorry." When he didn't speak for several moments, she added, "Don't hate me, Ed. There is much to explain."

After another long pause he said, "I feel sick, Amy. I really need to get off."

"No! Please don't. Please. I couldn't stand it if you don't let me finish. Please, Ed?"

"I don't think so. I really am sick to my stomach, Amy. I need to vomit."

"If you care for me at all, please don't hang up."

His voice was faint, almost inaudible. "Okay. First I need some water and sit down."

She told him about Carlo, how she loved him as a child, how special their relationship had been as teenagers. "He is my stepfather's sister's child. Carlo came to live with us after his parents were killed when we were both thirteen. We grew up together. When I came home after graduating from the university, I thought we might someday be.... Well, I can't explain that now, Ed. My parents were thrilled when they learned we were seeing each other regularly. It all seemed so natural."

"What happened to Camelot?"

"The usual things: other women, alcohol and drugs, his business, abuse, the penitentiary."

"Penitentiary? Abuse? What in the–"

"Yes, Carlo is in the penitentiary. Has been for three years. He is awaiting release soon. Any day."

"What about the abuse?

"It began with a slap when he came to my place drunk one night after I came home from college. He didn't have any respect for me after that–just someone else to mistreat. He was so involved with his work. The pressure on him kept building and he took it out on me."

"Why didn't you leave?"

"Oh, we never lived together, Ed. Not that kind of relationship."

"Okay. How much abuse?"

"Too much. He hit me more than once, Ed. I'd rather not go into that now."

"No! Please, Amy. Don't stop. Help me. I want to understand. Tell me!"

"It's not pretty, Ed. As I said, Carlo came over late one night, drunk. I protested and tried to throw him out. He beat me. He did it again months later. Maybe three times in all."

"Three times? Damn, Amy! Why would you stick around for that?"

"I know I shouldn't have. I thought I could help him. I have always been able to help. And I thought my stepfather would have gone into a rage and done something terrible to Carlo. So I didn't tell. It's hard to explain, and maybe I can't. Anyway, Carlo's rage kept getting worse. When I gave his pledge ring back–it was never an engagement ring, Ed. Just kid stuff. He went into an uncontrollable rage and I ended up with a broken jaw. I had to stay in the hospital a month that time."

"Wait a minute. *That* time? Were you in the hospital more than once from beatings?"

She laughed as though the comment amused her. "Yes, Ed, more than once. Mostly just for bruises and abrasions."

"I can't understand why you…. Help me understand this, Amy."

"None of the reasons could possibly justify the fact that I fantasized that everything would turn out okay. Being Catholic probably had something to do with it. Family pressure and our youth together. What my stepfather would do to him. I really can't explain it." She paused and then said, "I really believe Carlo hates women."

Ed's brow furrowed. The comment seemed completely out of context. "Explain, please."

"Carlo's mother made him nurse until he was almost ten. I think he hates all women for that."

"Ten? That's unbelievable. Still nursing at ten?"

"I know. It was bizarre. True nonetheless. Maybe some Old country practice. Something like that. He always smelled like a nursing baby and the other kids ridiculed him. Carlo was skinny and sang soprano in the church choir until he came to live with us. His mother coddled and protected him and his father despised him for being such a sissy. He needed me. I was the only one who didn't make fun of him. The other kids treated him terribly. He has certainly changed, though. My stepfather took Carlo into his business while I was away at school. When I returned from Europe, Carlo was an altered man. He was sarcastic, deceitful and cruel. Even the men working for my stepfather were afraid of him, and not because of his size but because he was so violent. It all seems like a nightmare now."

"When did you get away from him?"

"Oh, I never lived with him, Ed. I sent the ring back just before he went to prison. So, a little over three years ago."

"Why, Amy? How could you stick around after abuse?"

"Same answers: Catholic, family, pride, deserting in his time of need. Anyway, he posed no problems for me in prison. Well, other than I know now that he has me watched."

"Has? You mean even now?"

"Yes. I know for a fact that he keeps track of me."

"I need to know everything, Amy. This could blow up and have an effect on my career."

"Okay, but this will take some time." She paused, collecting her thoughts. "Carlo changed after I went off to Europe and Yale. I was away most of the time for almost six years. I believe my stepfather changed him. He kept Carlo by his side day and night. He bragged about teaching him to be a man. That's a laugh. Carlo can only pretend to be a man. He doesn't know how to be a man–just a bully. But Carlo and I were very close before I left home for school. After that we only saw each other a week or two during my vacations. He was changed; so different; so involved with work. Carlo loves power and my stepfather furnished power beyond anything you can imagine, Ed. Carlo had grown men working for him when he was only seventeen."

"I want to know more about that, but first, you mentioned women. Tell me about Carlo's women."

She laughed bitterly. "Oh, he knew all about women. Carlo had plenty of experience. I don't want to talk about that. Let's just say Carlo had some weird ideas."

"I want to know."

She hesitated. "No, Ed. It's not that important."

"I need to know, Amy."

"Okay, but not everything. For one thing, he didn't like my breasts. He made me hide my breasts. I have his mother to thank for that. He told me he hated women who looked like cows. I had to wear skintight tank tops around him. Women's breasts are ugly to Carlo. I couldn't make cooing noises...like a mother to a child. I couldn't wear anything low-cut or revealing."

"Sounds like he had some serious hang-ups."

"Oh, he does, and it got worse with time. I wondered sometimes if he might not be gay. He isn't. He just hates women."

"Including you?"

"No, just my body. We had some good times when sex was not involved. When he tries, Carlo can be very nice."

"But you said he consorted with other women?"

"Yes. He always had some bimbo to kick around, but you can be sure the poor thing didn't have a sign of breasts. They were all skinny little things."

She talked on and on. "He went to prison for tax evasion and some lesser counts of fraud and gambling. A ten year sentence eventually reduced to three."

Amy told Ed about her last night with Carlo, the night his family and friends gathered for a raucous celebration before he surrendered to federal marshals.

"I remember standing on the patio berating him, screaming at him: 'This isn't a victory, Carlo! What victory? You're going to prison for years!'"

"Did he hit you in front of everyone?"

"No. He just poured beer on me and said, 'You broads are all alike. You don't know anything. Prison to me is nothing. Just business. That's the way things are. I'll be out before you know it.' And then he poured another drink on me and everyone laughed.

"The trial dragged on for weeks after Carlo turned himself in to the federal marshals. He received a ten year sentence, but everyone believed his lawyers would beat the system. I don't understand why, but the major charges against him were dropped and his sentence reduced to three. Carlo wouldn't talk to me about his business, but the news media hinted at bribery and extortion.

"Our relationship was always on thin ice because of Carlo's business. I soon learned not to ask for specifics about his occupation, or where he went, or what he did. I knew enough by the time he came to trial to know that Carlo deserved to go to prison for much more than the charges against him. I suppose his narrow escape from a much longer prison sentence provided good reason for that last-night celebration.

"The men gathered around him like a hero. 'You'll be out in three, Carlo. Just part of doing business,' they said. 'Three years, tops,' his lawyer assured. 'I'll start the appeals process tomorrow. We're going to take care of you, Carlo. Don't worry.'

"Carlo was so confident. He said, 'That's what you get paid for.' He pinched the lawyer's cheek and slapped him playfully. 'They couldn't touch me,' he boasted. 'Dumb bunch of hicks.'

"I watched from the distance as Carlo went off to serve time in prison, much the same way other young men go off to war. The family kissed and hugged him and his friends gathered to clap him on the back.

"I thought Carlo would have a difficult time believing he'd won anything after the prison doors slammed behind him, even though they sent him to a prison for influential and affluent prisoners. The inmates call it The Country Club."

"How did he take it, Amy? Prison time?"

"I really don't know. I never visited him in prison, much to the dismay of my mother and stepfather. 'You owe him that much,' they told me. 'It isn't right to abandon him now. Not when he needs you most. How do you think it will look to others?' I told her, "How do you suppose the bruises on my face looked to others? What did the others think when I couldn't appear in public for weeks when my eyes were swollen and purple? She said, 'He was just a boy then. Things will be better this time. Forgive and forget.' No, Mother. I will never forget. How could I ever forget the last time?"

"What about the last time, Amy?" Ed was sitting on the floor, his back against the wall, cradling his head with one hand and the phone the other.

"Carlo flew into a jealous rage and beat me unconscious. I was in a comma for several hours and spent a month in the hospital with a broken jaw. All because Carlo thought I was too friendly with a grocery clerk."

"I can't believe it, Amy. He must be crazy."

"I think he is at times. The grocery clerk was just a fourteen-year-old boy, Ed. A skinny little boy. I protested and Carlo blew up. 'I've been watching you!' he yelled. 'I see how you look at other men! I know what you're thinking!' "He said things like that often."

"Damn, Amy. That's crazy. Didn't your stepfather know?"

"Maybe. Probably. But nothing changed. Anyway, I have paid dearly for being pretty, and around a man I probably knew was unstable, and for listening to my parents, and for being agreeable and feeling responsible. I have nightmares about Carlo even though he's in prison. I wrote him in prison once, Ed, to remove any thought of an engagement, only to regret the commotion it caused. Mother cried, the priest badgered me for weeks and my stepfather brought all of his considerable influence to bear. I held out long enough to win some freedoms. I gained the right to work, to have a place of my own and some reasonable latitude concerning independence. The family wanted to control my life, as always. Carlo's parole is imminent, Ed, and that hovers over me like a nightmare. I know my problems will begin all over again when he gets out. I am terrified, and right now I'm scared to death about us, Ed."

"What are you going to do? You can't go back."

"I know. I have had three fairly happy, uncomplicated years. Years of self-analysis, measuring my life against the lives of people I consider to be normal. People like Celia." She related much more to Ed. The call lasted two hours.

"Okay, I guess I'm up to date," he said. "Wait. Why didn't you tell me?"

"I wanted to have you in my life so much, and things happened so fast between us. I didn't have some devious design, Ed. Honestly. I never planned to mislead you. I didn't know I would care so much for you, and we haven't had the time together. It all happened so fast."

"Why did you decide to tell me now?"

"I don't want to lose you. I couldn't stand losing you, Ed, and now I may have ruined everything." Tears were streaming from her eyes.

"You haven't ruined anything. But didn't you think I had a right to know?"

"I know you did and do. But, Ed, I honestly didn't know that I would feel the way I do about you. I wish we could go back and do it over. I am so sorry."

"What do you mean? Was I just a fling or something?"

"Maybe, in the beginning. You were very interesting to me. Like no man I have ever known. You were my first intimate experience with a man other than Carlo, Ed. I'm not sure of anything now except I don't want to lose you and I'm truly sorry for letting things go this far before I told you about him."

"I never thought of you as a fling, Amy. Not once."

"That isn't fair. Those were never overt thoughts on my part. I was interested in you. I wanted to know you."

"Look, Amy, this is a lot to digest all at once. I'll call back later."

After the call ended, she crumpled to the floor and wept pitifully.

He called about midnight and they talked until nearly two in the morning. The tone of his voice scared her. He told her he that felt used and betrayed.

She left for Europe the next day, a day early, just to get away from the torment of waiting for another phone call. The buying trip sapped her time and energy, just not enough to suppress the pain of losing Ed. She found a letter from him upon return from the buying trip: a one sentence letter mailed from the Harpoons' spring training camp for rookies in Portland Maine. He wanted her to call.

She didn't pause to think.

*****

"I have to see you. I need to see you, Amy. Can you get away for the weekend?"

Amy's spirits soared for the first time in weeks. She had spent the most miserable time of her life in Europe, hating herself, suffering from a crippling depression. Her mind went blank as Ed spoke. She choked back a flood of tears, swallowed and whispered, "Yes. Yes."

"Great! I'll find a place. I have missed you more than I can say. I think about you constantly. This is great."

"That's good to hear. I can't tell you how distressed I have been, Ed. I'll be there Friday evening late. And, Ed?" Her confidence skyrocketed.

"I'm here."

"I'm starved for you. I need this so much."

They crushed together at the airport and Amy cried from sheer happiness. The long separation served as a catalyst for their affections. They went straight to the motel.

The night passed in outbreaks of conversation, laughter and passion. Ed didn't trust the feeling of happiness. He had forgotten how to laugh in her absence. Amy had returned to his life like a lost dream. They both cried when he asked her to forgive his insensitivity.

She said it first: "I love you, Ed. I have loved you from the moment we met. You are everything to me. I don't ever want to be without you."

"I love you, too. I have loved you from the time you came to the stadium to say thanks."

"That's exactly when it started for me, Ed."

She met and liked his friends the next morning at breakfast, and enjoyed watching the Saturday morning practice along with player and coach's wives. Ed arranged to be absent for the weekend, although the other players couldn't have friends or family.

"Just one of the perks of a veteran," he told her. "Anyway, this is a training camp for rookies. I'm here voluntarily to help with the new guys."

Despite the long night, Ed frolicked through the practice like a rooky. They went to dinner with a group of coaches that evening. Ed had to suffer the off-colored, good-natured comments from his teammates.

"We are all happy you're here, Amy," one of the men declared. "Old Ed hasn't been worth a damn. He's been a mean, moody son-of-a-bitch this year. It's good to see the old Conklin back. Yes, Ma'am, it's sure good to have you here."

They drove to a Lodge on the New Hampshire coast for the weekend. They had been apart for weeks, but the separation didn't affect the deep feelings Ed imagined and dreamed about during her absence. He loved her. She had filled his thoughts every waking moment during the long absence. The Amy Roman in his arms was everything he dreamed of: open and affectionate, loving and vulnerable, not to mention beautiful and intelligent. She touched and caressed, smiled and laughed. He felt good again.

Her eyes revealed everything. He knew exactly what she was thinking and how she felt. She made no secret of her feelings. Amy gave him confidence to be himself. He didn't need to maintain some fabricated image for her benefit, and he didn't have to impress her. Being with Amy was the easiest thing he had ever done, and the most rewarding. The loving relationship he had dreamed of for a lifetime unfolded in her company. Ed Conklin achieved happiness beyond his fondest wishes.

"I do love your body, Ed," she said, running her fingers through the hair on his chest. "I can't believe anything could be so perfect. To be honest, I never thought a man's body could interest me at all, and now I feel positively wanton. Do I embarrass you?"

"Hardly." He laughed and said, "I'm satisfied to know it's

good for something besides smashing into another man. I may never play football again."

Her mood changed late the last night of the weekend. "Ed, I want to be with you whenever it's possible. Is it too early to talk about that?"

"Not for me. I can't get enough of you. I don't ever want to be away from you again. Are you thinking about a living arrangement?"

"I am. Your place or mine?"

"Your choice."

"I have a nice apartment. Come live with me."

"I will, but you better be sure."

"I am sure," she said. "What about you?"

"I have never been more certain of anything."

"Okay. Let's do it. Will you keep your place?"

"Not if you think I'm hedging."

"No, Ed, that isn't a problem for me. Maybe you should keep it until we know for sure we are compatible."

He laughed. "How could anyone be more compatible?"

She returned to Boston, but flew to Maine again the next weekend. Ed moved in with her when training camp adjourned the following week.

*****

Harpy jumped and ran like a crazed demon when he recognized Ed. "I can't believe you kept that fool dog. I didn't mean for that to happen. I'm sorry."

"Don't be. He has become very important to me. I just couldn't let him go."

Their lives settled into a happy routine. Amy picked him up each day after practice and they began making the social rounds together. Ed fit into her group of friends naturally. Amy took great pride in him. They made the society columns nearly every week and were automatically included on invitation lists to the most prestigious parties. Ed Conklin and

Amy Roman were "a thing," one never to be invited without the other.

"Mother wants to meet you, Ed, is that okay?"

"Sure. Any time you say."

"She's having a family dinner this Friday. I know she planned it as an excuse to meet you. Are you sure?"

"Yeah. I think it's time." He didn't know much about her family, only that she preferred not to talk about them. He often wondered about her reluctance to share information, but decided not to press for details. "Do I need a briefing?"

She became pensive and shrugged. "Probably, but let's just wing it. My stepfather will undoubtedly come late and leave early. He usually doesn't have much to say around home. I expect you will find him to be a little strange. I'll let you be the judge."

The comment surprised him. "Your parents don't live together?"

"Not in the traditional sense. They aren't separated, but my stepfather doesn't spend much time at home. You'll understand more about that when you meet them." She hesitated and looked pensive. "You don't have to go, Ed."

He could have sworn she wished he wasn't going and didn't think she would mind at all if he declined. "It's okay. Let's go. Anyway, we have to do it sometime. What about Carlo? Will he be there?"

"I don't know. He is out on parole now, though, but I doubt if he comes. Would it be a problem if he does?"

"Not to me. What about him?"

"Carlo is strange. Everything has gone smoothly so far, but Carlo isn't predictable. There is no way he doesn't know about us, we are all over the society columns."

*****

Amy's mother met them at the door and stared up at Ed as if she had seen a living apparition.

"This is Ed Conklin, Mama."

"Oh, my. Such a big man. Such a big man." Her mother stared for too long before finally regaining her senses to lead them to a catered party in the walled courtyard behind the house. The gathering consisted mainly of her mother's female friends. Amy's stepfather arrived late as Amy predicted, accompanied by several men. Carlo also came, even later, with another entourage of men. A photographer busily recorded the entire event.

Carlo appeared to be an exact replica of Amy's stepfather, only short and slim with slick black hair. He was well-dressed and arrogant. Ed thought Carlo's movements seemed graceful, dainty, almost feminine. He also thought that if a man could be beautiful, Carlo was beautiful. The women loved him. He laughed and talked much too loudly. Everyone at the party catered to him. Carlo assumed an air of importance, slapping the men playfully, kissing the fawning women. He clearly believed himself to be the center of attention, breaking into conversations with impunity, dragging people away for private conversations. At least two men attended Carlo at all times. He was a king.

The party included an Italian band, playing mostly string folk music. The dances were alien to Ed. Amy begged until he joined her. He soon found himself in a circle of matronly women, obviously part of a performance organized to feature a lone male. *Him.*

*****

Carlo motioned for Amy to join him while the women circled Ed. She consented rather than create a scene.

"Who's the clumsy moose, Anna?"

"Like you don't know. He's just a friend, Carlo."

"Yeah, just a friend. That ain't what I hear. I know where you go and I know who with."

"Then why did you ask?"

Carlo's face softened and he whispered, "I want you back, Anna."

She turned to leave and he gripped her arm painfully.

"You're hurting me, Carlo. I guess that's typical for you, isn't it?"

"I don't want to hurt you, baby. I just want you back where you belong."

"Not in this lifetime, Carlo. I have someone else. I am exactly where I belong."

"Get rid of him."

"I don't plan to leave him, ever. I love him."

"Dump him! That will be better for both of you. Get rid of him. I'm serious."

"Not for you, Carlo. Not ever. Now let go of me."

His eyes narrowed into slits. He growled, "You are coming back, one way or another."

Amy pulled away. "No, Carlo. Forget about me."

His smile frightened her. Amy had seen it before–a mocking sneer that usually preceded something unpleasant.

"Don't fight me, baby. I won't lose you to any man, particularly some jock hick. You *are* coming back, and the sooner the better." He smiled at her menacingly.

*****

Ed escaped the circle of women and the dance ran out of steam. He noticed that most of the men remained in the background throughout the party, talking amongst themselves. The men spoke English. Most of the older women spoke either Italian or broken English. There were no young women present. The women watched him and giggled. Ed didn't need to be reminded that he and Amy were the source of their amusement. Amy took it all in good humor. Ed had to grit his teeth and concentrate on being pleasant.

"I'm sorry, Ed. This is much worse than I thought," she whispered. Amy worried and fretted about his comfort as the

111

party wore on.

She waited until her stepfather and Carlo were together before introducing Ed, and then retreated to the kitchen immediately and left the men alone.

The stepfather's limp handshake preceded some barely audible comment about the weather. He retreated to an easy chair to smoke a cigar and feign preoccupation with his fingernails. Ed took the older man's actions as an insult and the already uncomfortable atmosphere stiffened. He turned his attention to Carlo.

"So, Carlo, what do you do?"

"I'm in business for myself."

"Great. What kind of business?"

"Family business. You know–banking, investments, security, import/export, protection, stuff like that. No big deal."

"Banking?" Ed's curiosity stemmed from Amy's reluctance to say much about her ex. Carlo laughed sarcastically. Ed noticed her stepfather look up and frown.

"Yeah, we do some banking. Romano Savings and Loan. Yeah. Don't you like the way that sounds?" He laughed again and then suddenly became serious, as though he had no time for pleasure. "I've been reading about you," he said. "The paper says your team is supposed to be a contender this year. What do you think?"

Romano? Romano Savings and Loan? Protection? Security?

Ed speculated about the name but breathed a sigh of relief at the same time, having found football to be common ground with one member of her family. "I expect we'll make the playoffs again. We should do okay. Do you follow football?"

Carlo laughed again and glanced over his shoulder at two of his attendants. He said, "He asked do I follow football?" The two men exchanged knowing looks, as if they knew something Ed should know. Ed had seen it before–mockery and sarcasm directed at some poor bastard who wasn't in on the joke. He despised being the object of ridicule. The hair on the back of his neck begin to tingle. He was not going to like Carlo. Carlo grilled him for several minutes about football; mostly about the strengths and weaknesses of the Harpoon's coming schedule.

Carlo motioned for his attendants to assemble in preparation to leave, then turned to Ed and said, "We should talk more. I could use some tips."

"Any time." Ed didn't think he would ever see Carlo again socially. Ever.

Carlo moved closer, into Ed's comfort zone. "I mean it, man. We should talk. We can do business. I'll be in touch." He looked Ed directly in the eye, leaned in and whispered, "Anna is a Romano. You remember that. She will always be a Romano. You be good to her or I'll have you busted up." He smiled condescendingly and patted Ed on the cheek.

Ed's temper flared. He grabbed Carlo's wrist and wrenched it away from his face. Carlo winced as he tried to pry Ed's fingers away. Three overweight men rushed to his aid. Carlo stopped resisting and growled, "Better let go, friend." He glared as beads of sweat popped out on his forehead. Ed didn't release the hold. "I mean it, friend," Carlo added. "Either you let go or I'll have the boys make a mess of you. You wouldn't want to ruin the party, now would you?" He forced a pained smile.

"You don't know me, *friend*," Ed mimicked. "And if you ever touch me again, I'll break your damned arm and your fat friends won't be able to do a thing to help you." He thrust Carlo's arm away.

Amy had watched the entire sequence of events and rushed to place herself between the men before a physical confrontation took place.

Carlo backed away and pointed a finger at Ed. "We'll talk. We'll talk." He smiled scornfully and led his entourage from the courtyard.

The long drive back to the apartment was quiet until Ed

finally said, "Anna Romano? Is that your name? Is there anything else I should know?"

Amy looked puzzled. "I thought you knew. Oh, I'm sorry, Ed. I should have made it clear. I'm really sorry, but I honestly thought you knew. You said you googled me. That's how you knew where I worked and my numbers."

"Damn, Amy, what next? Why didn't you tell me about your family?"

She looked confused and studied him intently before saying, "You really don't know, do you?"

Ed's expression exhibited impatience. "What's the big secret? Come on, Amy, I'm damned tired of secrets."

Her confusion increased. "I just can't believe you don't know. Not after you investigated me in the beginning. How could you have missed that I changed my name? Are you the last person in Boston to get it?"

"For God's sake, Amy! Will you stop playing games."

"My name is Amy Roman, not Anna Romano. I changed my name at twenty-one, almost nine years ago, Ed. My family's name is Romano. My stepfather is Alberto Romano." She paused and watched his face for a reaction and saw nothing. "You do know who Alberto Romano is, don't you? *The* Alberto Romano? *The* Boston Don? He is on every internet bio anyone ever mentioned my name in. Hundreds of entries, Ed. Probably thousands! You Googled me and missed that?" She looked directly into his eyes and waited for a response.

Ed blinked. The information registered with stunning force. *Alberto Romano? The man behind the scene in Boston's Mafia? The Boston Don?* "You have got to be kidding, Amy."

"You know I'm not."

Ed pulled to the curb and turned to her. His expression reflected stunned disbelief. "Damn, Amy! Your old man is linked to gambling and narcotics and...." He slammed his hands down on the steering wheel. "Jesus! Why am I telling you that? You know everything! How could you keep such information from me? Do you know what this could mean to me?"

She nodded somberly. "I know about some of the allegations against my stepfather. That's why I chose to change my name."

"But why didn't you tell me?"

She refused to look at him. "I honestly thought you had to know, Ed. You said you googled me. Wait, I'll show you." She took her phone out of the purse and googled herself and handed the phone to Ed. "There. See? How could you miss that? Amy Roman is Anna Romano, stepdaughter of Alberto Romano. Romano is the alleged leader of the Boston Mafia. It goes on and on, Ed. I honestly thought you knew. How could you miss it?"

"Oh, Amy. I'm sorry. I wasn't looking for anything except how to contact you. My search stopped with OLDE CONCEPTIONS and your numbers."

"I'm not proud of my family, Ed. I have been separated from them for years. I haven't made a habit of thinking about them one way or another. Why should I tell anyone? I am Amy Roman, not Anna Romano, and I have been for years. I am *not* Anna Romano! My name is Amy Roman! Can't you understand why I don't tell everyone?" She turned to him and said, "Look what it has already done to us! I really thought you were just being kind not to bring the Romano connection up."

"I'm disappointed, Amy. I didn't think there were any more secrets between us. I'm really disappointed."

"Fine. Now you listen to me, Ed. I didn't have to invite you to that party tonight. I thought it was time you knew all about my immediate family, not the family business, and I wanted you to understand why I don't live there. I thought you should see for yourself. I was a Romano once, yes. I am no longer. Please don't let it ruin what we have. Can't you understand why I want to be separate from them? I am *not* a

Romano!"

"Well, maybe you should tell that to Carlo. What is it with him, Amy? Is he part of your old man's outfit?"

"Yes. A very important part. Carlo is dangerous, and I mean extremely dangerous, Ed. I really don't know much about the family business as women are not privileged to know. I knew enough, though, and separated myself from them deliberately, even the name. But I know enough to warn you about Carlo. I cannot caution you enough to be careful. Carlo is treacherous, Ed. He is the enforcer. The enforcer! If you don't know what that means, you should look it up. It was a mistake to manhandle him this evening. He won't forget. Not ever. He lost face. He lost respect."

Ed related Carlo's threats to him. "He acted like he was your father."

"He wasn't kidding, Ed."

"Be serious, Amy. What could he do?"

"Carlo is my stepfather's first line of defense. He is a vicious, cruel man, maybe even unstable mentally. I wouldn't put anything past Carlo, not even the stories in the news associating him with several murders. I know him well enough to assure you that he is not kidding. Carlo isn't interested in me, except that he lost face because I chose you. Carlo usually doesn't care about anyone, but he does have some strange ideas about me. He is treacherous, Ed. Please, don't cross Carlo."

Ed remained quiet and pensive at the apartment that evening, ignoring her efforts to repair the damage. Finally, in an act of desperation, she knelt at his feet and begged forgiveness. He embraced her and said, "Don't worry about us, Amy. I love you. I will always love you. I am not worried about us, but I am worried about my career now, and your safety. Pro Football will not tolerate a breath of scandal, particularly when the scandal involves gambling and drugs, and most particularly if the Mafia is involved. If the press ever gets wind of our relationship…well."

"We won't go back, Ed. I don't need them. I only need you. I will never ask you to be around them again. I just thought you should meet them."

Chapter Eight

ED

The Harpoons won the first six games of the season. Ed played a major role in the success. He had more quarterback sacks and tackles than any player in the league. Pro Football's most noted observers were already touting him as possibly the greatest defensive end in history–a shoo-in for the hall of fame. Boston's premier sportswriter summarized Ed's play as, "Dazzling. The Harpoons would definitely have lost four of the six games without Conklin, perhaps all six. Conklin already has my vote as the league Most Valuable Player even if he doesn't play another game this year."

His professional life made the headlines on the sports page at least once a week, but football came in a distant second measured against the joy he received from the love he shared with Amy.

"You have to meet her, Ma," he told his mother on the phone while announcing the relationship. "She makes my life complete. Everything is better with Amy. I cannot imagine being happier than I am."

Their wild, whirlwind romance matured and they began staying at home more often than not, enjoying the simple pleasures of being alone. Much to Ed's surprise and pleasure, Amy took an interest in cooking and exhibited genuine talent, usually opting for the more exotic recipes. Ed's huge appetite challenged her ability and understanding. He began to lose weight but didn't complain. The head coach did. Ed wouldn't have murmured a word of protest even if her cooking was terrible, but he managed to adjust on the sly, supplementing her diet with sandwiches and milk shakes while driving to and from work.

One evening in November, Amy appeared at the library door with an apron over her dress and flour smudged on her face. "Darling, I hate to bother, but would you mind running down to the store for some milk? I cannot finish this casserole without it."

*****

Three large, swarthy men were waiting when he returned to his truck at the convenience store. Ed recognized them as Carlo's associates. He remembered seeing them at the Romano party. Two of them circled to his rear while the largest and oldest stood between him and the truck, feet spread, arms folded.

"Just put that sack in your truck, asshole. You're coming with us." The speaker, the best dressed and most obese of the trio, waved a shiny automatic pistol toward a waiting sedan. The other two edged closer, a hand inside their jackets, ostensibly on or close to a gun, Ed surmised. Their faces didn't reveal a sign of emotion. Ed decided to ignore them and moved forward. The cold barrel of a gun pressed against his neck changed his mind.

"If you know what's good for you, college boy, you better start listening. This ain't no frickin' fraternity party. Now get in the damned car before I decide to shoot off your frickin' kneecaps." The other two closed in.

Ed didn't move. He saw the gun and heard the threats, but refused to take the situation seriously.

"You boys can tell Carlo for me to get screwed," he said and turned away. Ed didn't lose consciousness, not quite, but the crushing blow rendered him powerless. He dropped the groceries and slumped to his knees.

He felt the cold barrel of the gun press against his neck again and the fat guy said, "Look, you dumb bastard, all he wants is to talk with you. Now I don't give a shit if you walk or we drag you, but you are coming. Now get in the damned car."

His legs were too wobbly to support his weight and the three men assisted him to the car. They drove to a vacant parking lot a few blocks away where Carlo waited in a limousine with two more fat men with two more shiny guns. His captors opened the passenger side front door and shoved Ed in.

"Long time no see, college boy," Carlo said after the driver made it clear by waving his gun toward the front that that Ed should not try to look toward the back seat.

Ed heard a woman giggle and almost gagged at the sickening, syrupy stench of her perfume. His eyes were clearing by then and the ringing in his ears had subsided to a high pitched screech. The waves of nausea retreated and his thoughts began to focus.

"The boys tell me you weren't all that cooperative. That's too bad. You need to pay attention, friend, or don't they teach you manners in college?"

"What do you want, Romano?" He thought Carlo probably wanted to get even for the scrape at the party.

Carlo's blow hit him squarely on the ear with enough force to bounce his head off the window. Ed whirled to grab the gun. His angry response ended with the driver's gun barrel again jammed painfully into his neck. He couldn't hear out of his left ear after the blow. He felt Carlo's breath in his other ear.

"I ask the questions here, college boy. You just keep your damned mouth shut." He patted Ed on the face the same way he had done at the party, only with more force. "Now, let's get down to business. Get out, Irma. Get your skinny ass in the other car."

The woman complained bitterly. Carlo opened the door and shoved her out.

"Sometimes I don't think you're such a nice man, Carlo," she complained.

"Shut the hell up and get in that car. Dumb bitch."

Carlo closed the door and turned to Ed. "You know what the point spread for your game is this weekend, college boy?"

Ed didn't answer.

"It doesn't matter, I'll tell you. The point spread is three points, asshole. But I asked one of my bookie friends what the spread would be if you didn't play. Seems like you are pretty important, college boy. You know what he said? The game would go two points to the other team if you don't play. Isn't that interesting?"

Ed already knew what came next. "You're wasting your time, Romano." He braced for another blow.

Carlo laughed instead, an effeminate cackle that caused Ed to remember that Amy told him that she once thought Carlo might be gay. Carlo then sobered and screamed into Ed's good ear. "I never waste time, friend! *You* are wasting my damned time!" He grabbed Ed by the hair and pulled his head back. "You better listen to what I'm going to tell you, college boy." He pulled even harder. "I'm going to bet a bundle against the spread next Sunday. I'm going to bet like you aren't playing, friend. Do you know what that means or do I have to spell it out to you?" He yanked Ed's hair again and the driver jammed his gun deeper into his neck. "That means you are not going to play too good, college boy. You are not going to get to the quarterback and you are not going tackle the runners. You are going to have a bad day, my friend. A very bad day." He shoved Ed's head forward.

Carlo lit a cigarette and didn't say anything for a least a minute. When he spoke again, his words were so soft Ed could barely hear. "This is just business, friend. Don't take it personal. I'm just like any other businessman. I always need collateral in my business. You are going to be my collateral. If you play too well and I lose.... Well, I'll have the boys put you out of business for the rest of the year, maybe even the rest of your damned life. So, if you want to play football, and you like your kneecaps right where they are, you better be paying attention. Now get the hell out of here."

*****

Amy panicked when she saw the blood and cuts, and then burst into tears and cried inconsolably when Ed told her what happened. He didn't tell her everything, letting her believe Carlo had roughed him up over the incident at her mother's house.

"What are you going to do, Ed?"

"I don't know. I'd like to kill him."

*****

He lied to the team physician the next morning about having been in a bar fight.

"You may lose some hearing in that ear, Ed. A little too soon to tell. What the hell did they hit you with, a pipe? How many were there?"

"Four, Doc. Look, if it's all the same to you, I'd prefer this didn't get out. I'll play Sunday, okay?"

He did play. He played with more energy than ever before. He played like a mad man and the other team's quarterback paid for it with a broken shoulder in the first quarter of the game. The Harpoons won by twenty points.

Ed told Amy about Carlo's scheme after the game, and after deciding never again to keep anything from her.

"What are you going to do, Ed?"

"Nothing. I'm going on with my life as if nothing happened. I'm not going to be badgered by a bunch of fat goons."

Amy began to exhibit signs of stress. He caught her watching in the rear view mirror and peeking through the curtains at night despite his objections. She jumped nervously when their phones rang and begged to stay home at night. She couldn't sleep and began losing weight. Ed regretted the decision to tell her about Carlo's scheme.

"Amy, you have got to relax. Nothing is going to happen. Carlo won't do anything. It's just a scare tactic."

"You don't know him, Ed. Carlo won't stop until he wins. This is a game to Carlo. Just a game. He smashes people who get in his way. I think we should move, Ed. Please, let's move someplace where they can't find us."

"What good would that do? Anyone can find me. I'm a public figure. Anyway, I'm not going to let anyone push me around–particularly not that damned Carlo."

"Ed, Carlo called me," she confessed.

"When? Why?"

"A couple of days ago."

"Why didn't you tell me?"

"He wants me back, Ed. That's what this is all about. Carlo wants me back."

The announcement stunned him for a moment. "That's crazy, Amy! Is he nuts?"

"Yes, on both counts. I told him never to call again."

"And?"

"And, I guess we will see. Carlo is unpredictable. What happened to you is probably related to my rejection of his advances."

He heard Amy scream dreadfully the next morning after stepping outside to get the morning paper. Ed found her slumped against the door, a hand covering her mouth, staring at the Harpy's dismembered remains. The dog had been butchered and disemboweled. Blood and intestines were spread all over the porch and sidewalk. She begged him not to call the police.

"It won't do any good, Ed. You can't prove anything and Carlo will just deny it. He *wants* you to call the police. He *wants* to know you are upset. This is just a game to Carlo. I'm really frightened, Ed."

"I'm not going to sit back and take this, Amy. I'm going to see him. I'll settle this." He stood.

She threw her arms around him. "No! You can't do anything. Please, for me, just let it go. You can't do anything. This is his game."

"I can break his damned face!"

"No you can't. You can't get close enough to Carlo to touch him. He always has at least two men nearby, and they have guns, and they will use them. You don't understand, Ed. These people aren't like you. Believe me, you can't do anything. Don't even think about it."

Their phones began ringing at all hours of the night. They finally gave up and traded for new phones. Ed found his truck tires slashed and the windshield broken. Someone poured red paint on the sidewalk and wrote: "College boy".

"That's it! I know it's him! Carlo is the only person who ever called me that."

"The police won't think that is proof, Ed. Please, let's move. Let's get out of here."

He refused and Amy became visibly more distraught. Ed watched the dark circles spread beneath her eyes. She broke into tears for no reason. Their love life suffered. Ed came home late on several occasions and learned that she had called the Harpoon front office and the police. He refused to tell her why he was late, but she knew.

"I know you are looking for him, Ed. Even if you find him, it won't do any good. You are going to get hurt. I know how to do this," she said, suddenly brightening. "I'll talk to my father. He is the only man on earth who can call Carlo off."

"No! Absolutely not! This is my problem, Amy. Our problem. I don't want to get involved with your father. The answer is no! If this business with Carlo is getting to be too much for you, maybe it would be a good idea if you went someplace for a week or two."

"What are you planning?" She stood in front of him, hands on hips, glaring.

"Don't jump to conclusions. I am thinking we should probably move out, though. Look, Amy, Carlo is after me, not you. Maybe I should go back to burbs and live in my old place for a while to take the heat off of you. If I leave–"

"No! That's exactly what he wants! If you leave, I'm going with you. This is not about *you*, Ed. He is using you to get to me. Don't you see?"

"I won't run from him, Amy, but I don't want to see you get hurt because of my values."

"It isn't that simple, Ed. He isn't through with you. Carlo won't quit until he is satisfied."

"What in the hell is the matter with him? Doesn't he have anything else to do? Is he that hard up for entertainment? He isn't going to run my life."

"Yes he is, Ed. He already is. You don't know what you are up against. Carlo is unscrupulous. He is truly evil. Carlo is very important in the organization."

"That really pisses me off. Why do you call it an organization? Why don't you call it what it is? It's the damned mob, Amy! Your family is the Mafia."

"I know exactly what my family is, Ed, but you don't. Carlo is very central and he has plenty to do, but he loves to play games. He is enjoying this. This is just a game to him; nothing but an interesting sidelight; just something he does for fun. But the end game for Carlo is me. He has lost face and wants satisfaction."

*****

125

Amy travelled with Ed that weekend for a game in Los Angeles. They found her apartment trashed when they returned.

"That's it!" Ed exploded. I'm going to the police. I have had it, Amy!"

"You will be wasting your time. You have no proof."

"Amy! Are you with me or against me? Something has got to be done. I won't live like this anymore!"

"Carlo won't stop until you play his game." She averted her eyes immediately.

"I don't believe you said that. I can't believe you can even think something like that. How could you, Amy?"

She whirled and faced him angrily. "Because that's the only way you are going to get out of this, Ed! Because that's the only way you will ever get peace in your life, if you manage to live through what is coming. I can think about it because Carlo is going to destroy you if you don't do what he wants. I don't give a damn about Carlo, or football, but I love you. I don't want to see you hurt, and Carlo is going to hurt you, or worse. This is serious, Ed. This is what he does. This is his life. You have to understand that."

"And you don't think betraying my profession would hurt me? You don't know me very well, Amy."

"Maybe not, but I know what's going to happen. Carlo is going to destroy you. He is going to hurt you worse than you can imagine. Carlo is the devil."

Ed's anger diminished and a torrent of frustrations spun through his thoughts. "I want to know something, Amy. Are you still taking money from your father?"

"Why would you ask that at a time like this? How dare you!"

"I'll tell you how I dare. That job of yours doesn't pay enough to support your lifestyle, Amy. That's how I dare. You don't make enough money to afford a two-hundred-thousand-dollar car. And how did you get all of the jewelry? Where does the money come from for your clothes, Amy?

And this apartment? And how about the two club memberships, Amy? Where does all of the damned money come from?"

"I make a good salary and I get bonuses. I also get paid for playing with the Pops orchestra. I am not a principal player, so maybe not all that much, but I do okay."

"How much with the orchestra?"

Depends on how much they play. Last year I missed some, so maybe thirty-thousand."

"That helps. But the rest puzzles me. What, exactly, do you get paid for? What makes you so special? Look, Amy, I know what you do and I know how hard you work. Not very hard and certainly not full time. I don't spend money the way you do, Amy, and my job pays fifty times more than yours probably does, at least. You don't work an average of six hours a day, and you take days off any time you want. How does the gallery afford you?"

"I resent the implications."

"I'll just bet you do. Okay, one more question. Did you pay for that car? I want to know. That is one hell of an expensive car. Two-hundred-thousand probably won't touch it."

Her nostrils flared and angry tears formed, ready to fall. "That's none of your business. I work for a living, Ed. I don't have to answer to you, or anyone. I work for my pay. I don't have to answer those questions."

He nodded sadly and sat back. "That's what I thought you would say. Well, you're wrong! You do have to answer. Our lives are bound together now, Amy. So, like it or not, what you do and who you are and who you were affects me. Your old buddy Carlo is trying to destroy me, for Christ's sake, and you don't want me to report him to the police! I'm in this, too, Amy! Now, what about the damned car?"

She turned away, arms folded over her chest.

"I mean it, Amy. I want to know. Right now. This is important to me."

She turned back to him and shouted, "Okay! My stepfather gave me the car! Is that illegal? Is that what you wanted to hear?"

He shook his head. "That is absolutely *not* what I hoped to hear, Amy, even though I knew better. Now, what about the apartment? Does he pay for this, too? Am I living off money from your father?"

Tears started streaming down her face. She looked angry and miserable but refused to answer.

"May I take your silence to mean he does?"

Her eyes begged for relief. "Don't do this to me, Ed. I have tried to be independent, really I have. I don't think it's wrong to accept gifts from my own stepfather. Please don't be so mean."

His anger spilled over. "What else is there, Amy? What else should I know about you?"

"Isn't that enough?"

"What about your job, Amy? Does he own the gallery?"

She glared at indignantly. "No! I got that job on my own. I worked hard to get where I am, Ed. I have a major in antiquities and I am very good at what I do."

"You didn't answer the question. How much is your salary?"

"I don't get paid a salary. I get paid according to how much we sell. Some months are better than others."

"That's ridiculous. Do you get paid by check or in cash?"

"What are you trying to say?"

"You know damned well what I'm saying! Answer me!"

She looked confused. "Sometimes the bonus is in cash. Why is that important?"

"How much money are we talking about?"

"I don't really keep track of it."

"Come on, Amy. How much? Hundreds? Thousands? Ten's of thousands? How much?"

"That's none of your business."

"It shouldn't be, but it absolutely is. I don't want to believe my suspicions are correct, but I have been to your gallery, Amy. It's a nice place, just not that nice. Your gallery can't possibly be making enough to pay what you make. Come on, who owns the gallery?"

"I don't know. Is that important?"

"It would be to me if I worked there. It should be to you."

"Well, we are different. You can't judge me by your standards. I know Miss Hopkins manages it for someone, but I really don't know who it is. Do you know something I should know?"

"Not yet. But I am willing to bet that you can't find out who the owner is. And I would also be willing to bet that if you did discover who it is, it will be your stepfather."

His words shocked her. "You don't really believe that! That's fiction! That's just inconceivable!"

"Maybe. Maybe not. Why don't you ask?" He came to her and said, "I'm really sorry, Amy, but these things have been on my mind for a while. I love you with all of my heart, but I don't like what is happening to us. I have to know more than I do to make decisions about my life, Amy. I may have to leave football."

"You are going to leave me, too, aren't you?" She rushed to him and embraced with all her might.

"I am moving out, not leaving you. I think that would be best under the circumstances. Amy, I want to know when you find the answers to my questions, if and when you develop the courage to look. If my suspicions are correct, I would also like to know what you intend to do about it."

"Don't leave me, Ed. I cannot possibly go on without you. I don't want to live without you. I love you." She held tightly and wept.

"Amy, you know I love you beyond measure, but we can't go on like this. I can't go on like this. If my suspicions are correct, who you are and who you know and what you do involves me and my career. If word gets out about what Carlo wants me to do, and it will whenever he wants it to, organized crime will be linked to my career. I am going to the club general manager tomorrow and let him know about my relationship with you, and with Carlo. This could end up being a terrible scandal for the team, the league, and for me. As it stands, I am probably out of football anyway, Amy. If this business with Carlo happens one more time, I will definitely quit. That really doesn't matter to me financially. I am already well set for life. But it sure matters in every other way. So, let me know what you learn." He went to the bedroom, packed and left ten minutes later.

Chapter Nine

CRISIS

The moment Ed walked out, what little self-control Amy had remaining wilted. She pulled the curtains and collapsed to the floor, there to stay in a defeated heap, crying for hours in the darkened room. She called in sick the following morning and remained at home for the next week staring at nothing from the back window.

Ed dutifully answered her calls each evening after practice and listened quietly as she begged. He always ended the conversation by asking the same question: "Have you found out who owns the gallery? Do you know who is paying your salary?"

She stayed wide awake at night wrestling with the dilemma, finally deciding to confront the questions directly or lose Ed. She went to work the next morning, walked into Leitha's office unannounced and took a seat next to the desk.

"Leitha, who owns this gallery?"

"Amy, you look terrible! Are you sick?" Without waiting for an answer, she said, "What difference does it make to you who owns the gallery?" She clearly resented Amy's question.

"I have worked here for almost four years, Leitha, and I don't think that was an unreasonable question. I'm the assistant manager, after all. I should know and I don't."

"Fine, since you are so determined. We are owned by a corporate holding company. That is honestly all I know, and that's all you need to know. I suspect several owners are involved.'"

"What holding company?"

Leitha placed a binder of paperwork in the "out" basket, solemnly folded her hands on the desk and pretended to give Amy her undivided attention. "Amy, when and if you are ever the manager, you will need to know such things. However, for now, I really think you should concentrate on the little things that pertain to your own special interests. That is, if you can find the time to favor us with your services." She forced a phony smile.

"In other words, you aren't going to tell me?"

"You are so theatrical, Amy. This business isn't a soap opera. Anyway, why should you care about such mundane issues? Really, Amy, I am surprised at you. Perhaps you should concentrate more on your work. That should keep your mind busy. You have been absent quite a bit lately. Now is a good time to catch up on your paperwork and let me get back to my work." She fashioned a patronizing smile and closed the conversation by punching in a number on the house phone, dismissing Amy with a nonchalant flick of her wrist.

Amy felt discouraged and needed to be alone. Leitha's evasiveness gave Ed's accusations new meaning and she suffered an ominous misgiving that he was right. Her worst fears inched a notch closer to reality. She sat in her office brooding after deciding not to press Leitha for more information.

Maybe it's time I started doing for myself.

Leitha conveniently lived in a suite over the gallery, yet another coincidence now with significant meaning to Amy.

And the fact that she had never been invited to Leitha's place was another particularly noteworthy bit of information that tweaked her spiraling interest.

The fact is, I don't really know her at all.

They had been friends for years, but never once on a social basis.

I really don't know her. Leitha is an utter stranger to me. Why haven't I cared before?

Amy drove to the gallery just before midnight to find the street lined with limousines. Several men loitered near the entrance to the gallery talking and laughing with two cops in a patrol car. She recognized some of the men as her father's associates and drove on, returning twice in the next hour before surrendering her intentions. The next morning, she detected the strong odor of cigar smoke as she walked by the conference room next to Leitha's office.

"Who used the conference room last night, Leitha? It smells terrible." She had noticed the odor on several occasions, but, until now, it had not been noteworthy. "We need to get a cleaning service to purify it before it putrefies the entire gallery."

"I let some of the local businessmen use it last night. Mostly the city council guys, I think. They come here occasionally. The smell is awful, isn't it."

"We really could make better use of that space for some special gallery shows, don't you think? We don't need a conference room for gallery conferences, now do we? We never have meetings there."

Leitha never looked up from the papers on her desk. "I like things just the way they are, thank you. Maybe someday when you are the manager. Now, if you will, I'm busy here."

*****

Amy used her private key to enter the gallery late in the evening three days later after watching for almost two hours from a rented car down the block. Her night watch ended the moment Leitha rushed from the gallery to enter and depart in a limousine. The opportunity to snoop had taken two nights of waiting from six thirty until midnight. She closed the building's upper blinds and began the search by going through the files in Leitha's office, copying business names and addresses of every corporation she could find. She found Leitha's desk drawer locked, as expected. After deliberating the possible consequences of prying it open, she settled in favor of discretion.

Anyway, I can always come back some other time if I don't find what I need tonight.

After scouring through the office for almost an hour, she used the old credit card trick on the aging lock to Leitha's apartment. It worked, much to her surprise. She entered, trembling with excitement and fear, too nervous to breath normally.

Amy had never seen such elegant furnishings. "Good Lord!" she said aloud. This is unbelievable, and huge. This is opulence. What does she do with all this space? She crept from one room to another, nervously whispering reassurance to dissipate the mounting tension. She would never have guessed Leitha lived in the lap of such abundance. Her closets were filled with expensive clothes and furs, with at least a hundred pairs of shoes and expensive belts. *"No wonder she never wears the same thing twice."*

Amy rifled through the kitchen drawers and a small desk in the living room without finding anything important, and then turned her attention to the bedroom. The room didn't have a window to worry about, so she closed the door quietly, took a deep breath, and then flipped the light switch.

The world as she knew it disintegrated. "Oh. My God! Ed was right."

After collecting her wits, Amy didn't take time to analyze the fine furnishings, or the expensive Persian rugs, or the private collection of famous paintings–none of that mattered.

And then her breathing stopped, overcome by yet another revelation. She couldn't tear her eyes from the night stand beside Leitha's bed, where, with a single wilting rose draped over it, her stepfather's picture held the place of honor.

She stood rigidly, still as a statue, and stared. Her emotions altered dramatically during those moments, from the first staggering flash of recognition, to disbelief, to crushing acceptance, to amazement and ultimately to rage. She stood spellbound for several seconds as anger overpowered the paralyzing effect of her discovery. After that she no longer harbored doubts about her objective and methodically completed the investigation of Leitha's room with vengeance in her heart.

She found more of her father's pictures, always with Leitha, scattered throughout the room in drawers and albums, on shelves and in ornate frames on the walls. The pictures obviously spanned a period of many years.

Amy used her master key to open the conference room where she found Alberto's name on several corporation organizational wiring diagrams that she discovered in the only unlocked conference room file. She went to the courthouse the next day and traced the corporations as far as she could and her life continued to crumble.

I have been so naïve. A little girl playing at life. How could I be so blind?

Her memory was sketchy, but when concentrating on events leading up to her job with the gallery, she vaguely remembered that her mother had suggested the job might be open.

Might be? She knew it all along. My, God! I have been hand-carried through life.

*****

"I want some straight answers from you, Leitha."

Leitha sat bolt upright as Amy stormed across the office

the next morning after slamming the door. "You stop right where you are, missy!"

"Cut the bossy crap. I want to know why you hired me? Who told you to hire me?"

"I will not put up with that tone of voice!"

"Okay, Leitha. I am not angry with you, but I want to know who told you to hire me."

"I thought you were best qualified. Don't make me regret it."

"That's a damned lie! You hired me because my father told you to. You pay me too much because he gives you the money. You let me take too much time off, and when I am here you don't make me work. You have put on a pretty good front, Leitha, but I would bet you secretly hate my guts. Now, how long have you been seeing my father?"

Leitha sat back suddenly, her face unable to control the surprise of disclosure. "I don't know what you are talking about. Why are you acting this way?"

"Because it's my life, Leitha! It is *my* damned life! You have been manipulating my life! I want to know, just how long have you been seeing him? Tell me!"

"You don't–"

"Oh, yes I do! I went to your apartment night before last, and I followed you last night. I know you were with my father last night, Leitha. Does Sardino's mean anything to you? You had the house salad and white wine and my father had veal. And don't you dare try to tell me he didn't stay with you overnight. I know he slept here. Now, how long?"

Leitha's eyes narrowed as she glared at Amy. "Why don't you ask him?"

"I will if I have to, Leitha. Are you sure that's what you want?"

Leitha appeared to think about the alternatives and obviously reached the conclusion Amy supposed she would.

"Fine. I have known your father for more than twenty years, Amy. Or should I call you Anna?" She stood proudly and said, "I'm not ashamed of it. He belongs to me. I don't expect you to understand that, but I have loved him more than any other person. I hope you will not make life difficult for us."

"What about my mother?"

Leitha laughed contemptuously. "That is a laugh. Your mother has known from the very beginning. You are not the only one to find out and you damned sure aren't changing anything."

"I thought you were special, Leitha. You are nothing but a common prostitute."

Leitha's back straightened proudly. "That may be, Amy, but I take his money honestly. Do you? I know what I am and I earn every cent. Can you say the same? There is more than one way to prostitute yourself, Amy. Who is calling who a prostitute? Why don't you grow up and appreciate what you have? You will be much happier if you accept your stepfather for what he is. He is a good and decent man who has provided very well for you, Amy. Now, can we put this little soap opera scene behind and get on with our lives."

Amy wanted to scream, instead she simply turned and walked out. All of Ed's suspicions were true. She spent the night preparing for the next day. The moving van came early and left before noon with instructions to dump the load on her parent's lawn.

"We can't do that, Miss Roman. Look, we don't want no trouble. Know what I mean?"

"Would a hundred dollars help?"

"I don't–"

"Okay, then drop everything off at the Salvation Army."

"Okay, but they don't usually help us unload."

"Would two-hundred help?"

He took the money with a satisfied smile. She had packed one large suitcase and an overnight bag with essential items; everything else in the apartment went with the trucks: the clothes, jewelry and furniture. Everything. Amy left the apartment carrying the two bags with all of her worldly possessions. She kept nothing expensive, and nothing she could not have earned herself. She called Carlo and asked to see him.

"What's this all about?"

"It's personal, Carlo. I need to talk to you."

"We have nothing to talk about. I don't want to be bothered with a bunch of cheap crap from you."

They traded angry barbs, and then she lied and said, "I think you should see me, Carlo. I can't tell you on the phone, but it could be very profitable."

"Does it have anything to do with football?"

"Could be. Where, Carlo?"

"Do you know Sardino's?"

"Well, of course, Sardino's. Why didn't I think of that. Now, how do I get in touch with my father?"

"You ain't planning to make trouble, are you?"

"I am leaving town and I want to see my stepfather, Carlo. Will you help me or should I just walk in on him at Sardino's some evening? I'm sure he would love that." Of course Carlo would know about Leitha.

"You're leaving? What are you up to? I don't want you causing no damned trouble."

"Have you got a guilty conscience, Carlo?"

He laughed scornfully. "Okay, I'll tell him you're coming, but it's up to him. Anything else before you shoot yourself in the other foot?"

*****

She speculated that her father would be present at Sardino's, and then insured his presence by quitting her job at the gallery. Leitha didn't object.

"You have been a good worker, Amy. When Alberto first.... Well, suffice it to say, I thought you would be a spoiled brat, but you were a pleasant surprise. I will miss you,

Amy, and that's the truth. You will always have a position here should you change your mind. You haven't burned all the bridges with me. However, I think your decision is wise, based on the current circumstances. If you ever need a letter of recommendation...."

"No thanks. I intend to lead my own life from now on. I don't need or want your help, or my father's. Is he going to see me this evening?"

"You know I cannot reveal his intentions." Leitha held the office door open. As Amy walked through she smiled compassionately and said, "For what it's worth, Amy, he isn't planning to see me this evening."

Amy left the gallery with her pride intact, quite surprised by how civilized the meeting with Leitha had been. She left the hotel early that evening, allowing time to sit across the street from Sardino's and observe. She began to think the club was an exclusive meeting place for every well-to-do, Mediterranean, olive-skinned man in Boston, and supposed they were probably all associated in some way to her father's business.

Amy observed from the shadows as several limousines came and went, expelling passengers in a routine that amazed her. The performance never varied. Two men got out and scrutinized the street soon after the gleaming car pulled to a stop. They always talked with not-so-innocent bystanders for a moment–some of the bystanders were beat cops–and then returned to the car and held the door open for an older man. And then, with their ever vigilant and trusted lieutenants casting furtive glances up and down the street, the older men disembarked and quickly hustled into the smoky recesses of Sardino's. Her father and Carlo both received the same royal treatment.

*****

The room full of men stopped talking and laughing the

moment she entered. She stood for a few moment allowing her eyes to adapt to the dim light and the unpleasant sting of cigar smoke. The large table toward the back of the room attracted her attention. She took a deep breath and filtered through tables mostly occupied by men.

"Hey, baby. You lost?"

"Yo. Have a seat right here, baby."

The comments served to spur her anger. None of the men at her father's table stood as she approached, spiking her rage even more. At the last moment, the same two men who acted as escorts for her father earlier, intercepted her advance and blocked the way.

"You ain't welcome here, chicky."

"Get out of my way. I am Anna Romano." The men looked to her father for guidance and moved aside when he nodded.

"Anna," he said pleasantly. "I haven't heard you use that name in years." He smiled and added, "This is a nice surprise."

"I seriously doubt that. And, just so you don't get any ideas, I hope that is the last time I ever have to use that name, Father. Now cut the nice talk. I know this is no surprise."

All color drained from his face and his eyes narrowed dangerously. Carlo pushed his chair back and started to get up. Alberto stopped him with a raised hand.

"We handle family matters privately, Anna. Let's go to the back room."

"This is as far as I am going," she announced. "I just came to say goodbye." She threw the car keys on the table. "You have ruined my life, Father. You have meddled and destroyed my life. I don't want any more of your money, or your gifts. All I want from you is out. I want to be left alone. If either one of you," She paused and pointed to Carlo. "ever interfere with my life again, ever, I will make you regret it, and that is a promise. Leave me alone!"

Alberto didn't say anything. The room fell into a whispered hush as one man after another raised their eyebrows and glanced at each other in disbelief. Nobody ever said anything harsh to Alberto Romano.

"That's enough, Anna!"

His words spurred another outburst. "That's enough? Is that all you have to say? That's enough? You sit here with your fat friends and tell me that's enough? For the first time in my life, I'm going to tell you what is enough!"

Alberto glanced over his shoulder and nodded. The driver advanced immediately and held his chair. He folded the napkin neatly and apologized to his friends for the embarrassment and left the room by a back door.

"That's right," she screamed after him. "Run away! Don't let me interfere with your life!"

The room buzzed with muttered comments.

Amy waited until her father disappeared before turning her wrath on Carlo. "And I've had enough of you, Carlo!" She pointed an accusing finger. "Who gave you the right to intrude in my life? Ed had to leave because of you! I will never forgive you for that! Never! You have ruined my life! I warn you, Carlo, if you ever interfere with me or him again, I will make you regret it, and you know I can. I have hospital records and photos. Leave me and him alone!"

She stood her ground defiantly as Carlo approached. They stood face to face. His breath reeked of garlic.

"Why should you care about that dumb football player?" he said. "Anyway, I hear he dumped you."

His smile had always infuriated her. Carlo perfected the arrogant sneer as a child and it was now a permanent part of his personality.

"Nothing has changed between you and me, Carlo. We will never be together."

"You don't know that, Anna. You and I both know that you don't really care anything about that dumb hick."

"I love him, Carlo, and he loves me. You lost me years ago. Leave us alone!" She slapped him as hard as she could and fled the room.

Carlo went directly to the private room in the back.

*****

Alberto Romano wasn't pleased. "Carlo, what do you know about this friend of Anna's? The football player. What is going on with him?"

"He's just a big, dumb hick."

"You waste my time. Answer the question," he spoke irritably.

"It's business, Uncle Alberto. I got business with him, that's all."

"Ah, business. Of course. Many times I have told you, family and business don't mix. You should always keep family separate from business." He stared at the back of his hand for at least a full minute before returning his attention to Carlo. He sighed heavily and said, "I must ask you to do something for me. Anna has caused embarrassment in front of my friends. She is only a woman and doesn't know about such things as respect. My soul is sad because of Anna. Perhaps I gave her too much. Perhaps it's my fault, but what happened here tonight cannot happen again. Respect is an important thing, Carlo." He paused and stared directly into his eyes until Carlo shifted weight uncomfortably. "Without respect even the strongest wilt. I want you to go to Anna, Carlo. This business of tonight cannot happen again."

"What do you want me to do, Uncle? What am I.... How do I...."

Alberto replied angrily: "Do I have to get involved in every chickenshit detail? Just do it! You know how to do these things. I depend on you to take care of this matter with discretion. Don't disappoint me, Carlo. I don't want you to hurt Anna, but she must be made to understand." He slammed his fist on the table and said, "There will be no more embarrassment!"

*****

Amy soon tired of job hunting and took a menial position with another art gallery. The pay barely provided enough money for food and rent for a run-down, cold water flat. She learned to wash her clothes by hand and cook beans and spaghetti over a two burner stove. If Celia had not loaned some clothes, she would not have been presentable at work. Celia also demanded that Amy spend weekends at her home.

"I can't bear to think of you in the rat infested hole. Why won't you consider staying here until your feet are on the ground?"

"No, Celia. I have to do this my way. I won't be there long. I'm looking for a better job."

"Have you called Ed?"

"No. I don't think he particularly cares for me at the moment, Celia, and he has good reason. Carlo made sure of that."

"Carlo called me, Amy."

Amy's breathing stopped. "You didn't–"

"Of course not. He just asked if you were okay. Actually, he seemed very concerned."

"That's crap! Carlo has something up his sleeve. That rotten bastard. Well, at least I know he is still playing the game. I have got to get out of this town, Celia."

"What you have to do is get a grip on yourself. Are you becoming paranoid? He may be your ex whatever, Amy, but he is still family. Did you ever think for an instant that Carlo might be worried?"

"No. Not in this lifetime. Carlo is up to something."

*****

They were waiting in her flat when she unlocked the door, and obviously had been for some time. The place reeked of cigarette smoke. A huge hand covered her mouth as she reached for the light switch, smothering her voice before she had a chance to scream. When the light came on, two things were immediately apparent: there were three of them and the windows were covered with blankets.

She struggled fiercely for a moment before the awful smell of something like ether from a handkerchief held tightly over her face began to take her strength. She didn't quite lose consciousness, but weakened quickly and soon lost the will and energy to fight. The room spun. She wanted nothing more than to lie down and go to sleep, but they kept tugging and pulling her away from the door.

"Get her into the bedroom."

The bedroom looked different–so bright. A movie camera on tripods sat at the foot of the bed. She saw the camera but didn't understand its significance.

Why are the lights so bright?

"Get her clothes off."

They were so clumsy. She couldn't do anything to stop them. She just wanted to lie down and be left alone. The voices sounded as if they were coming from an empty barrel.

"Man, she's nice, isn't she?"

Someone pushed her arms away and clutched at her breasts.

"Shut up and do your damned job."

"Great tits, man. Look at these tits."

She vainly attempted to twist away. Rough hands pulled her back and she had to close her eyes to shut out the bright lights.

"I'm warning you, dipshit. You heard what the boss said. Keep your hands off."

"Don't worry. I ain't going to do nothing I ain't supposed to."

"Just shut up and get your damned clothes off. Let's get this over with. I hate shit like this."

She squinted into the light, watching the two younger men take their clothes off. The other man gave orders and worked with the camera. She observed the proceedings as an interested bystander, completely bewildered by the activities. The naked men fondled her and themselves until they were physically stimulated.

"Okay, the camera is running. Let's get this over with. Do it."

*****

"You poor baby. I'm so sorry, Amy. Okay, that's it! You are never going back to that dump. I won't have it! I'm going to call the police." Celia sat on the edge of the bathtub as Amy scrubbed.

"It won't do any good to call the police, Celia. There was no penetration. No semen. It was all faked for the camera. Carlo is going to use blackmail to keep me quiet. This was his way of controlling me." She sat in a tub of near scalding water and scrubbed ferociously. "I don't think I will ever feel clean again, Celia. You cannot imagine how disgusting and sick they were. I need more hot water." She sobbed and snuffled throughout the cleansing, barely controlling her voice. "I feel so violated."

"Did you know the men? Did you ever see them before?"

"No. But I know Carlo did it, Celia. I have never been so sure of anything. I threatened him with the hospital records. He neutralized a threat. This is so Carlo."

"Maybe if we went to the police you could identify the men. Why won't you call the police? I don't understand."

"Because I know it was Carlo. I embarrassed him and he is getting even. It's Carlo."

"Are you sure they didn't...."

"No. They did everything but that. Oh, God. And it's all on film, Celia. They tried to make it look like an orgy. They didn't complete the act, though, and that's why I know it's Carlo. Those men were not rapist. I don't think they enjoyed what they were doing. They were just doing a job. I'm sure it was Carlo's idea."

"What are you going to do, Amy?"

"What can I do? Life goes on. I'll get over it, Celia, but I'm going to get out of here as soon as I can save the money."

"I can help."

"No! I have to do this myself!"

Chapter Ten

JULIA SKELTON

Flickering shadows from a scented candle on the dresser illuminate the darkened room. A well-built young man is standing naked beside the bed, his attention on the slender naked figure of a woman writhing on the sheet. He appears ill-at-ease, frowning, uncertain, glancing around cautiously, evidently troubled. Tape covers the woman's mouth, her wrists and ankles are lashed to the bedposts with panty hose. Muted, tormented cries come from her taped mouth as she twists and struggles, her blonde hair spreading wildly over the pillow, covering most of her face.

"You asked for this, bitch," the man growls. "You've had this coming for a long time." He fondles himself, stimulating an uncooperative erection, and then abruptly settles his weight over her twisting body.

Her muffled screams fail to check his intent. She trembles and moans as he forces entry, and then slowly, in weakening stages, surrenders and lies motionless, helpless against the nylon tethers and weight of his body.

He proceeds methodically, mechanically, pounding into

her until paroxysms of release shake his body, and then he collapses, a dead weight. Scarcely moments after he finishes, she begins moving, hands clenching and unclenching, head thrown back, nostrils flaring, hips thrusting rhythmically, pressing against him aggressively. A low, animal moan escapes from deep within as she tenses and arches upward, shuddering. Moments pass as they lay motionless; nothing but the sound of their heavy breathing breaks the silence. The man stirs upon recognizing the sound of her fingernails tapping the bedpost. He rolls off and staggers to the bathroom, soon returning to stand over her while listening to the muffled sounds of her voice. "What? You want more?"

Her head rolls from side to side. *No.*

"Well, that's good, baby, 'cause I'm beat."

He unties her ankles, then her hands. She sits up rubbing her wrists, glaring at him, then rips the tape from her mouth and rakes his face with her fingernails, leaving cruel crimson welts on his cheeks.

"Lou, you stupid bastard! You didn't have to tie me so damned tight! You hurt me, Lou! I wasn't ready! Did you ever hear of preparation? Do you think I'm some barnyard animal? I wasn't ready! God, I hate you! Just get out! Get dressed and get out!"

He steps back, startled by her fury, touching his face tenderly, pouting and angered by her savagery. "Christ, Julia! What the hell is it with you? Look what you did to my damned face!" He draws his hand away from the stinging scratches and stares at the trace of blood on his fingers. "I just don't get it, Julia. You must be crazy."

"You were too rough, Lou! I'm not crazy. You are a damned moron! Now, get out!"

"Shit, Julia, I thought that's what you wanted! That's what you said. I only did what I thought you wanted me to do. This whole damned fool thing was your idea. What the hell!"

She pulls the sheet over her body and shrieks, "Just get out, you miserable bastard! Get the hell out and leave me alone!"

He is nothing to her, just another guy to use. She can find a man any time. She knows lots of men.

Lou gathers his clothes, slams the bedroom door on the way out and dresses in her living room, all the while confused and muttering. She listens until the front door closes as he leaves the apartment, then pulls the blanket up and goes to sleep smiling.

*****

The following morning, Julia enters the Federal Court building and steps through a door with her name and title drafted in bold, black script:

JULIA SKELTON
ASSISTANT PROSECUTING ATTORNEY

She nods to the woman at the desk guarding the door to her inner office. "Good morning, Edwina."

Her secretary, a well-dressed, middle-aged black woman, looks up and replies, "And a good morning to you, Miss Skelton." She appraises her young boss for a moment. "You sure look nice today. Life must be treating you good."

"Can't complain. Any messages?"

"Nothing much. Hagerty's been looking' for you." She nods toward a side door. "Waitin' in his office. You two up to something I should know about?"

"Probably not today. Get the Jensen file out of the safe, would you please?"

She steps through the side door and enters Wayne Hagerty's office. Wayne, a rather delicate little red-headed man, wider at the hips than shoulders, serves as her regular partner on major cases, and as her unenthusiastic escort at official appearances around town.

"Well, you look positively radiant, Julia." He winks suggestively. "Must be getting your share."

She flops into the chair beside his desk, leans back, smiles luxuriously and says, "And your share too, Wayne. Okay, enough about our sex lives. What's on today?"

"Just wanted to touch base with you on the Jensen thing before I get involved in something else. You still going after him?"

"Damned right. You get his phone bills?"

"Yup. Like you asked. I highlighted the calls you're probably going to be interested in." He hands her a manila folder.

She leans forward to take the folder, sits back and reviews the contents before whistling. "Wow! There is some good stuff here, Wayne. Looks like our boy is definitely talking to the Mob, doesn't it?"

"Yeah, he is undeniably talking to them. No doubt about that. Those highlighted calls are to Alberto himself. Sixteen just last month."

"You did good, Wayne. Have you asked for a phone tap?"

"Yup. The judge wouldn't buy it."

She looks up, a perplexed frown marring her unblemished face. "What?" She exhales like a disgusted teen. "Oh, no!" She buries her face in her hands and growls, "Okay, exactly what judge did you use, Wayne?"

He holds a folder between them as a handy defense. Hanson?"

Julia shakes her head dejectedly. "Oh, no! Please don't tell me that. Why didn't you try Judge Owens?"

"Tried to. Couldn't get him. On vacation." Wayne holds up his hand to restrain her predictable anger. "I know. I know what you're thinking. I should have waited. In my favor, though, I did call Owens' office. I did not call or ask for Hanson, Julia. Someone had to tell him we are after a tap. Anyway, he got wind of our request and took over on his own. However it happened, Hanson interceded. I'm sorry, but it really wasn't my fault. Someone told him, Julia. I know better than to call his office. Someone leaked."

Julia's anger subsides. She swallows the disappointment and says, "Okay. We will just have to try something else."

She sits back and groans, "God, I hate this racket! Is everyone crooked? Is the entire damned city government on the take?"

Wayne nods appropriately. "That's the way I read it. Sorry, Julia. I'll have to be more careful from here on. First, though, we need to figure out who ratted us out."

She stands and flips the folder on his desk. "Well, it was a good idea. We have to think of something else right quick or we're going to lose the Jensen lead. Damn, I do hate this business!"

"Why don't you get the hell out, Julia? I would if I were you. Take a position with a private firm. Hell, with your record, you could get on with anyone anywhere. Really. Why don't you get out? You've been here long enough. Things are going to get risky. Move out west."

"You know why I don't, Wayne. You know damned well why." She walks out and Wayne turns to his office mate, a young attorney fresh out of Harvard. "She's something, isn't she, Al?"

Al Coffey, prematurely balding yet still looking too much like an adolescent to appeal to any prestigious private firm, replies, "Yeah. She sure is something. Got to be the best looking attorney in this town. She going with anyone, Wayne?"

Wayne's laugh mocks the idea. "That woman leaves a string of broken men in her wake, Al. Don't even think about her. She is way out of our league."

Al takes the rebuff unconvincingly, lower lip protruding. "A man can dream. I'd give anything to.... Ah! never mind."

*****

"Come in, Julia. How nice to see you again. Please, have a seat." Doctor Rose Howe, middle-aged, bespectacled, hair pulled back severely, rises as Julia enters. The two women make small talk for a minute before the veteran psychiatrist says, "Well, enough chit chat, Julia. Where were we last?"

She sits and opens a folder, arranges her glasses and reads for a moment. "Oh, yes. Here we are. Your father. It seems to me you were somewhat hesitant to talk about your father." She closes the folder and looks up. "Do I need to remind you where we stopped last session?"

Julia grimaces, closes her eyes momentarily, takes a deep breath, and then opens her eyes extra wide to say, "No, Doctor Howe, I remember exactly where we were, all too well. First, let me apologize for the way I rushed out. I'm sorry about that."

"Thank you, but that is not important." Doctor Howe's pleasant smile does not take the bite out of her next remark. "I want you to tell me about your father, Julia. I believe it is important."

Julia's grim smile fades. She nods, sighs and says "Okay, I'll try." She smooths her skirt, unconsciously delaying to collect her thoughts. When she looks up again, her breath escapes in a resigned sigh. "This isn't easy for me. My father. Okay. Well, for starters, he is…was the only man I have ever really loved. He was everything to me, Doctor. Everything. I can't get over…I will never get over...." She covers her eyes and groans. "Oh, God, I am such a sorry mess. This is really very difficult. I just can't forget the way he died." She pats her cheeks fiercely, flashes a determined smile and then her entire demeanor changes as anger surfaces. "My entire life, every damned thing I do is dedicated to the purpose of avenging his death! I *am* going to prosecute the miserable...." She grimaces and shrugs to ward off Dr. Howe's disapproval. "I know, I know: I'm preoccupied. I know that." She forces a weak smile. "But I won't rest until I get him–them. I'm going to bury all of them. Every damned last one of them."

Doctor Howe's expression remains professionally fixed. "Who are *them*, Julia?"

Julia looks surprised. "Who? You know very well. The Mafia! The Mob. Everyone knows who killed my father, Doctor Howe. Everybody knows who and why."

"Really? Well, I don't know, Julia. Why don't you tell me? Why do you think they killed him?"

Julia looks frustrated, questioning. "Why? Because he was the only unshakable and honest attorney in the prosecutor's office. That's why."

Doctor Howe's eyebrows raise. "The only honest attorney? I see. That is an all-encompassing statement, Julia. Are you so sure he was all that different from other prosecutors?"

"Yes! I'm an attorney, for god's sake! What makes you think I wouldn't know?"

Howe, recognizing Julia's confrontational mood, sits back and folds her hands on the desk. "Please, try to control the anger. I am not the enemy and this isn't a courtroom, Julia. This is about you. I cannot help if you cannot master your hostility. Now, please, calmly, tell me about your father. Everything."

Julia smooths her face, forces an unconvincing, apologetic smile and says, "Sorry. I am not angry with you." Her strained smile fades. "Okay. After mother died, he became my entire life. We did everything together." She nods to reinforce the statement. "Everything. He was it. He was my life."

"How old were you when he...when you lost him?"

"Eighteen. Just out of high school. But I didn't lose him. They killed him, and they deliberately did it on the night of my graduation. A bomb under his car, all because he wouldn't drop charges against them." She glared. "And it worked! No one has taken up where he left off. The entire justice system is running scared. This whole town is running from them."

Doctor Howe looks thoughtful while tapping a pencil on the desk. "But not you?"

"No. I am going to get them. I am going to *finish* what my father started!" Julia laughs nervously and waves a hand to dismiss the intensity of her comment. "I know you think I'm obsessing."

The doctor nods. "It's one thing to admit obsession, Julia, quite another to consciously nurture it. Do you think it possible that this preoccupation with revenge is ruling your life?"

Julia laughs. "Oh, there is no doubt about that. Absolutely. Yes."

Doctor Howe flips through the file on her desk. "Okay, that information is helpful, but I really think there is yet a more conspicuous starting place. I want to go back to a comment you made during our last session." She looks over her glasses at Julia. "A very disturbing comment, I might add. Let me quote." She reads aloud: 'I don't hate all men, just most of them. I would really like to find someone, but I always seem to choose men I know I won't like; men I know I will *not* like.' Her gaze returns to Julia. "Will you please elaborate on that for me?"

Julia winces. "God. Did I actually I say that?"

The doctor nods, folds her hands again on the desk, and waits. Julia doesn't answer. Doctor Howe finally says, "And what about the history of abuse? The mistreatment of these men you don't like? You mentioned some pretty bizarre things, Julia. Aren't you afraid some exploited victim will harm you?"

Julia laughs derisively. "No. Remember, I intentionally choose weaklings. I can dominate the men I pick, Dr. Howe. That's why I choose them. No, I'm not afraid of being harmed."

Dr. Howe's eyebrows lift again. "Well, I view the pattern as more than a little bit alarming, Julia. I don't see anything good happening until you can forgive men, as a whole, for what happened to your father. Men are not the problem. I believe your attitude toward men is the problem." She sits back and frowns. "Now, I must ask the one question that has bothered me for several days. Hear me out, Julia. Please don't leave this time. Nothing can be solved by avoiding the issue. I believe this is extremely important."

Julia shrugs. "Sure. Go for it. Ask away."

Doctor Howe sighs deeply, thinks for a moment, then says, "What I must say next is difficult, even for me, so I know it will be much worse for you." She clears her throat and says, "Just how intimate was the relationship with your father?"

Julia stands suddenly and glares down at Howe. "What are you trying to say? I don't think I like the implication here, Doctor Howe. And I won't have it!"

Doctor Howe does not react at all. She taps the pencil against her lips, looks Julia directly in the eye and says, "I am on your side. Remember that Julia. Now, please have a seat. There is nothing to be gained by anger. I am on your side." Julia sits but does not relax. "Thank you, Julia. The reason I have asked, the reason I must ask, is because I believe there is much more to the relationship than you have revealed. Now, please—how intimate?"

Julia stands again. Instead of bolting, she closes her eyes, bows her head and begins to weep.

"Please sit, Julia. Let it out. Sit down for a moment, and then tell me. Let's finish this. Please, this is important."

Julia slips back into the chair, still weeping. Several moments later, red-eyed but moderately composed, she looks up, smiles grimly and says, "What made you think.... How did you know?"

"I am a psychiatrist, Julia. What did you say earlier? 'I'm an attorney, for God's sake. What makes you think I wouldn't know?' That works both ways. I am a psychiatrist. I know. I know, Julia. Now, I think it would be beneficial for both of us if you could talk freely to me about the relationship. And I think you must talk about it. Now, how intimate?"

Julia shakes her head miserably, tears still trickling down her cheeks. "I really loved him, Doctor Howe. I wanted to take care of him. What happened wasn't his fault. It was all my fault. He loved me so much. Really, it wasn't his fault."

"You were physically intimate?"

Julia looks away, stares out the window for several

seconds, and then, almost imperceptibly, nods and wipes the tear from her cheeks.

Doctor Howe presses ahead. "When did it start, Julia?"

Julia's head drops until her chin rests on her chest. "I don't know. About...oh, fourteen or fifteen, I think. But it was my fault. I started it. You have to believe that, Doctor Howe. He was so lost without Mother. All my fault. He needed me, and I loved him so much."

Julia's anguished sobbing prevents further discussion. The session ends and she departs. Doctor Howe turns her chair to the window and weeps.

Chapter Eleven

ED

———————————⌄———————————

"Hey, Conklin! There's some gal in the front office lobby to see you!" The assistant trainer didn't pause to elaborate.

Amy hadn't called in two weeks. Ed's fingers were suddenly ineffective as he struggled to pull a shirt on while running to the lobby. The woman in the outer lobby bore no resemblance to Amy. Disappointment smothered his excitement and expectations.

Crap! Now what?

"That's him, Miss," the receptionist said as Ed stopped short and turned, preparing to leave.

"Mister Conklin? Are you Ed Conklin?" The woman waved a large envelope, smiled brightly and headed directly for him.

He sighed heavily, taking time to overcome the disappointment before facing what he assumed would be yet another autograph seeker.

"Yes, Ma'am. I'm Ed Conklin. What can I do for you?"

She smiled brightly and handed him the envelope. "This is

for you. Special delivery. Bye now." She trotted briskly through the front entrance and entered a limousine waiting at the curb.

A limousine?

Ed opened the envelope and read:

TONIGHT. TEN SHARP.
SANDY'S BAR. WEST BIRCH STREET.
ANNA'S LIFE. DON'T SCREW UP.

He dialed her number while battling a swelling sense of urgency, only to have Amy's ominous recorded message introduce a new sensation. Panic. The message was not in her voice, just the standard phone company "Out-Of-Service" notification.

Has she moved out? I should have been there for her. Damned Carlo.

He had to get out of the uniform and hurry. The team had practiced under the lights in preparation for the coming Monday night game and Ed barely had time to make it to Sandy's before the ten deadline.

Anna's life? Don't screw up?

He tried to analyze the situation on the way but couldn't concentrate. *Whoever set this up knew exactly what they were doing. I don't have time to think. Amy's life?* He rushed into the bar without exercising caution, determined not to display any signs of nervousness.

"Yo, buddy! You Conklin?" The bartender caught Ed's eye and jerked his head to a door in the rear. Ed nodded and he went impassively back to polishing a glass. Ed paused and took a moment to survey the small gathering of customers. He didn't recognize a face and no one seemed interested in him. The back door was locked. He knocked. Someone on the other side opened the eye-level one-way window, and then snapped the lock. The door swung open. Ed recognized two of the room's several occupants as Carlo's men. Carlo's gun-wielding men.

"Have a seat, friend." The voice originated from an

indistinct figure in the background, partially shrouded in a fog of cigar smoke. "Right there. Sit" The dim form stepped forward and motioned to the two empty chairs at a small table in the middle of the room.

Ed recognized the speaker as the driver who had jammed a gun into his neck weeks before. He detected three other men in the shadows. "I'll stand," he countered.

"No you won't, friend. Now sit your ass down in the damned chair or we'll sit you down." Three men emerged from the smoke and converged in a semi-circle around Ed, pistols already in hand.

"I'll sit," he conceded nonchalantly.

The men withdrew into the veil of smoke to lean against the walls near the front and back doors. The driver remained close and said, "Just so you don't get some funny idea about what happens next, friend, I have a silencer on my piece and I'll blow your damned head off if you so much as raise your voice. Got that? Now, I'd advise you to just pay close attention and keep your damned mouth shut." He knocked on the back door and another man stepped into the room. The new player casually inspected the setting and stepped out to return shortly followed by Carlo.

"Hey, Carlo. What's up?" Ed wanted to ID the speaker. His phone was on.

Carlo sat across the table without removing his hat or topcoat. He took at least a minute to remove an expensive pair of thin leather gloves before inspecting them while ignoring Ed. "You cost me a bundle, college boy," he said, carefully folding the gloves before slapping them idly on the table. "I'm not happy with you." He gazed blankly at the gloves and then smiled at something secretly humorous. "But I don't want you to think us Romano's are too quick to judge." He looked up for the first time and fixed his eyes on Ed. "What do you think of that, college boy? Would you like another chance?"

Ed assumed an answer would be appropriate. "You already

know what I think." He maintained unblinking eye contact with Carlo.

"Yeah, but I better not hear you say it, college boy. I have waited nearly a month for another three point spread. Monday night is a three point spread. You are described, in all that sport page crap written about you, as a smart man, so you know what I expect, right?"

Ed glanced around the room without replying, having decided not to speak until forced.

"I know things haven't been too good for you recently, college boy, but if you screw up again Monday night on coast to coast television, things are going to get a lot worse. You can either do what I ask or kiss your ball playing career goodbye. It's that simple." He stood and gazed down at Ed. "This isn't some kiddy game, college boy. You screw this up and people are going to get hurt, and I mean hurt bad." He glared malevolently and then smashed his fist on the table. "I'm through screwing with you!"

Ed spoke before Carlo reached the door. "What about Amy?"

Carlo paused. "I don't know anyone named Amy." He left the room without looking back.

*****

Ed drove like a madman in his haste to get to the apartment and call Celia. "I have to know about Amy, Celia. Is she's okay? This is important. Please."

"Yes, she's okay, Ed. Why do you ask?"

"I tried to call her tonight, Celia. Her phone has been disconnected."

"I know."

"Do you have a new number, Celia? She doesn't have a cell now."

"No number yet, but I wouldn't give it to you if I did. Look, Ed, I would really like to help you, but my allegiances are with Amy. She asked me not to say anything to you. I'm sorry."

He went to Amy's old apartment the next day, and then to the art gallery. Amy had quit her job and vanished. No one at the gallery knew anything.

He played a lousy game on Monday night, but the Harpoons won and beat the spread anyway. His conscience tortured him through a long and sleepless night following the game.

Carlo got to me. I took a fall. I didn't try.

*****

They were waiting in his apartment after practice the following Thursday. Carlo with two of his men casually fooling around with their pistols. One holstered his gun and frisked Ed. He took his phone, turned it off and threw it on the couch.

Carlo said, "I would have lost money again, college boy."

"I don't control everything, Carlo."

"I appreciate what you're saying, friend. You were bad, just not bad enough. Oh, don't worry. I didn't have any money down. I don't like to gamble. I only bet on sure things. I didn't have that much confidence in you, so I bet the other way. The next time will be different. I am going to get the money back that you already blew, and I intend to get it back this weekend, college boy. All of it. Just thought you might want to help me out."

"Don't gamble on me, then."

"Oh, it ain't going to be no gamble, friend. This time I'm going to make sure you do the right thing." He stood, retrieved an envelope from an inside jacket pocket and flipped it on the table. "I got a copy of that with the league commissioner's address on it, just in case you screw up. Oh, and there is a great video of those pictures if you are interested." He smiled and led the entourage out.

The envelope contained copies of betting IOU's with Ed's signature. He wrote his name on a blank piece of paper and compared the handwriting–a fair match. Someone had done a good job of recording bets on Harpoon games–allegedly his bets. The paperwork covered a period of two years. He thumbed slowly through the first packet of pictures. The images were circled and numbered, and the numbers matched names written on the back. Each name had additional information appended. Joseph Ceppa (Alleged Bookmaker). Alphonse Guardino (Alleged Bookmaker), and so on. Each picture included Ed, smiling and shaking hands with each man. They were all identified as Mafia connected. The pictures looked authentic because they were. In fact, Ed had shaken hands with each man at Amy's mother's party.

The second envelope of pictures weakened his legs. He had to sit before he could finish thumbing through them. He didn't want to believe what he saw.

This can't be true. Why would she...? How did Carlo get these?

He forced himself to look again at each print. Her eyes were always closed, looking away from the assaulters.

Something is terribly wrong here.

*****

He called Celia and demanded to know about Amy.

"She's fine, as far as I know, Ed. Why are you bothering me?"

"Because I don't think she is fine. Something terrible has happened to her, Celia. I'm sure of it. I need to talk to Amy. This is important, Celia. I'm going crazy. I have to see her. Please don't say no, Celia, because if you do I.... I'm sorry. I am so desperate. Please."

"Call me back in the morning."

He wasted another night pacing and worrying. The whole world seemed to be closing in, but his primary anxieties were centered on Amy. He called Celia before eight.

"She doesn't want to see you, Ed."

His knees buckled and he slipped down the wall and sat on the floor. The sickness in the pit of his stomach expanded to compete with the ache in his chest.

"Are you there, Ed?"

"Yeah. Did you tell her I...."

"I told her. Look, she's hurting, Ed. Her life has been turned upside down."

"I know. Carlo is involved, Celia. Amy is in trouble. What happened, Celia? I know you can tell me."

"You also know I won't."

"Look, Celia, I have to see her. This isn't about getting her back. There is much more to this than I can tell you. She is in real danger and she is being used."

"Oh? Do you know something?"

"Enough to know she is in serious trouble."

She didn't answer right away. "I think you may be correct. She is being evasive with me. How can you help her?"

"I can't unless I can find her. This may be about life and death, Celia."

She didn't answer for the longest time, and then her voice sounded strained. "I feel trapped Ed. I'm not sure of my loyalties. Okay, she comes here sometime in early mornings. Very early. She has a job now. My kids leave for school at seven with Bud. After they leave, Ed." The phone went dead.

Ed asked for a day off, pleading sickness. He plotted a schedule for the coming days. He needed to make some major life changes and everything depended on Amy. He couldn't do anything without knowing about her.

*****

Celia hugged him affectionately. "What happened to you two, Ed?"

"Amy didn't tell you?"

"Not much, except she doesn't think you care about her anymore, and that Carlo got a little out of hand."

"A little? God, Celia, there is far more to it than that. He is using her to force me to throw games."

"I wondered about that, but that's between the two of you. She is going to hate me for bringing you here, so I'm not saying another word. You two can work things out for yourselves. I really don't know anything, okay? She is very different, Ed. I almost don't know who she is now. Good luck." She paused. "And don't you ever come back here, Ed. I don't want my family used as pawns in your messy life. Got that?"

He nodded, and then waited in the shadows on the porch until Amy's cab pulled away. She froze when he stepped into the light and a package fell as she covered a distressed expression with her hands.

"Ed?"

"Yup, it's me."

"What are you doing here?" She swiftly recovered from the initial surprise. "I didn't ask for you. You shouldn't be—"

"What's going on, Amy?"

"I'm doing fine. You don't need to worry about me." She lifted her chin.

"What about the pictures, Amy? Tell me. I want to know."

"Oh, no. Please not that. Oh, Carlo." She turned away as her previously fabricated demonstration of independence faded before his eyes. Her entire body sagged in defeat and tears began falling without a sound to indicate she was crying.

"Carlo gave me some pictures, Amy. I want to know about the pictures. How did he get those pictures?"

"I don't want to talk about it. They came to my room last week."

"Did they—"

She whirled to face him. "No! No, they didn't, Ed! They didn't hurt anything but my pride. It was all for show. Carlo wants to control you through me. That's what this is all about.

I wondered what that miserable bastard would do with those pictures. I just can't believe he gave them to you. That miserable...." Her eyes blazed defiantly. "But don't waste your time worrying about me. I'm fine."

"I'm sorry, Amy."

"Is he getting to you though me? Did he use those pictures to pressure you?"

"Yes. He gave them to me, but there is more. We need to talk."

"So talk."

"Not here. Come with me."

"Why should I? What more is there to say? Anyway, I have to be at work." Amy's shoulders and chin came up proudly again as he approached, but her eyes and a swelling smear of tell-all tears revealed a different account.

"This separation isn't working, Amy. My life is unbearable without you. I thought he would leave you alone if we separated, but my leaving hasn't helped either of us. Come with me, Amy. I need you. I don't want to go on without you. You are my life. I will gladly give up everything for you. Everything."

Celia found the note taped to the kitchen table:

DON'T WORRY ABOUT ME
I AM WITH ED
I'll CALL

*****

They gathered her few belongings and went to a motel for the night. Before sleep came, they had talked about events during their separation and made plans for the future. They both cried after making love, clinging together desperately.

The next morning brought tremendous changes in their lives. They packed Ed's truck in the dark and drove through back streets until they were certain nobody could have followed. Ed took a small apartment with a garage in

Rockport, a northern suburb of Boston not too far from the stadium.

"This is the best we can do until this mess is straightened out, Amy. We are going to have to maintain a low profile."

"I'm not worried about me, Ed. You are going to be out in the open, though. Be careful."

"I'll see you this evening. I have much to do."

He called Uber for the trip back to the stadium and went straight to the head coach's office. Ed didn't say anything, just walked in and gave him Carlo's packet, without the pictures of Amy.

The head coach, a short, stocky ex-linebacker with a crew cut, after briefly examining the packet, exclaimed, "Christ, Ed! How did you get yourself in this mess?" He had flipped through the copies of betting slips and IOU's, laying one after the other on his desk, along with the pictures associating Ed to the mob.

"I have never in my life bet on a football game, Coach. You know me better than that."

"Oh yeah? Well what in the hell do you call this!" He slapped his hand on the evidence.

"I'm being set up. Why do you think I brought this forward? Do you think I would tell you if any of that was true? Come on, Coach, I could use some help here."

"You got that right. Okay, Ed, this is for damned sure way out of my pay grade." He dialed the general manager and related the problem. "You are to meet with the GM this afternoon, Ed. He said the owner is also going to be there. All right, I'm scratching you from practice for the day. We sure as hell have to get this taken care of first. Christ, I hate to see something like this happen. This could end up being hard on everyone, Ed."

The owner and GM listened attentively as Ed unveiled the story. Ed had known them both since they joined the organization and knew the owner didn't know much about football. His background was real estate, but he had surrounded himself with a quality staff. The Harpoon organization had not suffered from his lack of knowledge. He wore silk suits and sweated profusely, even in cold weather, a short, ugly man with the puzzling reputation of being a ladies man. He took great pains to hide severe scars of adolescent facial sores. Ed had never liked him. They treated each other with guarded civility.

The general manager spoke first. "You claim to be framed, Ed, but how in the world did you get involved with the mob in the first place?"

"That's a long story, Sir."

"No doubt, but I expect we should probably hear it, don't you?"

"Yes. It all began after I met a girl several months ago. Maybe you remember how we met. She is the woman I pulled from a flaming car wreck. That's how I got the burns on my back. Her name is Amy Roman, but I didn't know that she had legally changed her name years before. Her given name was Anna Maria Romano. She is Alberto Romano's stepdaughter. You know, *that* Romano. The Mafia Romano."

The information registered on the general manager's face. "Holy crap!" he exclaimed. "Didn't you know? You had to know who she was, Ed."

"I didn't. Not until after the party where those pictures were taken. She told me then."

"So she set you up? Is there more?"

"No, Sir. I mean, no, she didn't set me up. She didn't have anything to do with it. She was once involved with a guy named Carlo Romano. I'm sure you also know that name. He is a nephew of her stepfather. She dumped him while he was in prison. Carlo is the mastermind behind all of this. He is fabricating the evidence to blackmail me, looking for a betting edge."

"Holy…. What a mess. Okay, Ed. Leave us alone here for a few minutes. We need to talk. Leave these photos with me. I'll keep them here in the office safe."

Thirty minutes later the receptionist told Ed to forget practice and go on home. "He will speak with you again tomorrow morning, Mister Conklin. He doesn't want you to practice with the team today and he wants you to come back to his office tomorrow morning about nine."

Ed arrived at the apartment late after carefully weaving an impossible trail for anyone to follow.

Amy flew into his arms. "I have been so worried about you. I'm scared to death, Ed. How long is this going to last?"

"I don't know, but I can go on forever as long as you're here at the end of the day. I told the management almost everything. I feel better about them knowing, Amy. What is happening to us is not a secret anymore. Maybe things will begin to clear up. Maybe this will take Carlo's influence away."

*****

The GM seemed to be genuinely happy to see him the next morning. "Come on in. Have a seat. Make yourself comfortable." He waited for Ed to settle before continuing. "Okay, first of all, I want to commend you for coming forward. You did the right thing. Now, here is how we are going to handle this unfortunate situation. Don't you breathe a word of this to anyone, Ed. That's important. Not a word. If this ever gets out the media will ruin us. Not a word. I want you to go on as if nothing happened. I have already informed the coach that the information is bogus and you have been cleared of suspicion. I am going to handle this matter personally, so you don't need to worry about anything."

Personally?

"What about Carlo? He isn't going to stop."

"Oh, I think he will. A word here and there will probably quiet him down. I have contacts, Ed. You just go on with your daily routine as if nothing happened. Leave everything to us." He spun the chair toward the window and spoke with his back to Ed. "Are you still seeing that Romano girl, Ed?"

I have contacts?

Ed pondered the question before answering. "What contacts?"

The GM hesitated way too long to suit Ed.

"Oh, some local law enforcement types. What about the girl, Ed?"

"Her name is Amy Roman and she doesn't have anything to do with this."

"Maybe not, but I think you can see how a football player's relationship with a known gangster's family would look to the media. What is the new buzzword now? Optics? Perhaps you should become more discreet with relationships. Anyway, you need to think about it." He came around the desk and offered his hand, ending the conversation.

*****

Ed continued his covert conduct, sneaking back and forth from the apartment each day. He arrived at the stadium two hours before the game Sunday to find a note taped to his locker. He went directly to the GM's office.

"You aren't playing today, Ed. Don't bother suiting up."

"I thought...."

"Yes, I know. I didn't want to bother you with the details, but I have decided that it won't be wise to have you play today. I simply cannot take the chance. You know how serious charges of bribery and gambling are. I can't take the chance."

"But I thought–"

"Don't you worry about a thing. That's my job. You will be listed as a late entry to the injured list. I have already taken care of it with the team physician. You just go on home, Ed. Watch the game on TV. Take the weekend off and enjoy yourself."

"What about next week? What if they contact me again?"

"We can worry about that when the time comes, if it comes, and I don't believe it will."

Chapter Twelve

DECEIVED

Ed sat in front of a TV at his apartment and winced as time ran out and the Harpoons lost the game by one point. The odds maker's point spread had been three points. The spread was predicated on the likelihood that Ed Conklin would play. No one in the Las Vegas gambling establishment had any idea he wouldn't play until too late to change the spread.

The team's GM called Ed in on Monday and reinstated him.

"I can't find any reason to doubt your word, Ed. This whole thing has been nothing but a pack of lies." He waved the packet of betting slips, IOU's and pictures. "As far as I am concerned, this doesn't exist. I'm sorry this state of affairs ever happened to you, Ed. There is one thing, though. We need to keep this little matter in-house, so I'm going to hold on to the evidence, if you don't mind. I'll feel much better knowing where it is and that it's safe. The media would have a field day if this ever got out. This needs to stay between you and me, Ed. Let's make sure it stays that way. This stuff is potential dynamite." He made a meticulous ceremony of placing the packet in his safe.

Ed went back to practice amid the cold stares of sullen teammates. They made it transparently unmistakable that they suspected he had not been hurt or sick. Their open hostility and disapproval infected the teams normal exuberance throughout the day. Even his closest friends kept their distance.

The team lost importance to Ed. Life with Amy filled the void, at least until the next note arrived in his mail box at the stadium offices on Thursday. The threats and demands were the same: Carlo wanted to insure his bets. The note contained two major changes to add additional pressure to Ed's predicament. He read the directions carefully.

"Your contact will be Falcon. Follow instructions and no one gets hurt. I know you have been talking to the team's suits. Don't contact any authority again or I will take you down. Big money and lives at stake this time–your life and my money. I sure hated to hear about your mother's house. A shame that had to happen."

Ed wadded the note and threw it in a waste can in front of the receptionist's desk and rushed to an empty meeting room to call his mother's number. He frowned as a recorded message droned through the customary-out-of-service spiel. *Out-of-service?* He quickly called his mother's next door neighbor and paled as she related news.

"That's right, honey. Your mother's house burned real early this morning. Still dark out at the time. It's just a terrible thing, her being away and all. The house is totally ruined, Eddy. There is not one thing left worth saving. The police and fire department say arson is the most probable cause. They found two gas cans right off, right out there in the front yard. Now Eddy, you know your mother never had any use for gas. Someone deliberately burned your mother's home. Some of my siding got warped, and a couple of places even melted."

"I will see about your house repair, Mrs. Burns. Don't

worry about that. I will take care of everything for you as soon as I can get there. You go ahead and have it replaced and let me know what it cost."

His mother was living at a rest home, almost comatose most of the time. She probably never would learn about the fire. Ed needed to go home Monday after the next game and take care of insurance and municipal matters.

The news only added to his present dilemma. His thoughts remained focused on Falcon. He started to leave the building, but quickly returned to the office trash can and sheepishly retrieved the note to add to his records, along with the copies of material from the packet in the GM's safe. Ed sat in the truck for several minutes, deliberating about reporting the Falcon note to the GM. He decided to talk to Amy first and headed for the apartment.

Is there really a Falcon? Or is this just Carlo's way of adding pressure?

He noticed the car in the rear view mirror and made several experimental turns before his suspicions altered to reality. Rain clouds brought darkness early so he couldn't see the car or the occupants clearly. He watched it pull to the curb a half a block behind after he stopped at a grocery store. Ed had deliberately parked beyond the store so he could walk back toward the tailing car in near darkness. He wanted to take a look at the occupants. The two men inside made a show of nonchalance as he walked by. He delayed several minutes in the store, long enough to inspire one of the men to come in and investigate.

"Hey! You looking for me?" He stepped around the shelves and faced the surprised intruder.

The man recoiled nervously, stabbing for what Ed assumed to be a weapon beneath his topcoat. Ed hadn't planned a physical confrontation, but couldn't wait to find out if his misgivings were correct. His fist connected solidly with the man's chin and the poor devil crumpled, out cold. A nearby woman screamed and ran down the aisle, alerting the entire store. Ed needed only a moment to consider what his next dilemma would be–the cops–then reached into the man's coat and removed a pistol. He raced through the produce storage area at the rear and into the alley, then to the street in front of the store. He approached their car from the shadows and snapped the passenger door open before the driver had a chance to reach for a weapon.

Ed displayed the pistol and growled, "Get out! Nice and slow."

The driver heaved a resigned sigh and stepped out. "You're making a big mistake here, friend," he said, raising his hands without being prompted.

Ed removed the driver's gun after forcing him to spread-eagle on the hood. He threw both guns on the front seat and locked the car doors with the keys still in the ignition. He made a show of observing the license plate.

"Tell your boss I am going to report everything to the authorities. Right now, you probably should get inside and see about your friend. He looked just a little bit woozy when I last saw him."

The driver shrugged indifferently and shuffled off toward the store.

*****

"We have to move, Amy," he announced the second he walked in. "Carlo is still looking for us. They followed me tonight."

"Did something happen?"

He told her about the confrontation.

"Oh, Ed," she moaned. "You just made things so much worse. Now Carlo will be forced do something to save face again. You don't know how he is. Do you think he knows where we are living?"

"Maybe. It would be just a matter of time. Let's pack and get out of here. We stayed too long."

Amy didn't object. They were gone within minutes to become fugitives in yet another apartment in another part of another suburb. Ed went to see the team's GM the next day and laid the Falcon note on his desk. He didn't mention that he had a copy.

After studying the evidence for a few moments, the GM said, "I will need to add this to the evidence in the safe, Ed."

"Okay. So, now what?"

"This creates a new dimension, Ed. I need some time to think this out. Come back and we'll talk. I'll wait for you here after practice."

"I have to be honest with you, Sir. This is ruining not only my life, but everyone around me. They burned my mother's home yesterday. I'm going to the police."

"Damn! I'm sorry to hear that, Ed. Before you go to the authorities, I wonder if you can hold on a bit longer? Maybe I can get to the bottom of this. I have contacts. Are you sure Romano burned your mother out? Is there any proof? Don't jump to conclusions."

He has contacts?

Team practices provided no relief. Ed couldn't concentrate and his teammates were a brooding, contemptuous lot, no longer playful or friendly. He returned to the GM's office that afternoon in low spirits.

"Okay, this is how we are going to handle the problem, Ed, if in fact there is a problem. We simply cannot allow anyone to influence the outcome of a game with threats, now can we? I want you to disregard the note for now, but report back to me the moment anyone attempts to contact you again about.... Well, you know. I seriously doubt anything comes of this, Ed. These things do seem to pop up occasionally. Just part of the game."

Part of the game? My mother's house burned.

"I don't take threats like these lightly, Sir. They are ruining my life. This isn't something that just popped up and I seriously doubt if it's going to get better. People I care about are involved now. If this doesn't stop, and I mean soon, someone is going to get hurt. This is serious and I think we should go to the authorities. And you should probably come with me."

"What authorities?"

"Probably Federal, don't you think? Maybe the state Attorney General? The FBI? Someone on the federal level."

"I'm not saying we shouldn't take it seriously, Ed, and by all means protect yourself. Okay, let me get with the owner so he has a chance to agree before this gets out of house."

The Saturday practice didn't amount to much more than a photo opportunity for the press. Ed had to field several questions about missing the previous game and his physical readiness for the Sunday game. The practice recessed early so the players had time to pack before flying to Kansas City that evening.

*****

He found the apartment door unlocked and a note on the kitchen table.

DON'T MAKE ME HURT HER
DON'T GET ANY DUMBASS IDEAS.

Amy was gone. He could find no evidence of violence and her things were not missing–just Amy. He ran to the garage to see if she had taken the truck. It had not been moved. Ed ran to check the nearby grocery store, then to the meat market before returning to the apartment to check again before calling Celia.

"No, I haven't seen her. Is something wrong, Ed?"

"She's gone, Celia. All of her things are still here. I think Carlo has her. Must be Carlo." He read the note to her.

"That's horrible! Do you know what's going on, Ed?"

"Yeah, probably. I can't talk to you about it yet, but I'm sure it has to do with Carlo and gambling. I have to hurry to make the flight to Kansas City. I'll be in touch."

The moment he put the phone in his pocket, it rang.

"Conklin, you better listen to this." He heard a coarse male voice in the background and then Amy's voice.

She had to snuff back tears before speaking. "Ed, I'm okay. Don't worry about me. I'm–" Her voice trailed off into the distance and he heard scuffling sounds.

"You got the idea, college boy? If you do right in KC tomorrow, I just might let you see her when you get back. You gotta do good, though. Real good. I have big money on the table."

The phone went dead. The thought of calling the police lingered only momentarily. *What would I tell them?* He felt nauseous. His hands shook so violently that it took extra time to pack.

Ed made the flight on time and pretended to sleep. He didn't want to be bothered, not that anyone wanted to talk to him. His teammates were still treating him like a leper. He called Amy several times from Kansas City and received no answer. The night seemed to last forever. He felt terrible the next morning and vomited after breakfast. She didn't answer his calls from the ball park before the game.

*****

"I'm Falcon."

The official's whistle had just stopped the action after the first play from scrimmage. The voice belonged to Benny Oldham, an opposing lineman Ed had known and respected for years. Benny's disclosure came as they separated from hand-to-hand combat after the whistle blew to end the play. Ed couldn't believe Oldham could be a part of something designed to ruin him, and possibly professional football. He angrily tore Benny's hands away from his jersey as they stood helmet to helmet jostling. Oldham noticed the referee approaching to quell the fracas and said, "Pay attention, Ed. I'll tell you what to do."

After that, directions always came at the end of a pass play or when Ed and Oldham were naturally close to each other. They, whoever the nebulous "they" were, apparently provided information to Oldham by hand signals from the Kansas City sideline. Ed watched Benny survey the side after each play. Falcon gave the information on critical third and fourth down plays, usually as the opposing team approached scoring territory. Ed's assignments were always easy: "Fall down; block the wrong direction; put up token resistance." The instructions were clear-cut.

"Your hole next play, Conklin. Shift left." or, "Stay outside, Ed." or, "Coming through your slot. Hit the dirt."

The Chief's ran though Ed's area of responsibility all afternoon as he floundered through the game in a trance. He didn't think about right or wrong, or morality, or anything other than his anxieties about Amy. After one botched play, the Harpoon's defensive coordinator grabbed his face mask and screamed at him in front of eighty-thousand fans in the ballpark and millions watching the game on national television.

"What the hell is wrong with you, Conklin? Get your head out of your ass and play ball! You're killing us!"

Ed could only hang his head and wait for the nightmare to end. Kansas City won easily. Everyone ignored him again on the flight back, and that suited Ed just fine.

*****

He rushed to a quiet place in the Boston airport lobby to call Amy again, for at least the tenth time that day. She didn't answer. She didn't come home that night. Celia didn't know anything and Ed didn't know how to contact Amy. *Do I wait or call the cops?*

He went to see the team's general manager first thing the next morning. He needed help and didn't know where else to look. The GM didn't ask him to sit.

"I'm afraid there is more bad news, Ed"

"About Amy? What? Have you heard something?"

"No. The commissioner's office called this morning. They are convening an investigation on you into allegations of gambling."

"But I.... Wait a minute! How did they get that information?" He felt a sinking sensation and the added confusion further crippled his bewildered thoughts.

"Apparently they received a copy of the same packet you gave me, Ed. They now have copies of the IOU's and betting slips you gave me, and pictures of you with those bookies. I'm sorry, but I'll have to suspend you, Ed. Don't worry, the suspension will be temporary. Should only last until the league office gets to the bottom of things. I'm sorry, Ed, but I also must separate you from all Harpoon facilities and further practice with the team. I suppose you should just go on home and wait. I'll call as soon as something turns up."

"This is unbelievable. Who sent that information to the Commissioner?"

The GM gave him a brotherly clap on the shoulder and said, "I don't know. Hang in there, big guy. The Commissioner will soon get to the bottom of it."

*****

Ed drove back to the apartment in a daze. His last conversation with Amy before her disappearance materialized from the jumble of thoughts. She had been explicit. 'You can't fight him, Ed. Carlo is crazy and he wants revenge. You took me from him. That's what he believes and that's what this is all about. Carlo doesn't care about money. He wants to ruin you.'

He remembered telling her, 'He probably already has ruined my career. This is all so unbelievable, Amy. I'm not just going to sit on my butt and take it. I will not roll over and play dead for Carlo.'

'You are too proud, Ed. You can't fight him or the organization by yourself. You don't have any idea what you are up against. You can't fight them. They will probably kill you if you become too difficult. Let's just leave, Ed. Let's get as far away as possible before it's too late. Let's leave right now. Please?'

Of course she was right. He wished now that he could go back and handle things differently. He had answered, 'No! I'm not going to be run off by a bunch of damned hoods. I won't run. Not from any man.'

She had cried that night, vomited repeatedly and cried. She cried while he paced.

"Where can I find him, Amy?"

"You cannot be serious! Please don't try anything. They will kill you, Ed. This is no longer a game. This is life and death. Your life and death."

"That's right, it's my life. Our life, Amy! And it is *not* a game! Anything is better than doing nothing. I can't just sit by and wait while he ruins our lives."

"You don't have any choice, Ed. You cannot fight him."

"The hell I can't! Come on. Where can I find him?"

She refused to answer. "I wouldn't tell you that even if I knew. That would be like sending you to your death."

His anger had flared. "Are you with me or against me?"

"I love you, Ed. I want you alive. Carlo has an army."

"You are protecting your damned family from me. Tell me how to find him, Amy! I want to end this business."

"No."

He stormed out, and then apologized to her hours later upon return, tired and wet. Now he was beginning to understand just how much she knew about Carlo. Her warnings had proven to be accurate. He knew that couldn't fight them. Too late. Now he would handle everything differently. Now was too late. Ed realized he should have quit the team and taken her far away. Too late.

*****

The headlines blazoned the news the next day.

HARPOON PLAYER INVESTIGATED FOR GAMBLING

Ed Conklin, the Harpoon's All Pro defensive end is being investigated by NFL officials for alleged gambling offenses. League representatives refuse to reveal the information that led to the announcement. Conklin is suspended temporarily pending results of the investigation. Conklin is not available for comment. Unofficial reports link Conklin to a football betting ring presently the subject of an intense investigation by league officials and the FBI. The Harpoon front office has declined comment, referring all questions to the commissioner's office. Conklin is to appear before the commissioner sometime this week to answer allegations.

*****

Ed called the commissioner's office and scheduled a meeting as soon as he read the paper. He left a note for Amy and departed for the league office in New York that afternoon. The meeting took place in a conference room with a flock of the commissioner's legal advisors present. An official directed Ed to sit alone on one side of a huge, green felt-topped table to face the pack of attorneys and the commissioner. The commissioner never smiled, instead motioned toward a chair and said, "Sit down there, Mister Conklin. Looks like we have much to talk about. Where is your counsel?"

"I don't have anything to hide. Why would I need counsel?"

"Your choice, but under the circumstances...." He looked apprehensive.

"I'm good, Commissioner. Let's get on with this. I can always retain counsel."

The meeting concluded at midnight and the entire group reassembled the next morning. When the inquiry finally ended, Ed had been thoroughly grilled, mostly about his connections with the mob. He listened to the same echoed questions hour after hour without complaining. Ed handled the examination calmly and courteously until near the end. He finally became indignant and stood.

"All right! I've just about had it! All of you have missed the point! Why in the hell don't you ask *yourselves* some pertinent questions? Why haven't you asked yourselves how Benny Oldham already knew what the next play would be? Doesn't that strike you as being important? Someone had to tell him or signal what the next play would be. Someone on the KC coaching staff had to tell him. Someone who knew the next play maybe? He looked toward the sideline after every play. Don't you think that's important? And don't you wonder who sent the falsified betting slips and IOU's to you? Surely you don't think I sent them, do you? Look, I'm not hiding anything. This is obviously a set-up. Why don't you believe me?"

"We are asking the questions here, Mister Conklin. We believe you have been treated fairly under the circumstances. Look at it from our viewpoint."

"Your viewpoint seems pretty damned one way to me. Look, fellows, I didn't try to keep anything secret and you know that. I kept my team advised from the very beginning."

"That's *your* story, Mister Conklin. We cannot find any evidence that supports your story. Where is the evidence? Your general manager and owner deny any previous knowledge."

The news stunned Ed. "What? No! I cannot believe that. They can't deny previous knowledge. That is just not possible! They were both in on it from the beginning. I told the GM everything and he has the packet of information in his safe."

"Yes, but that's your story, not his. The bottom line is, he denies it and you have openly admitted affiliations with a known gangster's family, Mister Conklin. And that is, as the pictures, signatures, IOU's and your own words tell us, that is indisputable."

Now I'm Mister Conklin.

"I told you how that happened. My affiliation with the Romano family was innocent."

"A nice story, but it doesn't alter the facts. Now, let's get back to what we do know. Did you or did you not take a dive Sunday? And did you knowingly associate with a member of the Romano family? Did you attend functions with the family?"

"You know I did. I said so. I told you everything. I did it willingly and innocently, not criminally."

The commissioner stood and said, "I suppose you would like us to believe that, but unsavory facts do keep surfacing, Mister Conklin. Whether or not the threats and messages you allege are true cannot be proven. We have no evidence to support you."

What the hell is going on?

"I told the general manager everything! I don't understand what is happening here. Are you sure the GM and owner denied knowledge? If they did, they lied to you. What about the coach?"

"We only know what we have been told. You tell us one thing, your owner and general manager say something else. Surely you can understand our predicament. We haven't talked to the coaching staff yet, but we are not finished investigating. Please bear with us until we finish."

"About taking a fall. I admitted that and you know I didn't have any choice! If your wife or daughter's life was at stake, what would you have done? I did what I had to, and I notified the team ahead of time."

"They deny that. And you didn't notify law enforcement authorities, did you?"

"Didn't you read the damned note? They had Amy! What

would you have done?"

"I am not the issue here. Your story is pretty far-fetched, Mister Conklin, don't you think? You must admit that from our viewpoint your version may be conveniently contrived. Obviously we must take that possibility into consideration. What we do know so far is very damaging, both to you and for professional football. No player in the history of our league has ever been accused of throwing a game, Mister Conklin, let alone freely admitting such actions. Professional football has been free of suspicion insofar player gambling is concerned. Heretofore, there has never been a hint of such violations, but we can't say that any more, now can we? This is a low point for professional football, Mr. Conklin. The entire league is now involved in a media circus. Baseball had its betting scandal, and now it appears we are going to have ours. Place yourself in my shoes, Mister Conklin."

"You are not listening to me. Listen to *me*! I am telling the truth!"

"We will take your information into our decision, but you do seem to have some unusual connections, Mister Conklin–unusual and extremely disturbing."

"That simply is not true! I do not have any connections with gamblers or crooks and neither does Amy. My affiliation with her was and is legal and innocent. Carlo Romano is using her to blackmail me. Can't you see that?"

The commissioner called a halt to the proceedings. "We plan to look closely at all aspects of your story. I simply cannot reinstate you at the moment, not until these allegations have been dealt with. Are you still living with Romano's daughter?"

"No, sir. She is missing."

The commissioner looked up. "You say she is missing? But, do you happen to know of her whereabouts by any chance?"

"Of course not! I said she's missing! That means I don't know where she is. That's why she is *missing!* I think

Romano has abducted and is holding her."

"Really?" He took a quick look at the others seated around the table. They all exchanged skeptical glances and shrugs. "I see. Well, you must admit that also seems pretty far-fetched."

"I am and have been telling you the truth. She is missing."

"Abducted, you say? By whom?"

"I believe by Carlo."

"Aren't they from the same family? Cousins? Well, no matter. I think it would be prudent if you separated yourself from any hint of impropriety for the time being, and that includes contact with all members of the Romano family. I expect there will soon be a grand jury hearing concerning these allegations, Mister Conklin. So, you see, this matter, legally, is out of my hands now that the FBI and IRS are involved. Tax evasion and illegal gambling are federal offenses, you know. Take a room nearby and keep me informed of your whereabouts. Good day, Sir."

The league office announced Ed's suspension to the news media that afternoon. The commissioner's office called the next morning.

"We will wait to see how the gambling and tax evasion charges against you develop, Mister Conklin, after that we will make a decision about your National Football League football future. Keep us informed of your whereabouts."

"What charges?"

"I take it you haven't read the morning paper."

The news crushed what little spirit Ed had remaining. The IRS had picked up the information about his gambling connections and their Tax Fraud Division would soon submit evidence to the court system, along with possible recommendations for a Grand Jury trial. If so, the federal district prosecutor would probably call for a grand jury to deal with allegations of tax evasion and illegal gambling. Ed's professional and personal life had fallen apart and his legal troubles were multiplying by the day.

*****

Ed drove to Boston the next morning and went straight to the apartment to wait. He grabbed his phone the second it rang. "Thank God," he said, the moment he recognized her voice. "Are you okay, Amy? Where are you?"

"I'm okay, but I don't have time to talk. I can't see you again, Ed. Please don't try to contact me again; not ever. I mean that. Not ever. I am alone right now and only have a moment. For your good and mine, Ed. Stay out of my life."

His initial elation crumbled. "I don't understand. Tell me where you are. I'll come for you. Amy?"

"No! I can't see you again, Ed. Please take care of Harpy for me. Goodbye." Her voice sounded subdued and strained. She hung up immediately, leaving him begging the silence for answers.

Harpy? Why did she mention Harpy? She knows Harpy is dead. She's trying to tell me something.

*****

"Where is she, Celia?" he demanded the moment she opened the door.

"Well, nice to see you, too, Ed. Amy isn't here and that's all I can tell you. You don't need to hang around here waiting for her, either. She doesn't come here anymore and told me she never will again."

"Is she okay?"

"How the hell would I know?" She stared at him, refusing to give the slightest hint of compassion.

"I'm not her enemy, Celia. I love her. Why won't you tell me about her?"

"That's all very nice, Ed, now if you don't mind, I'm busy."

"Tell her I–"

"No! I will not be caught between you two! Leave me out

of your problems, Ed. I am not a messenger and I don't want you coming here again. Stay away from my family. I don't want those people you are involved with coming around here looking for you or Amy. Can't you understand that?"

He nodded sadly and said, "You're right. I'm sorry, Celia. For everything."

A tremendous weight fell over his life as the final ray of hope vanished. He felt defeated, alone, betrayed and forsaken, all at the lowest point of his life. Celia stood implacably, arms folded, feet apart, staring at him dispassionately. He gestured helplessly and said, "I'm sorry. I don't know what to do, Celia."

Celia's eyes filled with tears as he turned away. His shoulders were stooped as he shuffled down the walk like a beaten old man.

*****

She spoke into the phone moments after watching his truck disappear. "Ed just left. I did just as you asked and I feel perfectly miserable. I feel like a damned traitor, Amy. I sure hope you know what you are doing. I have never seen anyone so despondent. He looks terrible. His entire life has been destroyed."

Celia listened to Amy's response with her eyes closed, tears streaming steadily. She nodded and said, "I know. I know. Me too, honey. I'm so sorry. Will you be okay? Do you need me?" She listened again and said, "No, Amy. If you want to know, you ask him. I won't do it for you. Please don't ask. If you want his numbers, all you have to do is ask."

*****

His grand jury hearing convened the next week. The prosecution lawyer presented his reasons for indictment and the jury, nineteen members, listened and asked questions. By law, there were no defense lawyers or a judge present, only a prosecution representative to assist with the process. The jurors asked questions and sought evidence. Their findings would be sent to the requesting prosecutor who would, if they recommend indictment, probably call for a trial. Either a bench trial with judge alone, or a jury trial with defense attorneys, prosecuting attorneys, and a judge present, depending on Ed's choice, if it went to trial.

Ed believed their questions would be easy to answer. He planned to start from the beginning and simply tell the truth about everything. He disliked the assisting prosecutor immediately, an imperious older attorney nearing retirement, assigned by the prosecutor in charge to support the jury. He featured a mop of wavy silver hair and a pair of Ben Franklin glasses on his bulbous alcoholic's nose. He also played constantly with a conspicuous mole on the back of his neck. Ed noticed everything about him while suffering through hours of jury questioning.

"Yes, I see, Mister Conklin, but where are these notes you say this Carlo person gave you?"

"I gave them to the team general manager and owner. I suppose the GM still has them, except the last one. You have that copy."

"I see. But the owner and general manager deny any such transactions. Let's say, just for the hell of it, that you *did* give the GM the information you so obviously want the jury to believe you did. If that's true, then why didn't you give that final message to him?"

"Because I thought Miss Roman would be endangered if I did. She has been abducted."

"Oh, yes, that–the alleged abduction. I presume you meant Miss Romano?"

"No, dammit! I meant exactly what I said! Her name is Amy Roman, and the abduction isn't a figment of my imagination. She would never leave by choice."

"Please, Mister Conklin. No more outbursts." The

prosecutor didn't appear to be all that upset and continued. "We are all in this together. Tell me, Mister Conklin, where is Miss Roman now?"

"Are you people listening to me? She is missing! I don't know where she is!"

"You don't know. How convenient. Have you been in contact with her?"

"She called earlier this week but wouldn't, or couldn't, tell me where she was. I could hear someone there with her. She seemed frightened. I know something is terribly wrong. I honestly don't know where she is."

"Indeed? Well, is she or is she not abducted?"

"I'm certain she is. I don't know where she is and she didn't or couldn't say. She did call but wouldn't tell me anything, other than to let me know she was okay. I think whoever has her was with her. Someone was. She got shut off." His confidence began slipping. The day went like that, hour after frustrating hour, ending with an another overnight recess. When the jury met the next morning, his torment continued.

"Mister Conklin, there seems to be some rather puzzling inconsistencies in your story."

"I told you the truth."

"So you say. Well, perhaps you can explain why your owner and general manager would disavow knowledge of the notes you contend were given to them by you? In fact, they refuse to accept responsibility for any knowledge whatsoever. How do you explain that?"

"We have been over that several times. I cannot explain it. I absolutely did give them the notes and they have known about everything from the very beginning." His voice trailed off as the implications sank in.

"I see. Well, perhaps you can understand our predicament here. We have problems corroborating your story. There are some extremely serious discrepancies and, I might add, some rather significant irregularities in your personal relationships.

Is that all you have to say?"

"It is. That's all there is to it."

"Very well. Thank you, sir. That concludes our questions You will be informed of our recommendations to the prosecutor, probably no later than tomorrow noon. Please make yourself available at the Federal Marshal's request.

He stood when the jury filed in at noon the following day. The prosecutor made the announcement.

"Mister Conklin. You have given the jury no choice as to their verdict, however, they have limited their recommendations to the governing prosecutor for an indictment against you for income tax evasion. Some jurors believed you should also be charged with gambling, fraud, and for accepting bribes. Enough members of the jury spoke otherwise to limit their recommendation to one charge. The jury's decision is final. You need to prepare yourself to defend against the recommended indictment for tax evasion. We respectfully encourage you gain the services of a good attorney."

A federal marshal escorted Ed to the courthouse for arraignment. His troubles continued to spiral out of control. The news media ran the article that evening and he made headline news the next morning.

CONKLIN INDICTED FOR TAX EVASION

Chapter Thirteen

CARLO

⎯⎯⎯⎯⎯⌄⎯⎯⎯⎯⎯

"Hello, baby."

"Carlo?" She dropped the sack of groceries and retreated down the walk. Carlo's men stepped from the shadows and blocked the way before she could run.

"Don't look so surprised. You must have known I would come to get what's mine." He pulled her roughly into the apartment. "You boys wait in the car. I'll be a few minutes here."

"How did you find me?"

"You can't hide from me, baby. Helicopters can follow you anywhere. I've known where you were all along. Just been waiting for the right time. That would be now."

He locked the door and positioned himself so she had to go through him to escape. Carlo threw his topcoat on a chair, peeled off a pair of thin leather gloves and placed them on the coat. He smiled self-confidently, stepped closer and reached out to touch her. When the back of his fingers brushed her face, Amy swept them away angrily.

"I want you out of here!" she screamed. "Out! Right now, Carlo! Get out!"

"Not until I get what I came for." His movements were slow and deliberate, forcing her into a position with no escape, smiling as he countered her every move.

Amy tried not to show it, but she knew he was going to hurt her. "You have no right to invade my house, Carlo!"

His stalking closeness was frightening enough, but her terror intensified as she recognized the look of pure hatred on his face. She had seen it before.

"You remember the rules, don't you, baby? No strain, no pain."

"No, Carlo. You can't do this!" Her back touched the wall just as his fist crashed against the side of her face. Amy staggered and regained her balance just before a second blow smashed her to the floor. He pulled her up by the hair and imprisoned her against the wall, his fingers now fastened tightly around her throat.

"Don't you ever tell me what I can and can't do," he whispered fiercely. "You have screwed with me for the last time, Anna."

He ripped her blouse off as she fought against the strangling power of his grip. His fingernails dug deep into the flesh of her neck until she couldn't breathe. Amy fought frantically but his fingers were too strong. The light began to dim before he released the grip. Amy's legs buckled and she collapsed gasping for air.

"If you still want to fight, that's fine with me, Anna. But I'm not leaving without getting what I came for. Your choice."

Amy sat up and massaged her throat for a moment before answering, "You go straight to hell!" She didn't comprehend much after the first numbing kick to the ribs and only vaguely remembered the endless beating, and being raped, and that Carlo had showered to remove the blood before returning to stand over her. She lay on the bed in a fetal position barely able to see him through bloodshot eyes. She watched as he dressed and stood over her again. She was too numbed to care. He rolled her over roughly and spit on her before stepping to the door.

"I'll send one of the boys after you tomorrow. Get your shit together and be ready. Playing time is over for you, Anna. From here on I play for keeps. If you care at all for yourself or that dumb ballplayer, you better start paying attention. This is my last warning, Anna. No more games. If you don't do right, someone might accidentally die."

"You can rape and kill me, Carlo, but I will never go with you."

He smiled triumphantly and replied, "Sure you will. You belong to me, Anna. You should know better than anyone that you can't fight me. I ought to kill you for what you have done to me, and maybe I will someday, but that can wait. I'm taking you back."

Amy recognized that her options had run out. "You don't want me, Carlo. You just don't want someone else to have me."

He rushed back and yanked her off the bed. A vicious kick to the stomach brought a short period of unconsciousness. Carlo was still there when she recovered and the nightmare continued.

"You better learn to keep your damned mouth shut and listen, woman. You *are* coming back to me, Anna. You know that, so don't fight it."

"Never!"

He laughed contemptuously and pinched her cheek. "I warn you, Anna, I'm just about out of patience. Okay, I'm going to make it easy for you to understand, so listen good. If you don't come back on your own, I will *make* you want to come back. You wouldn't want me to do that, would you? You know I can."

"I will never come with you, Carlo."

His slap ruptured an eardrum and blood ran down her neck.

She flinched as he drew back to strike again.

"You still thinking about that damned football player, Anna?" He hovered over her menacingly.

She knew better than to antagonize him further.

"You'll forget him, Anna. I'll see to that. Anyway, he ain't worth a damn now, Anna. I fixed him good. He is one washed up football player."

When she didn't answer, Carlo unlocked the door and prepared to leave.

"Just one more thing. You just think you still want him, Anna, and that's a real shame because you belong to me. You have always belonged to me and I want you back. If you don't come back to me, Anna, of your own free will, you can kiss that damned football player goodbye, and I mean permanently. You know exactly what I mean.

"You be settled in my house by dark tomorrow or I'll have the boys take care of your football player, Anna. You know I mean it, so do the right thing. Get your butt home where you belong. Ciao, baby."

"Why, Carlo? You don't want me. You don't love me. Why?"

"I warn you, Anna, this isn't a kiddy game. You just be there tomorrow when I get home." He walked out and left the door open.

She didn't have to think long. The game was over and he won. Amy didn't go home, though. She went to the hospital in a cab with his lieutenants following.

*****

The doctor entered the room and closed the door the day before he released her. "I know you say it was an accident, Miss Roman, but I have seen hundreds of injuries like yours during a long career. You have been beaten viciously. I *know* that. I have also reviewed all of your previous medical records. You may never regain full hearing in that damaged ear and there is still evidence of internal bleeding. Only time will tell if you can have children. I am going to bring the authorities in, with or without your permission."

Amy panicked. "No! Don't you dare! There are things you don't know. He will kill the man I love if you interfere." She turned to stare out of the window.

"This is serious, Miss Roman. Your medical records indicate a history of abuse. You have been in more than once for the same type of injuries. I hope you are frightened by what I must say next, but I must inform you that the evidence all points, with absolute certainty, that you are in mortal danger. You will probably die from another beating."

Her eyes remained locked in a vacant stare. She answered listlessly, "Thank you for your concern, Doctor. That doesn't matter. The only thing that matters is that he doesn't kill my friend, and he will if I don't go to his home. He is a stone cold killer, Doctor. He will kill anyone who gets in his way. So you see? I no longer matter."

"I think you matter," he said, becoming irritable. "And you are going to be killed if this pattern continues. Don't you understand that? I cannot say this strongly enough. He is going to kill you!"

"I know that, but I'm already dead so it doesn't matter." Her eyes glazed.

"What? What are you saying?"

She faced him and smiled feebly. "It doesn't matter about me any more, Doctor, because I lost my life weeks ago. My life is over and nothing matters to me anymore." She favored him with a weary smile. "Please stay out of my life or someone I love is going to be killed. I am begging you. Please."

*****

Amy went to Carlo's home by taxi and surrendered her life, gratefully embracing the solitude. Carlo didn't come around for two weeks and Amy never opened the shades or left the house. She married Carlo after the bruising and cuts could be hidden with makeup, and shortly after Ed's indictment. The marriage would have happened sooner but the internal bleeding persisted.

*****

"Hello, Leitha."

Leitha looked up from her work, clearly surprised, and said, "Why, Amy. What an unexpected pleasure. To what do I owe this honor?" She calmly tapped a stack of invoices into order and placed them in the out basket.

"I know I don't deserve anything from you, but I would like very much to come back to work."

Leitha's mask of control almost cracked. She cleared her throat and said, "I see. I take it then that you have spoken with your father?"

"You know I haven't. I'm sorry about the way I left, Leitha. You didn't deserve such poor treatment from me. You were always decent and kind. I'm sorry."

"Why have you decided to come back, Anna?"

"I need to keep busy, Leitha. I need to work."

"You are going way too fast for me. This is all so sudden." Leitha spun the chair away to reach for a glass of water and sipped while facing away from Amy. Moments later, with an oddly satisfied smile, she faced Amy and said, "Could I delay any decision until later, Anna? You must know that I need to speak with your father about this. Surely you can understand my position? Leave your number with the secretary, Anna, and I will let you know." She smiled cheerfully and busied herself with another invoice.

"Thank you. I hope we can be friends again, Leitha. I promise you won't regret it. I'm sorry for everything."

Amy didn't fail to notice the look of pleasure on Leitha's face each time she called her Anna, nor did she miss the smell of cigar smoke as she passed the conference room on the way out. Leitha called in midafternoon and instructed her to meet with her father at Sardino's that evening.

*****

She kissed him platonically and took the lone seat across the table. His lieutenants retreated into the background as he inspected her with narrowed eyes through the billowing cloud of cigar smoke. She might just as well have been one of the throng of hapless debtors who came by to pay protection money.

"So, the prodigal returns. You look terrible, Anna. You should gain some weight."

"I'm sorry for everything, Father. I have been very childish. Please forgive me."

His eyes, cold and distant, were totally devoid of compassion. Amy had voluntarily placed her life at his mercy and now had nothing left to do but wait quietly for either a fatherly endorsement or the noose of unsympathetic authority.

"The gallery manager asked for my advice."

"Yes, I know."

"Why do you come to me?"

"I thought...." She suddenly realized that he probably wanted to maintain his association to the art gallery a secret.

"Why, Anna?"

She felt trapped. He had to know everything. Leitha would have told him about the break-in and the questions about gallery ownership. "I thought the family should consent if I work."

He leaned close and his voice hardened. "You have meddled, Anna, and I don't like family problems."

"It will never happen again, Father. I'm sorry."

"I expect complete loyalty."

She recognized the opening and breathed a secret sigh of relief. "I know that, Father."

"You are a Romano."

"I understand, Father."

He sat back and nodded with satisfaction. "No more silly independence. Romano women do not embarrass the family."

"No, Father." She kept her eyes down submissively. "Everything will be just like old times. I promise to make sure of that." She cringed at the inescapable vision of Carlo's anger.

"Good. What about the football player?"

She looked away quickly so he couldn't read her eyes. "That ended before I married Carlo, Father."

"Good. You should be with your own kind, Anna."

"I know, Father. I am home now."

"Good." He watched her face for tell-tale signs of discomfort as he presented the keys to another expensive automobile. He had known this moment would happen from the time Leitha called to tell him. Amy swallowed her pride and took the keys, and with that concession drifted back into the role of a subservient daughter.

"Is that all, Father?"

"You may go, Anna, but remember–no mistakes." His eyes narrowed and he took a long draw on the cigar. "I never forgive disloyalty, Anna, but you are family. You must earn your place in the family again."

Leitha called and Amy began work the next day as a floor clerk, dusting and walk-in customers were her only responsibilities. Leitha treated her like a stranger.

*****

Carlo returned the next week and flew into a dark rage when she told him about the job.

"You didn't say I couldn't work, Carlo. Anyway, Father said I could."

"You used the old man against me! He has no right! You are my wife! You should have asked me first! Damn you!" He approached with clenched fists.

"Are you going to hit me again, Carlo?" She didn't flinch or back away. "I don't think my father would like it if he knew how you treat me, and he just might find out if you ever hit me again."

Carlo could barely control his anger. He breathed deep and fast for a moment and seemed to relax by stages, but his face was still contorted with anger. His fist dropped and he said, "He don't know anything and if you know what's good for you, you sure as hell won't tell. Don't ever threaten me again. You know what I'll do if you ever say anything to your old man about our private life? Sure you do. You won't say anything. Not when that lousy football player's neck is on the line."

"My father isn't stupid, Carlo. He knows more than you think. Maybe not quite everything, but more than you think. What do you think he would do if he knew you beat and raped me? I wonder what he would do if he knew that, Carlo? I wonder what he would think if he knew the only reason I am with you is because you threatened to kill Ed? What do you suppose he *will* do if I tell him you beat me more than once? And what if I show him the hospital records and photos? He warned you after the first time, remember?"

"You can't threaten me. I don't give a damn what he thinks!"

"Oh, sure you do, Carlo. He runs your life just like he does mine. Why don't you tell him to his face that you don't give a damn what he thinks?"

"I want your ass at home when I get here!"

"That's too bad, tough guy. Father gave me permission to work."

"I won't release you, Anna. You know that."

"I don't intend to walk out, Carlo, but I do have his permission to work."

"Shit!" He stomped out and she didn't see him again for weeks, and then found him waiting one evening when she came home from work.

"I moving back in," he announced.

"It's your house, Carlo." She ignored him and went to the kitchen.

"I want things to be the way they were, Anna." He followed and blocked her movements.

"That isn't saying much. As in, the way they were when? When were things between us that good?" She refused to look at him.

"We could be good together if you come to your senses."

"Not in this lifetime," she snapped.

"Don't piss me off, damn you." His eyes narrowed and he inched closer. "I want you back. All of you."

She sighed wearily and said, "So, I'm back."

"No, you're not. You aren't trying, Anna. You haven't kissed me and you haven't made love to me. How long do I have to wait?"

She glared at him and exploded. "What did you expect? Am I supposed to act as if nothing happened, Carlo? I will never forget what you did! You made me a prostitute! You forced me to trade my life away and now you expect me to give my body and love to you and act as if nothing happened!"

"I can make you forget him if you give me a chance."

"I'm not thinking about him," she lied. "And there is nothing you can do to make me like you, let alone love you."

"Don't make me mad, Anna. I'm warning you."

They bickered for several minutes before Carlo lost patience and shoved her to the floor and started dragging her to the bedroom. She fought against his strength for a moment before submitting lifelessly. She lay perfectly still making no effort to protect herself as he vented his frustrations with deliberately halfhearted kicks and punches. She didn't cry out, refusing to give him any satisfaction. He pulled her up. She turned away so he couldn't kiss her on the mouth. Tears streaked her face.

"Shit!" he exclaimed, terminating the performance. "I

could screw a damned knothole and get more pleasure than I can get out of you. You ain't worth a damn!" He threw her down again, turned her over with his foot and kicked at her stomach. She avoided the brunt of the blows by rolling beneath a coffee table, doubled into a fetal position to protect her body.

*****

Her mother visited the next day. "Your father worries about your marriage, Anna."

"*He* doesn't worry, Mother. *You* do."

"When are you going to have babies, Anna? You don't want to wait too long."

"I don't want a baby."

"You should settle down and have babies, Anna. It isn't natural for a woman to be barren. A baby will make you feel better."

"Maybe someday," she said, hoping the small concession would appease her mother.

"Someday you will be too old. Thirty is already too old. You will dry up if you don't start soon. Is that what you want, Anna?"

She lost her temper. "Yes, Mother! That is exactly what I want! Now please leave me alone and stay out of my private life!"

*****

Amy followed the evening news with intense curiosity, remaining abreast of Ed's problems. Her heart ached for him. She felt helpless. Her commitment to shield Ed was uncompromising. She fought a never-ending, almost overpowering urge to pick up the phone and establish contact with him. Common sense prevailed–and fear.

Celia wanted to help, but Amy wouldn't let her in. Carlo

wouldn't allow Celia to visit in his house. Celia could not understand Amy's voluntary return to a man she loathed and spurned. Their timeless relationship cooled. Amy called Celia occasionally, but never from home.

"What happened, Amy? Two months ago you were in heaven. What happened? Talk to me! Who are you? I don't know you any more. What has Carlo done to you? I know something is very wrong and you aren't sharing."

"You wouldn't understand."

"You may be right. Look, if I can't be a friend in your time of need, then–"

"You can't, Celia. You wouldn't understand and I don't want you to try. I'm sorry. Please don't ever call me at home again. Carlo doesn't want you calling and I'm sure he knows every word we say. Always use the cell."

"Why are you avoiding me?"

"Things change, Celia. Please help me the only way you can. Let me go."

She began withdrawing from Celia and her life settled into a monotonous routine of work at the gallery, coming home on time, and dreading Carlo's periodic appearances.

Amy abandoned all social activities and Carlo saw to it that she didn't have a chance to get out alone. He gave strict orders about where she could go and who she could see, and the dark sedans in her rear view mirror and across from their house reinforced the substance of his intent. The cars usually sat in plain view under the streetlight across from her house throughout the nights.

"No, Carlo. I don't feel like it," she complained when he arrived home drunk and pulled at her skirt.

He flew into a rage. "I don't give a damn how you feel! Get up those stairs and get your clothes off!"

"No, Carlo!"

He knocked her senseless with a crushing blow to the stomach and she regained consciousness in a pool of blood on the bathroom floor, naked and cold. She crawled and fell down the stairs. One of the men in the car across the street saw her collapse on the front steps and delivered her to the hospital. Amy returned home from the hospital a week later and discovered a pair of Carlo's bloodstained shorts still in the clothes hamper. The bedspread was ruined by blood stains. She had gained days of reprieve from Carlo's vengefulness, and also time to reach a positive decision regarding the rest of her life.

Amy returned home a different woman–never speaking, never smiling, never objecting to his advances. After a month of careful attention to everything he desired, except how she looked, Amy moved her clothes into a downstairs bedroom. The bedroom faced the beautiful courtyard in the back yard, a much better view than the car parked across the street day and night. Carlo didn't object to anything, except the way she looked.

"You look like a goddamned bag lady. Get cleaned up! Fix yourself! You look like shit! Who the hell would want to touch you?"

Amy finally had a shield against his lust. Carlo couldn't tolerate sloth and filth. He left her alone and stayed away for days at a time–enough time for Amy to nurture the birth of a plan. She would find a way to stop Carlo.

Chapter Fourteen

THE TRIAL

E d's life continued to disintegrate. The team suspended him without pay, his commercial endorsement contracts ended, and then his mother died. Her funeral took his mind away from the tax evasion trial for a week before that ordeal began again.

The FBI and IRS entered the fray, holding him captive for days with meetings and questions. Through it all, his lawyer appeared unconcerned, almost nonchalant, often acting as the Devil's Advocate. Ed complained, "You know, Norm, it would be helpful if I thought you believed me. I feel isolated, like I'm out here on a limb by myself."

"Hell, you know I believe in you, Ed. I'm just trying to take the other side during the preliminaries so you have a feel for what to expect and how to counter."

"Okay, now let me tell *you* what I expect, Norm! I expect they are going to try to hang my ass for something I didn't do. Look, this is all pretty simple to me: they have to prove I did something I didn't do. I think this whole mashup is that damned simple. Their entire case is tied to pictures that prove nothing except I attended a party and some bad guys were there. They have to prove I was involved with those people and they can't do that because I wasn't. They are relying on forged IOU's and betting slips. All we have to do is prove the signatures aren't mine, which shouldn't be that hard, Norm, because they aren't mine! Can't you get a handwriting specialist to confirm that much?"

"I'm working on that."

"You have all of my financial records. Doesn't that prove I didn't make money betting?"

"Not quite that simple, Ed. They will counter by presuming the money you made betting is hidden in some offshore account. Can you prove it isn't?"

"Where? And wouldn't they have to prove that, too? Wouldn't they? And they can't because there isn't any damned extra money! Come on, Norm! They can't prove anything! Shouldn't that just about wrap it up? I am innocent until proven guilty, right? Isn't that the law?"

"I wish it were that simple, Ed. They are sure to bring in witnesses who will swear you were involved with the Romano family. You can absolutely count on that."

"So what? Even if I was involved with someone other than Amy, and I wasn't, that wouldn't prove tax evasion, would it?"

"No. I believe we are going to beat the tax rap, Ed, but I would like to see you get out of this with your good name intact. That's what worries me."

Ed sighed heavily and said, "Well, I don't think that is about to happen. Do you?"

"Nope. Sure doesn't look good."

"Okay. Let's concentrate on one thing at a time. Is it even remotely possible that I could be convicted for tax evasion?"

Norm shrugged and shook his head. "I really don't think so, Ed. I don't think they can prove anything. Have you decided on a trial by jury or a bench trial?"

"No. What do you think?"

"All right, if you were guilty, I would say go for a jury. But, under the circumstances, I think a judge is probably your best bet. A judge probably won't be swayed by the emotion of some flashy prosecuting attorney. So, I would advise that you ask for trial by judge."

"Okay, do it. Let's get this tax indictment business out of the way so I can begin to worry about what comes next."

Norm sat back and gazed thoughtfully at Ed for several moments before asking, "Have you been in contact with her, Ed?"

"No. I don't know where she is. I can't find her and her phone is off or destroyed."

"Okay. Have you even tried to contact her?" He frowned in disbelief when Ed looked away before answering.

"Of course I have. I have tried every way I can think of to contact her. I got nothing, Norm. She is missing and it's killing me!"

"Dammit, Ed, you have to let her go, at least for now. She is nothing but trouble for how you look to the public, and maybe even to a judge. Let her go, man! I'm serious, Ed. I cannot guarantee anything if she is still in your life. She's a Romano, and that's all anyone needs to know to convict you by association."

*****

The longer the preliminaries lasted, the more Ed worried about Norm's cavalier attitude about his defense. He contacted a well-advertised law firm to ask for an opinion about how to contact handwriting experts. After developing a comfort zone with the firm's attorney, he also confessed reservations about Norm.

Before the attorney gave an opinion, he said, "I am a football fan and familiar with what is happening to your career, Mister Conklin. The news is swarming with it. I feel for you. From what you have told me today, and in all honesty, I must tell you that I do not believe you are receiving adequate representation. There are at least three excellent and well-known handwriting experts in the Boston area. My firm has abundant experience with them if you need numbers. You not only need a couple of genuine experts–the more the better–in court to present their analysis. I also believe you could use a more established and determined attorney to represent your overall interests. I am booked for weeks or I would like to represent the case for you. Would you like a recommendation?"

"Yes. I am worried about my guy. Please."

"Very well. You could try the Gruber Group. Great name, right? I am very familiar with that firm. They may be new guys in town, but I believe you will benefit substantially from their enthusiasm and determination. I can attest from some depressing experiences with them that they are very sharp. Both of them topped their law school class at Yale and I have recently been on the losing end of two of their cases. They are brothers, by the way. Very competent. I urge you get their services if at all possible.

Ed gave the Gruber Group a call and after one meeting fired his lawyer to retain them as counselors. Their first action was to ask the court system for an accelerated date for Ed's trial. The United States Attorney General, providentially a great football fan, intervened, more politically than legally, and the Gruber brothers won their first battle.

The preliminaries for his case had already dragged on for weeks as Ed continued to lose weight dramatically. His daily routine centered on meetings and preparations for the coming trial. His nights were a series of restless naps interspersed with long, exhausting runs through the darkened streets. His waking hour thoughts, when not involved with the coming trial, centered on Amy–agonizing over and worrying about Amy. Ed Conklin, the best and toughest defensive lineman in professional football, teetered constantly on the threshold of tears. When his thoughts drifted to Amy, as they did almost every waking moment, he wept, sometimes uncontrollably. His weight dropped and he didn't care. Ed Conklin no longer looked like a football player, more like a hollow-faced drunken derelict. His eyes were empty, buried in dark, cavernous basins surrounded by the ever deepening creases on his face, a face filled with problems and worries that he couldn't share with anyone. He stopped shaving and changing clothes.

Ed didn't have a life. His world seemed to be on an accelerating road to ruin, and then everything changed in a twinkling. Ed Conklin regained a reason for living and once again felt the excitement of hope. The everything that changed life for Ed happened just after midnight during another of his exhausting late night runs. His entire existence changed immediately after he crashed into a shadowy figure on the sidewalk a block from his apartment, knocking the other person sprawling.

"Are you okay?" he asked, bending over to assist the fallen man after the incident.

The unlucky fellow sat up and brushed himself off. "Yeah, I'm probably okay. You are Ed Conklin, aren't you? I hoped to catch you here tonight."

Ed sensed danger and stepped back, looking around for others. "Who wants to know?" He pulled the pint-sized man on the pavement to his feet.

"Can I please have a moment of your time, Mister Conklin? My name is Don Hagerty."

"Sorry. Have we met? Am I supposed to know you?"

"No, and no. I am an Assistant Federal Prosecutor." The little guy continued to dust himself off and moved farther into the street light to present his credentials. Ed approached cautiously to examine the card. He recognized the guy's face. "Haven't I seen you hanging around the courthouse?"

"Possibly. I spend a lot of time there."

"You're out late, Hagerty." The tiny attorney was overweight and nearly bald, probably only in his early thirties. Ed had noticed him around the court building. "What are we doing here, Hagerty? This meeting is no accident, is it?"

"No. I am not here by accident, Mister Conklin. I have recently become familiar with your nocturnal habits. This meeting is intentional."

"Okay, you found me. What's this all about?"

"My boss wants some time with you. Tonight. Right now. We have important information that involves you. She wants to talk."

She?

"You could catch me around court a hell of a lot easier than this."

"Well, yes, that's true. However, we are not involved with your case and should not be connected publicly with you at this point in our investigation. What we want to speak to you about is something separate from the legal circumstances you are presently involved with. I really think you should give her some time. All in your favor, believe me." He practically begged. "I think you will agree after you hear her proposal that she has your best interest in mind. All good, I promise."

Ed began to relax. Hagerty posed no threat. "First things first. Who is she?"

Hagerty looked around cautiously. "Would you mind stepping around the corner with me? We should not be seen together. Someone could end up connecting dots before we are ready to start."

"What's the big secret?"

Hagerty glanced up and down the street nervously. "I really shouldn't be seen in the open with you. I can't explain here." Beads of perspiration had popped out on his forehead. "We need to get off the street. Please." He pointed to the corner.

Hagerty's anxieties were making Ed nervous. "Look, friend, if you have something to say, spill it. I need to move on."

Hagerty summoned strength and came near assertiveness. "No. Not here, Mister Conklin. Please, come with me. Just around the corner. This won't take long." Hagerty backed into the shadows. "I guess you probably already know that every move you make, day and night, is being observed. You should also be aware that your phone is probably bugged."

"How do you know that?"

"Not bugged by us, but we have ways to know. Now, please come with me. This won't take long."

Ed was puzzled. "You have referred to we and us. Who is waiting for me? Is that why we need to move?"

"Yes. And we are not the only organization interested in you, but I doubt if that comes as a surprise. Come. Please follow me. The car is around just around the corner." He gestured down the block and led the way.

Ed followed at a discreet distance and soon joined Hagerty in the back seat of a car with the engine running. The driver remained silent and drove around for a few moments, turning corners unexpectedly, driving down alleys until she spoke for the first time. "I think we are clear now. No one is following." She parked between two cars on a dark street.

Hagerty spoke first. "None of this is my idea, Mr. Conklin. Meet Julia Skelton. This is her idea. I'll just wait down the block, Julia. Flash the lights when you're ready." He stepped out.

She offered her hand over the seat and said, "I am Julia Skelton, Mister Conklin. I am an Assistant Federal Prosecutor. What I want to talk to you about is not your present tax circumstances–not specifically anyway. I am on to something much more important for both of us, not just for me. You are implicated however."

"Implicated in what? What makes you think I'm involved in…well, what?"

"You are definitely involved, as you will soon see. I need your support because you are, like it or not, involved. Listen to what I have to say for a few moments and you will understand."

He couldn't see her face. She smelled good–some not-too-subtle fragrance. "Look, I'm really not interested in being involved in anything else right now. I have my hands full as I am sure you must know. I need to stay centered on the tax trial."

"I am not going to interfere with that," she said. "But I am willing to bet that you will be all in about helping me after I tell you what I am working on. Just a little of your time? This won't take long. You can make up your mind after you hear."

He settled back. "What the hell. I can't sleep anyway. Okay, you got the ball. Go." He watched as she angled the mirror to observe him.

"I am pretty sure that I can prove that you were set up," she said, watching for his reaction.

Ed laughed cynically. "No kidding? So what else is new?"

"Can I call you Ed?"

"Why not? Sure. What do I call you?"

The woman in the mirror appeared to be blonde, and perhaps about thirty. "My name Julia Skelton. Hagerty and I work out of the same office."

"What's your interest in my case? Is what you are doing official?"

"As I said, we are not interested or involved in your tax case, Ed. However, I am very interested in the reasons for your troubles. Look, I don't know everything yet, but what I do know is extremely sensitive. People are going to get hurt if I don't handle this correctly. I must be assured that you will be prudent with the information I am going to share with you. What I disclose here must stay just between the two of us. Hagerty doesn't know what I am going to tell you, and no one else does. There is also considerably more that I cannot reveal just yet, but I must have your word on complete secrecy. Right now. Before I say more. Your word."

"What makes you think my word is good? No one else seems to believe me."

"Okay, I'll level with you. What if I told you that I know for a fact that you were set up by the mob? The Mafia?"

He could see her eyes watching in the mirror. "If you know something like that, then why in the hell am I going through all of this trial crap?"

"What I have learned is recent, Mister Conklin, too late to stop your present court progression, but I know you are clean and with your assistance I can and will prove it. However, that is the least important part of what I am doing. What I am doing is incredibly sensitive. Important and powerful people are involved, and there are also some extremely dangerous people in the mix. I hate to admit this, but I believe there may be a leak in my office or in a local judge's office. Some information recently got out. That could be a problem, but not for you. What do you think? Are you interested?"

"Do you know who leaked?"

"Not yet, but I will. Are you in?"

"I'm interested. Go on."

"I need your word about secrecy."

"My word is good. You can trust me."

"All right, then, away we go. First of all, you need to know that the owner and general manager of your football team are involved with organized crime, as is the NFL commissioner's office, whether they like it or not."

"You have got to be kidding."

"No, I am absolutely serious. I am also pretty sure members of our city government may be involved in peripheral ways. Last, but certainly not least, certain eminent members of the judiciary might be also connected–not for criminal offenses that I know of yet–more like sins of omission, like looking the other way."

"Meaning?"

Her eyes glanced to the mirror again. "First I have to know where you stand." She waited for him to make eye contact. "I need to know if you are going to help me. My career is on the line, and maybe more than that–maybe my life. And to be perfectly honest, maybe your life."

"My life? That's interesting. Maybe a little bit disturbing, but interesting. Okay, I need to know more, like what the hell is going on, in a few words."

"Okay, but it is critically important that you know how serious the information we are dealing with is. If you breathe a word, if you so much as think out loud, someone could get hurt. Nothing, Mister Conklin, you can say nothing on the phone–any phone ever–and nothing written down. You cannot talk to anyone about this other than to me. Actually, and there can be no doubt about this, someone will be killed if what I am working on ever goes public or becomes known to the wrong people before I am ready. That's all I'm going to say for the time being. Now, are you in?"

His brow furrowed and he stared out of the window for several moments before answering, "Let me see your credentials, and Hagerty's."

She flashed the headlights and Hagerty came running.

Ed studied their ID's and driver's licenses before agreeing. "Okay, I'm in. Well, at least until I tell you I'm not in. Call me Ed."

She asked Hagerty to step out and drove away, concentrating on the road ahead. "I have discovered some fresh information, Mister Conklin that...excuse me, Ed, that I believe will guarantee your complete exoneration from the indictment you have been charged with, and everything else that has been concocted to ruin your career. Still interested?"

"You bet. Go ahead."

"Okay, hang on to your hat. I have good reason to believe the Harpoon's owner, general manager and perhaps some other team officials are involved in a betting scam with the local mob. I know for sure that you were used as part of that scam. I also have very good reasons to believe that you are innocent and with your help I can prove it. I plan to jail the perpetrators of the betting ring, and in consonance with all that, I plan to clean out the entire local organized crime organization."

His interest peaked. "Okay, I'm still in."

"Oh, there is one more thing that will no doubt interest you. Do you know that Alberto Romano is the secret owner the Harpoons? I believe you know who he is."

Chapter Fifteen

JULIA & ED

E d's thoughts lingered on Julia's revelation for several moments. "Romano? Who the hell is Paul Jensen, then, if he isn't the owner?"

"Contrary to what you have been led to believe, Jensen is absolutely *not* the owner of your team. He is a stand-in, a paper pretender, a front man. Alberto Romano is the owner. Jensen has worked with Romano for the past twenty years, albeit through several layers of insulation usually involved with real estate. Lots of real estate. I can and will prove that Alberto Romano is the Harpoon owner. I have traced the corporate window dressing he uses to insulate his name. I can also prove Jensen is Romano's man. Jensen gained prominence in real estate, but the money for his successes came from Romano. Jensen is nothing but veneer for mob business. Romano owns about half of Boston through go-betweens like Paul Jensen."

Ed wasn't convinced. "Come on! I seriously doubt if Jensen is tied to organized crime. The NFL would know have to that, and they are really picky about connections with the mob. I can't believe anyone could fool the NFL commissioner's office for long."

"You might think so, but it hasn't been that long, Ed. Do you know when Jensen bought controlling interest in the Harpoons?"

"About two years ago."

"Bingo. That's right."

Ed reached for the door handle. "Sorry, but I still can't buy it. I need to think about this. Drop me near my apartment, will you?"

Julia sighed, picked up Hagerty, drove to a spot near Ed's place and parked the car in darkness beside an old brick warehouse. "We didn't think you would come to us that easily, Ed. Would you help us if I can prove what I told you to your satisfaction?"

"I need hard proof."

"Fair enough, but that isn't the answer I need."

"Look, who is in charge of this investigation? I want to talk with someone higher up."

The two attorneys exchanged uneasy glances. Julia turned and Ed saw her face for the first time. She appeared to be no more than thirty, with long, brown hair and appeared to be very attractive, at least in the poor light.

"And, while you're at it, I need to know exactly why you are involved and how," he added.

"Okay, Ed. The truth is, there is no official investigation, yet. The two of us are pulling this together alone right now, for security reasons. We alone are putting this together for the time being, but we won't be alone much longer. I have enough evidence to bring the FBI in, and that will happen soon."

Ed's reservations deepened. "What is this, some kind of a bootleg operation?"

She nodded. "In a way, I suppose it is something like that," she admitted, pleading for understanding with her eyes.

Ed exhaled expansively. "Okay, what, exactly, is your

interest here, Julia? Why are you doing this? What's in it for you?"

"Justice?" She didn't appear to be certain.

He smiled cynically. "What? Justice for me, or you, or who?"

"I willingly admit I am primarily doing this for me. Yes, this is for me, but the justice I am seeking is also for you. I can clear you, Ed. Above all, what I am attempting to do is for justice. Absolutely."

"Ah, justice. That means there is more to it than you and me."

She turned away for a moment before observing him again in the mirror. "Yes, Ed. There is much, much more."

"Well, are we going to spar all night?"

She started the engine and pulled away. "You're right, of course. This fencing is getting us nowhere. We had to start somewhere though, didn't we? Okay, will you meet me tomorrow?"

"Why?"

"Just meet me at the central library downtown and I will provide the answers to your questions. Will you do that? You owe it to yourself, Ed. I promise you won't be sorry."

He didn't hesitate. "Sure. I am still in, Julia, but things better clear up tomorrow."

She gave rendezvous instructions and released Ed on the sidewalk where they stopped him earlier.

*****

Ed stood in the doorway of the microfilm room at the library late the next afternoon looking for her. Julia wasn't there. He checked the clock and headed for the information desk.

"Over here, Ed! Over here!" Julia waved and smiled from across the room, motioning to the chair next to hers. She was a slight woman, almost too thin, and not quite so attractive as Ed remembered. Enormous, thick, circular glasses covered a major portion of her face, giving her the comic appearance of a myopic bug. She had apparently worn a wig the night before to hide her short, blonde hair. Although surprised by her appearance, Ed liked her better without the wig. She was pleasant enough to look at, and wholesome, the old-fashioned all-American girl-next-door. Her smile inspired trust and provided a welcoming doorway to friendship. He liked what little he knew of her.

"Nice to see you again, Ed, and thank you for coming. I wondered if you would. Have a seat." She motioned to a chair in front of a viewing screen where several reels of film were already stacked in readiness. "Were you followed?" she asked in an offhand manner, almost as if unconcerned.

"No, I did as you asked. I'm sure no one knows I'm here."

"Good. But for future reference, they sometimes use helicopter surveillance. Be wary and always believe they are following and watching you."

"They?"

"Yes. You will soon know more than you probably want to about who they are." She switched the machine on and maneuvered the controls efficiently. An old copy of the Boston Globe whirled through the viewfinder in dazzling flashes, stopping at a date almost seven years earlier. It was obvious to Ed that she had done it many times before. Julia faced him. "All right. Last night you asked why I'm involved. This is why." She pointed to the screen. "Read."

Ed studied the picture above her finger. It was familiar. He had seen it before. The caption beneath the photo explained everything:

FEDERAL JUDGE ASSASSINATED.
JUDGE HAROLD SKELTON MURDERED BY A REMOTE CONTROLLED CAR BOMB. AUTHORITIES SUSPICION ASSASSINATION LINKED TO SKELTON'S RECENT INVOLVEMENT WITH MAFIA CASE.

He read the entire article, noting the murdered judge's

family consisted of one daughter in her final year of law school. Julia Skelton. After he finished, Julia rapidly operated the viewfinder, stopping automatically when another applicable article appeared. She knew the newspaper reports by heart. Ed understood the entire story when she finished. Her father's murderers were never caught. The active case had been discontinued due to a lack of evidence.

"I'm sorry, Julia."

"Now you know why I'm involved. I doubt if anyone will ever be brought to justice for my father's murder, but I know who did it. Your owner did it, Ed, or someone in his organization. The Romano's killed my father."

"And you have some notion about getting back at him through me?"

She turned the machine off and faced him squarely. Ed didn't detect any sign of humor or uncertainty in her expression. Her eyes were no longer friendly and warm. "With or without you, Mister Conklin–Ed, I am going to take these people off the street. Sooner or later, I'll get them. All of them." Her chin rose proudly, challenging a response.

"All right, but why me?"

"Because, Mister Ed, you are already in the middle of something that could be valuable to me. Unfortunately for you, and luckily for me, you were in the wrong place at the wrong time and they needed an advantage to bet on. However, you now do not have much to lose and perhaps everything to gain if you are willing to assist me. I desperately need you, Ed. You may be the key to breaking their entire organization."

"Okay. But why are you doing this by yourself?"

"I'm only alone until I get enough proof–until I'm sure the powers that be cannot just sweep me under the rug. Romano has unbelievable...no, unimaginable connections. He can have me stopped through government contacts if I don't manage this investigation perfectly, and I need to have it incontestably solid before bringing it to the justice system. As you know, he is dangerous and protected by layers of men who will and have killed for him. He also has layers of officials who shield him. Officials at city, state, and even federal levels, Ed. They protect him not because they want to, but because he has them dead to rights on something that he could use to ruin them if they didn't."

They sat perfectly still for several seconds. Julia waited like any good salesman who has just delivered a closing line. Ed pondered the consequences of commitment.

"Okay," he said. "With one stipulation."

"Name it."

"You have to call me Ed. No more Mister."

Her face gradually wrinkled into an ecstatic smile and tears pooled in her eyes. "You will never be sorry, Ed. That I can promise. Thank you. Thank you so much." She reached across and touched his arm reassuringly.

"Now what, Counselor?"

"I have a strategy, but you must be sure of yourself, Ed, because some of what I do will be very dangerous and possibly a little bit of a legal stretch. I don't want to mislead you by portraying what I plan as a walk in the park."

"I don't care. I need to do something. Anything is better than what is happening to me. Let's do this."

They established elaborate plans for meeting places and times, code names (his was Eagle), periodic new phones with no names, addresses or contact numbers on them. Julia had everything arranged in advance. Ed's confidence in her ability escalated. She was no college kid out on a lark. They initiated the first phase of Julia's plan the next day.

*****

Ed walked right by the Harpoon general manager's protesting secretary and took a position in front of his desk. The frustrated secretary followed him into the office and explained, "I'm sorry, Mister Houk, but he wouldn't wait."

"Thank you, Alice. Please close the door and leave Mister Conklin to me." Houk glared at Ed until the door clicked shut behind the secretary, and then he erupted. "What in the hell are you doing here, Conklin? You are suspended! Now get the hell out of my office!" He reached for the phone.

Ed clamped his fingers over Houk's hand on the phone and said, "Let's get a couple of things straight, Paul. If you touch that damned phone again I'm going to stick it where the sun never shines. And you can turn that inter-office speaker off, too. Do it right now before I rip the damned thing out!"

Houk flipped the machine off, stood and edged to a more secure position behind the desk. "You have no business–"

"That's where you're wrong, Paul. I want answers and I'm not leaving until I have them! You just sit down and listen for a damned moment." After Houk sat, Ed moved around the desk and sat on it facing him. "First of all, you are a lying son-of-a-bitch," he began. "I trusted you and you betrayed me. What is it you said, 'Don't worry about it, I have contacts?' I'll just bet you do."

Houk's face flushed to a motley crimson. He had no stomach for a physical standoff with an angry person of Ed's stature and unconsciously exposed the stress by nervously scratching his arms. Ed noted the white scratch marks and derived some satisfaction from his position of dominance. His previous knowledge of Houk had not revealed such vulnerability. All doubts about his chances for success faded. Houk would crumble.

"Don't worry, I'm not going to harm you, Paul, although I should tear your damned head off. Now, where are those betting slips and IOU's I gave you?"

"I don't know what you are talking about."

Of course he would deny. Julia expected that.

"Yeah you do, Paul, and I want them back. Right this damned minute. Now!"

"I don't have them."

Ed reached into his pocket and retrieved a miniature

recorder. "Sure you do. It's all right here." Ed now understood why Houk never played poker with the team. His face registered surprise and confusion. His eyes darted from Ed to the recorder, and then to the inter-office communication machine.

"That's right, Paul, I recorded our conversations. You didn't think I was dumb enough to hand those IOU's and notes to you without insurance, did you? It's all here." He shook the recorder in Houk's face and smiled. "So you see, Paul, I've got you by the balls. Now, let's start over, shall we?"

"You're bluffing."

"There are only two ways you can find that out, Pauly boy. You can either listen to your lies in front of the commissioner, or you can give me what I want and listen to it here."

"What do you want?"

"I want that packet I gave you."

"Why? What good will that do?"

"For starters, it belongs to me. And if you still have it, that will also prove you didn't send it to the commissioner and I won't have to beat the crap out of you. I doubt if you have it, though. I think you sent it to the commissioner."

"I swear that's not true."

"Prove it. Open that safe." Jensen was already sweating. Ed could almost see the cogs turning in the little fat man's head. "I'm not going down by myself, Paul. If this tax evasion trial gets me, I'm not going down alone."

"You can't intimidate me."

"Sure I can. I have this recording" he said, again waving the recorder under Houk's nose.

"That wouldn't be acceptable evidence."

"Maybe not in a courtroom, but I bet the other league owners and the commissioner will think it's acceptable. Are you willing to bet your career on it?"

Houk scratched and perspired as the stress literally poured

from him. "I don't have the packet."

"You are a damned liar."

"Even if I did have it, what assurance would I have that you didn't copy that tape?"

"None."

"I would have to have a guarantee."

"No deal. Take it or leave it."

Houk meditated for a moment and said, "Come back tomorrow."

"What for?"

"I need time to get the packet."

"No deal. It's right there in your safe. I watched you put it in there."

"It's not there now. It's in the bank."

"Bullshit! When did you take it out?"

"What difference does that make? Someone else must have sent the information to the commissioner. So what difference does it make? I didn't send that packet to anyone. It's safe at the bank. "

"Open the damned safe!"

The office door burst open and two burly security men followed the secretary in. Ed allowed them to escort him from the building without creating a scene.

Later, Julia's eyes remained closed as she listened to the listening device Ed had worn to the meeting with Houk. She listened over and over again, remaining impassive long after the recording finished.

Ed wanted to scream at her. *What do you think? Did I do okay? Say something!*

She made several notes and listened to the tape again, only then did she look up. "It's good, Ed. This is very good. He bought that recording bit. I'll keep this and have copies of your conversation with Houk made while you are in Kansas City. Good luck to you there."

*****

The Kansas City assignment took longer than Ed expected. Benny Oldham didn't have a listed phone and Ed had to wait outside the stadium and follow him home.

"Hey, ace! How you doing?" Ed yelled after getting out of the car in Oldham's driveway.

Oldham apparently didn't recognize Ed until he stepped from the rental car. "Conklin? Is that you, Ed? What the hell are you doing here? Man, you done lost a bunch of weight, Ed. You look like hell. Are you okay?"

"I've been better."

"Hey, I'm sorry about your tax trouble. That's a bummer."

Ed was well aware that Benny hadn't offered to shake hands, and they were old acquaintances, all the way back to college. "I need to talk to you, Benny."

"Sure, Ed. Shoot."

"Not here. Can we go someplace?"

Benny returned after speaking to his wife and they drove to a local bar. Neither man said anything on the way. Once seated, Ed said, "How did you get involved, Benny?"

Benny's brow furrowed and he glanced around the bar. "What the hell are you trying to do, Conklin? You know the damned rules."

Ed played along. "Just tell me how you got involved with betting, Benny?"

He shrugged and said, "Probably the same way you did. Look, Ed, I'm sorry you got caught, but I'm still clean. Leave me out of it."

"Were you betting with or against your team, Benny? How did the bookies get to you?"

"I bet some. Sure. We all do, right?"

"No. Not right. Did you lose? Is that how they got you to go along?"

"What do you think? You know how this shit goes down. Christ, man! You know we ain't supposed to be talking about this stuff. You trying to get me killed?"

"Who else is involved, Benny?"

"No way I'm going there. Look, we been friends a long time, Ed and I hate to say this to you, but you are poison, man. Hell, I could be out on my butt for just being seen with you. Forget it." He scooted across the booth preparing to leave.

Ed restrained Benny with his hand. He had to think fast. "You know what this is, Benny?" Ed pulled a miniature mic out of his shirt. Benny's face lost all expression.

"You miserable...."

"Not so fast, Falcon. This is the same mike I had on during the game."

Benny's face contorted in horror. "What? You recorded the damned game? Dammit, Ed! I didn't have any choice that day. You know that, man! You know the deal. They had me same as they had you. Aw, shit, Ed, what are you trying to do. I'm getting the hell out of here. Stay out of my life. And remember, I could let them know about this. You know what will happen if I do. Leave me alone!"

Ed didn't attempt to stop him.

*****

Julia complemented him the next day on a tremendous success.

"I didn't think it went all that well, Julia. Hell, he really didn't say much."

"This is plenty, Ed. Plenty." She smiled brightly. "And now we wait. And you stay the hell out of sight, Ed"

"Just like you said."

"That's right. Don't go back to your apartment–now or ever–at least until this wraps. They are definitely going to come after you now, Ed. It's life and death time. Stay out of sight."

"Is that all? Are you through with me?"

"Maybe. Maybe not quite. I might need you again, and

soon. But you are much more valuable to me alive, so use your head. Now I want to talk to you about the Anna Romano."

"Her name is Amy."

"Sorry. No offense. I want you to start from the beginning and tell me everything about her and your relationship. I need to know everything, Ed. Everything. This is no time to keep anything from me. And then you get out of this town."

"I have to be here for the tax trial."

"Of course, and we will need to plan security for that. But first, take this phone. It's time for new phones all around for both of us. And remember–no numbers or addresses on that phone. Leave nothing on that phone to connect us. If you have to call, you are Eagle. Don't use my name. Now, we need to be ultra-cautious during your trial. You will be well protected if you follow my instructions to the letter. Okay, now start at the beginning with Amy. Don't leave anything out."

Ed relived his time with Amy. Julia took notes in shorthand and asked questions. The conversation lasted two hours.

"Thank you, Ed. I know this hasn't been pleasant. She is special, but I knew she would be. Maybe things will work out for both of you."

Ed thought he could read between the lines. "What more do you know about Amy?"

"Some. Not enough yet. More than you might suspect, though. I have been using the local FBI office to track her. They are in this with me now, by the way. I will soon have national FBI support. This thing is going down, Ed." She smiled happily.

He leaned forward, senses alert. "Then you must know where Amy is?"

"I do." She looked grim and shook her head and groaned. "God, I hate to be the one to tell you this, Ed. You better prepare yourself for what comes next." He didn't react, so she said, "She is married to Carlo Romano."

His breathing stopped. "You cannot be serious." He nearly fainted and had to bend over and breathe deeply.

Julia didn't wait. "Absolutely serious. She is living at his home now and working her old job at the art gallery."

The news sickened him. "Oh, please don't tell me this is true. No!" His eyes watered. "Julia, something is terribly wrong. She would never marry him without–"

"I know, Ed. Yeah, I know. Sorry, but now don't you dare go near her. Stay away, Ed. It would be dangerous for both of you. Carlo is watching and listening twenty-four seven. She can't wiggle without him knowing. So, no calls, no snooping, no nothing. You stay away from her or you might get both of you killed. Promise?"

"How long have you known?"

"A while. Don't ask. Promise to stay away!"

"I promise, and I will. Is she okay?"

"Again, don't ask, Ed. You just stay away from her. Right now you need to get out of this town and keep your phone charged. I'll be in touch. I may need you for something. We are on the way, big guy. The plan is working. The mob big guys are going nuts as we speak."

"What makes you think that?"

"You, Ed. It is all about you and those two recorded conversations of yours. They are holding their breath waiting for that information to come out at the trial." She clapped and smiled gleefully. "I'm telling you, Ed, this is going down and there is nothing they can do about it."

"How about you, Julia? Do you need protection?"

"No. I'm good. They don't know I'm behind all of what has and is about to happen to them. Their world is crumbling as we speak and they can hear it. And guess what, Ed? We are now listening in on some of their big guys. The Fed FBI team is pretty good at intercepts. I sold it to the local bureau office and they are also on board now. I am keeping my office and the state attorney general guys completely out until I have this deal locked up. Ta DA!"

Chapter Sixteen

JULIA & ED

Alberto and Carlo Romano met with three of their trusted lieutenants to discuss Conklin's visits to the Harpoon's general manager and with Benny Oldham.

"This thing with Conklin is getting out of hand," Alberto announced.

"I got a handle on it," Carlo said.

"What handle? What makes you so damned smart all of a sudden? Don't you see what's going down? They are getting inside, Carlo. They are inside! I don't see where you got a handle on anything. Not just the locals, Nephew. The feds are inside now. The damned feds! And you got a handle on it?"

Carlo's usual arrogance faded in the wake of Alberto's glowering moodiness. He tapped a cigarette on the table thoughtfully, taking time to answer. Too often he had seen the older man's temperament provoked by weak answers. "Conklin is bluffing. I'm bettin' that recording he threatened Houk with don't even exist. Conklin is bluffing."

"Is that all you got? You are betting that he is bluffing? A bet? A bet is nothing but a guess. Am I supposed to feel relieved?"

"We don't have a problem, Uncle. That meathead from KC didn't tell him anything, either. I'd bet Conklin bluffed about recording him, too. Hell, there is no recording. We would already feel the heat if they had us talking like that."

The old man shook his head sadly. "You don't feel the heat, Carlo? I feel it. You're going to end up behind bars again if you can't feel this heat. Okay, let me ask this: Why would Conklin bluff even if he doesn't have recordings? Something deeper is going on, that's why. You don't really think that football player is smart enough to do these things on his own, do you? Someone is steering. That's heat, Carlo! Now, do you know who the heat is?" His eyes narrowed and he stared Carlo down. "I didn't think so."

"I know he ain't all that dumb, and I been paying attention, Uncle. I keep a tail on him. We would know if he was hooked up with the law." Carlo's gut began to churn. He had seen his uncle lead men to destruction by asking questions he already knew the answers to.

"You're a fool, Carlo! He's working with someone, I tell you! Any halfwit can see that! Dino!" He turned to face Dino (The Hachet) Donelli. "Tell him, Dino."

"Conklin's working with the feds, Carlo. That's for sure. I got a guy inside. Donelli made the announcement softly. He couldn't afford to offend Carlo. "The feds are building something, but we ain't sure what yet. May not be anything, but maybe something about that ballplayer's tax thing."

"You're guessing, Dino! You don't know shit!" Carlo was still smarting from his uncle's outburst.

"No guess, Carlo. Like I said, I got a mole at the Fed prosecutor's office. He never made no mistake before, so I gotta take it serious."

"What do you know, for Christ's sake?" Carlo's fury mounted. He realized that Donelli had spoken to Alberto without warning him first. Donelli made him lose face.

Donelli knew it, too. He also knew Carlo wouldn't forget

and gestured, palms up, shrugging submissively. "I just do my job, Carlo. I gotta do what I gotta do." He nodded toward Alberto.

"What do you know?" Carlo yelled irritably.

"You know...things. The guy knows that this prosecutor has handed out some body bugs. He knows names and phone numbers they use. He knows times some vehicles were checked out and where they went. He knows what files they are looking at down at the court house, things like that."

"So?"

Donelli's confidence began to return. "This young girl prosecutor is a Skelton, Carlo. She's Judge Skelton's kid and she's a damned Fed prosecutor now. That's who and what she is. I think maybe she's doing this on her own, though. She ain't on no official investigation, at least not yet. But I think she's piling up evidence. You know, files, organizational charts and diagrams. She's building something. Probably gonna ask for some heavy help if she gets evidence."

The anger suddenly drained from Carlo's face and his expression sobered. "Files? What files exactly?"

"You know. The cops and feds got files on us. On you, Carlo. Probably all of us. I got word from the mole that she's looking at the suspended case her father was working on when you took him out."

Alberto slammed his fist on the table. "A mistake, Carlo! I told you that judge would come back to haunt us. That was a mistake! Don't screw with the Feds! There are other ways." He motioned for Donelli to continue.

"I know she's been talkin' to that football guy, Conklin, Carlo. She's askin' around about some of our business. She been to the courthouse diggin' through corporation records. You know, stuff like that. She's messing in our business."

Carlo glanced around the table at the other men. One by one they averted their eyes rather than meet his penetrating scowl.

They all know Alberto cut me out! Donelli wouldn't do this on his own.

Carlo bore the look of a man betrayed, frantically searching for support.

Alberto saved him from further embarrassment. "Enough of this. All right, now we got to do something about her, Carlo, and that dumb little fat shit she's working with. I know he's been okay, but he could be a problem. Anyway, I don't trust him. He looked to Donelli for assistance.

"Hagerty, boss? You sure? He's been pretty reliable."

"Yeah, that's the one. I don't think she has the big guns in on it yet. She's way out alone on whatever she's working on, but we can't just wait to see if she brings the heat."

Carlo saw the opening. "You want I should take that Hag guy out?"

Alberto held up a hand for silence. "Yes, and that dumb player from Kansas City, too. Too bad. He did the right thing reporting Conklin's visit, but we don't know what they got on him. We can't take a chance if we don't know. We got some holes with this betting thing of yours, Carlo. So, it's your baby. Take care of it."

"Okay. What about Conklin? What about the girl Fed?"

"Not yet. Too much publicity. I'll let you know. You need some muscle?"

"I could use Dino."

Alberto turned to his trusted lieutenant and said, "Work with him on this, Dino. This needs to be taken care of before we lose control. Make them think twice about pressing me."

*****

Two days later, Ed read about Benny Oldham in the sports page–shot three times at a stop light in a drive-by shooting. The killers got away. The next day Julia called and tearfully told him about Hagerty.

"They got him, Ed. The bastards killed him in his sleep. They smothered him and the neighbors didn't hear anything."

"Damn! I'm really sorry, Julia. That's too bad. Now what?"

"My apartment was broken into while I was in Washington. I don't think they are out to get rid of me; probably just putting a scare in to let me know they are tracking. Things are getting spooky. I knew that would happen, though. Part of doing business."

"I think you should get some help, Julia."

"You are spot-on, Ed, but I am a step ahead. Help is on the way. I have been using the local Bureau some of late, but now the big guys from DC are in. That's what I was doing in DC, Ed. The big heat is on the way! Now, are you still in the game?"

"Damned right. What do you want me to do?"

"Nothing right now. Just stay out of sight and safe. They must have someone on the inside, Ed. Hagerty and Oldham can't be a coincidence. I hate to even think like this, but Hags might have been the possible leaker. I know he had some gambling problems. Hope I'm wrong. I am pretty sure they know we are onto something, Ed. Too many things are bubbling up. I'll be in touch. Watch out for yourself. They damned sure are either watching or looking for you."

Julia's cavalier attitude surprised Ed. She seemed indifferent to the danger. He wondered if she had resigned herself to the inevitability of dying. He also wondered about her trip to DC and felt relieved to know she went for help. They met again in the middle of the night a couple of days later and she mapped out a new strategy that left nothing to chance. Ed had always been uncomfortable with her decision to accomplish the investigation alone, outside of the prosecutor's office, until she had the information needed to turn it over to the her superiors. Her recent decision to bring the FBI in made him feel much better.

"Now, I want you to tell me about Amy again, Ed. From square one."

"What? I thought we covered this before."

"We did, but I need to be sure. Start from the beginning. I'll just close my eyes and listen this time. Forget you ever told me about her before." She reclined and closed her eyes. "Every single minute, Ed. Everything. I need to know her like a sister."

Ed repeated the entire story. Julia occasionally asked questions. She seemed more interested in little things: Amy's family history, her attitude about Alberto and Carlo, everything she ever revealed to Ed about Carlo and mob activities. She seemed most particularly interested in Olde Conceptions. They parted before daybreak with Ed more than somewhat worried by Julia's concentrated interest in Amy.

Chapter Seventeen

JULIA

A my's life had settled into the monotonous routine of going to and from work, crying herself to sleep each night, and worrying about the next time Carlo appeared and chose to vent his wrath on her, and Ed–always Ed. She refused to be angered by the constant company and presence of Carlo's accomplices, always watching, parked across the street from the gallery, in the shadows down the street from Carlo's home, and in her rear view mirror–always there. She no longer hated them for being there. Two of them had saved her life by taking her to the hospital after Carlo's last assault.

She never complained to Carlo about the men, preferring that he believed she didn't know. She never called Celia, but best of all, Carlo seldom came to the house. The last time he visited, nearly two weeks before, he demanded sex. Amy submissively took her clothes off and lay spread-eagled on the bed, face turned toward the wall, waiting for the unavoidable, resigned, miserable and detached. Carlo was insulted. He poured a drink over her naked body and stomped out. Amy took some pleasure realizing that she had found yet another defense other than how awful she looked, now adding lifeless, bored submission to her defenses.

Almost two months after Amy saw Ed for the last time, Leitha left her with one other clerk to watch the gallery during the noon hour. A frumpy woman with a shawl over her hair entered and wandered aimlessly through the pottery section. She approached Amy the moment the tinkling warning bell rang to signify departure of the gallery's only other customer.

"Can you help me, Miss?"

"Certainly. What can I show you?"

The woman seemed nervous, first glancing around the showroom before asking, "Are you two alone here?" She nodded toward the young salesman staring out the front window, and then held the vase up to the light, pretending to study the colors.

The back of Amy's neck tingled. *Is this a robbery?*

Her associate whistled to get her attention and said, "Hey, Anna! I'm going across the street for a sandwich. Be right back. Okay?" She waved him on and turned her attention to the customer. "Just you and me now, but the others will be back any time."

The woman shifted position until Amy was facing the rear of the store, then said, "Try to act natural, Amy."

Amy?

"I'm not here to harm you. Try to act natural." She handed the vase to Amy and smiled. "How much is this one? I have always admired Chinese glassware."

Amy's heart was racing. "What do you want? Who are you?"

"My name is not important. Are there listening devices in the gallery, Amy?"

"I really don't know."

She whispered, "All right then. Now I want you to listen carefully because this is important. I am Ed Conklin's friend.

No!" She whispered. "Don't act surprised. Try to act natural." Then, in her normal voice, "Is this a real Chinese vase?" She handed the vase to Amy and picked up another.

The mention of his name chilled Amy. Her heartbeat skyrocketed. She wanted to grab the woman and ask about him. *No, don't bite. This is just Carlo playing game. He is testing me. This is a trap.*

Amy collected her thoughts, replaced the vase and took another from the shelf. "No, that one is from Mexico. This is Chinese." She whispered, "Did Carlo send you?" Amy tried to act natural, but her hands were trembling. "If Carlo sent you, you can tell him that I didn't fall for it. Who are you?"

"Are we alone? Can I talk?"

Amy's suspicion continued to mount. "Say anything you want."

"Listen to me, Amy. I have to know for sure that we are alone. Are we?" She demanded Amy's concentration by smiling while returning the vase to the shelf.

Amy didn't know what to do. She wanted to ask about Ed but needed some assurance that she wasn't being set up. "I am the only person here at the moment."

"Can anyone see us through the office windows?"

"Yes, but no one is up there right now."

"Is that a one-way window behind you, up there on the upper level?"

"Yes."

"Does it have a camera? Anything? Are there other cameras?"

"Yes and yes, in every corner on the ceiling. Who are you? What do you want?"

"We don't have much time, Amy, so listen carefully. First, Ed is fine. I must talk to you in person. Alone. Not here." She smiled and kept the pretense of being a customer.

Amy's breathing held while she thought. She wanted so much to believe. "I don't know you and I think you should leave. Tell Carlo I didn't fall for it."

"Okay, I'm going to leave, Amy. I slipped a note with my number into this vase." She replaced the vase on the shelf. "I want you to call me. Now listen so you will know that I am telling the truth: They killed Harpy on your front porch. You spent a two weekends with Ed at the Elk Head Lodge in New Hampshire. You were planning to be secretly married this April in Vegas. Ed has a birthmark above his right hip. You exchanged suggestive greeting cards." She looked up to observe the expression on Amy's face. "No! Don't act surprised. Stay cool."

Amy stared at the woman for a moment, too stunned to speak, then swallowed and nodded.

"Call me when you can. I will try to find a safe place talk, Amy. I cannot tell you how important it is that you talk to me. Now, just so you know, Ed is also working with me." She held the vase up to the light and spoke loud enough that a microphone, if any, could pick up her voice. "I would dearly love to have this piece, but it is really too expensive for me. I just can't afford it." She returned the vase to Amy. "Thank you, Mrs. Romano."

Amy controlled the urge to shout, "Wait!" as she watched the woman leave. When the tinkling bell stopped ringing, she rushed to the sales office to make sure no one had returned, and then wiped the two vases off while collecting the crumpled note. The paper had a seven digit number–nothing else other than "Commit to memory and destroy ASAP. Do not fail us."

She floated on air. No one but Ed could have known Harpy's name, or about the lodge, or Las Vegas, or the unusual greeting cards. Only Ed knew those things. Her excitement overflowed. *Ed is okay. He sent that woman. Am I going to see him?*

She grew solemn. *What am I thinking? I can't see him. Carlo would know.* Her excitement began to wane. The afternoon crept by while she stealthily studied the phone number until she was absolutely certain there was no way to forget. She would remember that number the rest of her life. She flushed the paper and breathed a deep sigh. *Now what? Is this a trap? It could be. No. How could anyone else know those things? Who was she? Oh, God. What is going to happen?*

The usual car followed her home and remained, as always, parked in the shadows down the street that night. She saw it right after turning out the bedroom lights and watched for three more hours from behind the curtain, occasionally witnessing the flare of a cigarette lighter. They were still parked in the same place when she stepped from the alley just after midnight, entering the street two blocks west of the house and beyond Carlo's men. She hurried to a home that had a sign for school kids. A safe place in time of trouble. A portly young woman finally came to the door, rubbing sleep from her eyes. "What is it? Are you in trouble?"

"Yes. I need to make a call and I don't have a phone. Can you please help me? I am desperate. Please help me."

After a moment's indecision, the woman asked her in and stood between Amy and the door before producing the phone. "No longer than a minute. Then you need to go. If you are in danger, I will call the police."

Amy dialed the number. "I'm glad you called, Amy. This is a recording. Sorry, but I can't take chances, either. I am trying to help Ed and desperately need your assistance. If you decide to help, you will soon learn that I am your perfect contact. I will take your silence as a positive signal and arrange to contact you soon. Please be careful. This number will be disconnected after your call. You have thirty seconds after the beep to if you decide to leave a message."

Amy didn't reply after the beep. She ran back through the ally, slipped through the backyard window, checked the car across the street, and then cried herself to sleep. Tears of relief.

*****

A much younger woman with long dark hair came to the gallery the following morning and asked a clerk for 'The kind young woman who helped my mother with a vase yesterday. I believe her name is Anna. Is she here?"

Amy had nervously observed the door all morning and watched as the woman entered the gallery. She remained in the distance until the other clerk relayed the information that the customer had asked for her by name. This woman seemed much younger and better dressed.

"I assume you are on commission, Anna. That's the reason I asked for you." She smiled and refrained from making eye contact.

"No, I don't work on commission, but thank you for being so considerate."

They talked about the vase until the other clerk wandered out of hearing distance.

"Are you okay, Amy?" She asked, nonchalantly inspecting the vase.

"Yes. I'm fine."

"Good. I know you took a great risk last night. I take it you are interested?"

"I am, but they are watching and listening. I am not free."

"Yes, we know."

We?

The young woman smiled and compared the vase to another, steadily maintaining a detached demeanor. "We have to be careful. When can we meet?"

"That's a huge problem. Who are you?"

"A friend who will never betray you. I am Ed's friend."

"Is he all right?

"Yes, he is. Ed is safe." They played a charade with the vase again, smiling, acting their parts. "We need to meet, Amy. Tell me when and where. This is very important–life and death important."

"Enough to risk my life?"

"I am certain, when this is over you will agree that it was."

"Maybe I can get out to the alley late at night again." She had to think quickly. "Meet me in the alley behind my house after midnight."

"Not tonight. Wait until tomorrow. Tomorrow will be safer, and I need time to survey the area before we meet." She looked up and smiled. "Okay, I'll take it." Then she whispered, "Tomorrow, then?"

"Yes, after midnight," Amy whispered. Then aloud, "Would you like to have this wrapped?"

"No. I will take it unwrapped, thank you. Thank you, Anna." Then quietly, "Two short whistles."

*****

Amy wore a dark jumpsuit and black walking shoes for the meeting. Her nerves had been on the edge of breaking all that day. She was tired and needed to wait for breath after slithering over the wall at midnight. Her heartbeat accelerated as she stepped cautiously into the alley. The whistle came within seconds. She moved toward the sound until a whisper attracted her attention.

"Over here. Behind the fence."

The two women crouched behind a wooden fence and remained silent for a full minute, listening. Amy's breathing returned to near normal. She recognized the woman after her eyes adapted to the dark.

"We have to hurry," Amy whispered. "Who are you? I am trusting you with my life."

"And I am trusting you with mine."

"You can trust me."

"I know. Ed told me I could."

Ed? "Is he here?" Amy looked around hopefully.

"No. This is between you and me. Ed doesn't know."

"I don't understand."

"Ed would never approve of me using you. I know him

well enough to know that he wouldn't want you involved. My name is Julia Skelton and I am an assistant federal prosecutor."

Amy's breath caught. "Oh, My God."

"I know how you must feel. We need your help. Amy."

"We? No! I can't–"

"Shhh. Hear me out, Amy. This is for you and Ed. He needs you and so do I."

"I can't help him! What could I do?"

"I need information that you may have knowledge of. And you may also know how I can get information that I need to help you and Ed."

"I don't know anything."

"You may not think so, but yes you do. First, I want to know what you found when you looked into the conference room at the gallery."

Amy was puzzled and thought for a moment before saying, "Ed told you about that?"

"He did. He didn't know enough to help me, though, but I believe you do and can. I desperately need more information about what goes on in that room, Amy."

They spoke in hushed tones for five minutes before Julia said, "Now ,you better get back before someone misses you."

"But how can I do what you ask? I simply cannot bring that paperwork. There is too much."

"Here, use this camera." Julia presented what looked like a silver compact. "It's very simple. Practice with it when you have the chance, and then keep it in a safe place. You will need some suitable light for decent pictures. At least as much light as you can get. The battery is good for thirty-six exposures. Use one or two for practice. After you get the pictures and I get the camera back, you won't be actively involved with me again. I desperately need to know what kind of information is in those files." She handed Amy another slip of paper. "Commit that number to memory and destroy it. That is the number to my personal phone. Here, take this phone and use it only once, and that will be to contact me. We both have clean phones now. No one can trace us. Call when you are ready, Amy. Throw that phone away after you use it. Don't take it anywhere with you except to make the call. Keep it well hidden until you need it. Someplace no one will ever find it. Destroy it if you can after the call, but make sure no one ever gets that phone. Never use your name while dealing with me. You will be Swan. Remember that. Swan. I might want to ask you to testify, but you don't have to if you don't want to. Would you do that?"

"I don't know. That sounds so dangerous. I just don't know. Let me have time to think about that."

"It would be dangerous. Believe me, I know. They killed my father and my partner. I am certain they are trying to kill me."

"My, God!" Amy covered her mouth. "Who are they?"

"I expect you know. Now, I am not important. *You* are important, though. *Ed* is important. Can I count on you? This may be the most important thing you ever do. Please? I need those pictures"

Amy was well aware of the pressure Julia had introduced by including Ed. "I don't know. Let me think about it. I just don't know if I can. I will call as soon as I do, if…."

"I know you well enough to know that you will try. Time is important, Amy. As quickly as possible. Now you better get back. Be careful."

Julia watched her go with mixed emotions. Amy had not refused. She had taken the camera and phone. If they fell into the wrong hands, Amy would never be able to justify why she had them. Julia would then lose everything she had worked for. Everything depended on Amy. Julia crept from the ally and spent yet another night in yet another hotel room using yet another Uber.

*****

Two days later, Leitha ordered Amy to stay with another clerk to watch the gallery during the noon hour. Amy watched as the car carrying her stepfather and Leitha sped down the street. She turned and told the clerk to go to lunch. "No more than thirty minutes, Aubry. And I could use a chicken salad sandwich. See you." He thanked her for the break and walked out pecking at his phone. She ran to Leitha's office and grabbed the keys to the conference room and file cabinets, and then back to the gallery floor to watch and wait for her heart to slow. After gathering courage, she ran up the stairs as fast as she could. The key worked. She rushed from one file to another, opening and photographing the first folder in each file, and then selecting three more folders at random, then on to the next file. Five minutes later, she returned the keys and waited in the gallery for Leitha's return. Her heartbeat and breathing didn't return to normal for ten minutes.

*****

Amy called Julia that afternoon on the way home in yet another Uber. She had decided after her visit with Julia not to use her own car for fear of possible secret listening and tracking devices and had taken it for an oil change before work. "This is Swan. I did it. When can we meet?

"Oh, thank God. I was so afraid for you. Tonight. Same place, same time. Will that work for you?

"I will try. If something doesn't seem right, I will try every night from now on until we meet.

"Good. Now destroy that phone. I'll see you. No more chances for you, girl. Well done. Don't take chances."

Their meeting that night lasted no more than ten seconds, just enough time to pass the camera.

"Julia said, "Act as normal as you possibly can from here on, Amy. I expect some radical changes are going to take place very soon in your life in the coming days. When it happens, and believe me you are going to know, get out in a hurry. And I mean out of this town. Someplace safe and secret." She turned and departed before Amy could ask why she had to leave town.

*****

It took the FBI two days to study the file photos and secure a judge's authorization to raid the Gallery's conference room. The raid took place in the middle of the night. A team of fifteen FBI agents confiscated every file.

Amy noticed the commotion a block before she arrived at the gallery on the way to work the next morning. Television remote trucks lined the street, now blocked off by police cars with warning lights flashing and cops positioned everywhere. She drove to a nearby park, called for an Uber, placed the keys under the floor mat and locked the door. She ordered the driver to, "Take me to the federal court building, please. At once."

Julia was not there. Her secretary had no idea where she was or when she would be in. Amy didn't wait. She called another Uber, went directly to the bus station and took the next bus to Portsmouth New Hampshire, and from there to the Elkhead Lodge, the emergency meeting place she and Ed had playfully adopted during his summer practice session. The two best weeks of her entire life. She would wait there.

*****

The FBI located and imprisoned a dozen upper echelon mob members, not including Carlo or Alberto. The two Romano men received a tip late in the evening before the raid. Someone told them that the FBI was forming a unit armed and dressed like a swat team. They didn't wait or contact other members of the mob. Alberto went by way of helicopter to Maine that night, and then on by car into Canada. After he learned of the raid on Television the next morning, he flew on to Italy, landing there the day after the raid, to disappear. The

American government asked for his extradition immediately. Carlo was intercepted by the State Patrol in southern Maine for speeds in excess of one-hundred-and ten miles an hour. He died in the ensuing gun battle.

Chapter Eighteen

THE TRIAL

E d's trial has been fast-tracked by the U. S. attorney General, a well-known and enthusiastic professional football fan. He interceded and ordered the trial pushed forward to keep from interrupting the NFL schedule. Neither the defense or prosecution objected. Ed moved in temporarily with Don Gruber while the Gruber brothers planned his defense.

Ed heard the news about the FBI's midnight *OLDE CONCEPTIONS* raid from the federal marshal who picked him up at a Don's home the day his ordeal in court began. He could hardly contain his excitement.

Julia! Julia came through!

His eyes glistened, this time with tears of joy. He desperately wanted to rush to Amy and could hardly keep his thoughts on the business at hand. Maybe his life was taking a turn for the better.

While sitting in place at court waiting for the judge, Kirk Gruber rushed in and reported Carlo's death and Alberto's escape. Before Ed could learn more, the Judge stepped in.

"All rise!"

The trial began. Ed's thoughts seldom drifted from Amy. His attorney noticed and elbowed him to pay attention to business at hand. Ed could not stop wondering how the news about Carlo was affecting Amy's life. He agonized, wishing he could hear something, anything, about her status, wondering if she even knew the news, but most of all, desperately wishing to be anywhere but trapped in court. The trial droned on somewhere in the recesses of his mind while Amy's circumstances remained the center of thoughts, thoughts he could not break away from. The trial droned on somewhere in the monotonous distance.

Amy.

Don elbowed him again and whispered, "What the hell are you thinking about, Ed. You look like a zombie. Come on, man, keep your mind on the trial. This probably isn't going to take long. Stay with me."

The morning session started routinely, like most trials, mostly listening to judge directions and admonitions before taking an early break for lunch. The prosecutor turned out to be, much to Ed's surprise and disgust, the same attorney who led his Grand Jury procedures. During lunch, he mentioned his distress to the Grubers.

Don said, "Well, you have to know it's one of two things, Ed. They are either extremely confident, or they have already thrown in the towel. I will tell you, with great confidence, that I think they are just putting in their time. The prosecution is riding this one out, Ed–just treading water. Old Charlie isn't all that concerned about how this is going to end. So relax. He has already thrown in the towel and that's going to be the extent of what happens here today. He has nothing. So quit worrying."

"Okay. So what is going to happen?"

Don scoffed. "Nothing bad. This is just for show, Ed. A waste of time. Look, we had a pre-trial meeting, as you know, to present our witness lists. I can tell you, for a fact, that old

Charlie is dead in the water and he damned well knows it."

"Are you really that confident?"

"Absolutely. They cannot prove one damned thing, Ed. We have them by the gonies and they have thrown in the towel. Charlie is just going to go through the motions waiting for it to be over. I bet anything we could ask for a mistrial after his opening remarks."

Ed was surprised. "You really aren't thinking of doing that, are you, Don?"

"No, but I bet we could get a mistrial within thirty minutes if you want it. If you like, I'll let you know what I think after we get started and after I have a solid feel for how this is going. Anyway, asking for a mistrial will be your call."

"No, Don! No! I want this trial to go the distance. I want the judge to hear everything and I want his verdict. I want him to tell the whole damned world what happened. I want a trial verdict, Don. No mistrial!"

"Okay, okay. Don't get upset. I'm with you, Ed. Just theorizing here. We are absolutely going to do this your way. Kirk and I agree with you and plan to see it all the way through."

*****

The judged tapped the gavel and the afternoon session began. "Mister Prosecutor. Let us get started. Your opening statement, if you please."

The prosecutor stood behind his desk, where he stood during his segments throughout the remainder of the trial. He never once approached the witness stand or the judge. "Thank you, Your Honor. The prosecution will prove beyond a reasonable doubt that the defendant, Edward Conklin did, with deliberate intent and malice of forethought, defraud local, state and federal governments of taxation he was and is legally compelled to pay." He sat down.

The judge, ambushed by the brevity of the opening

statement, glanced up from his notes, appearing to be more than a little perplexed. He cleared his throat and said, "That's it? That concludes your opening statement?"

The prosecutor almost stood, just not quite, and said, "Yes, Your Honor. I yield the floor." He sat.

The judge stared at him for several seconds before shrugging. "I see. Well, highly irregular and possibly a wee bit casual, if you don't mind me saying so. Highly irregular. "Very well, then." He shrugged, turned to the defendant's table and said, "The Defense has an opening statement, I presume."

Don stood and replied, "Yes, Your Honor. The Defense will prove that the Prosecution cannot prove my client guilty beyond a reasonable doubt, or any other doubt whatsoever. The defense yields the floor." He smiled and took his seat.

The judge, now clearly irritated, shook his head somberly and said, "Gentlemen, that was the most unusual start to any trial I have ever witnessed." He glanced back and forth to the two attorneys, apparently hoping for some clarification. After a deep sigh and another shake of his head, he said, "Well, all right then, gentlemen, let's try it your way. He turned to the prosecutor. "I suppose that you know that it is now your turn to present evidence, Mister Prosecutor. Would you by any chance have questions for the accused? Would you by any chance have physical evidence? Do you by any chance have witnesses? Anything at all? I am almost certain you must be aware that I am required to make a judgement based on evidence, and that includes *your* evidence, Mister Prosecutor. Oh, sure you do. Now, if you please, can we get on with it. You have, as you seem fond of saying, the floor." He sat back, still frowning, glaring at both attorneys.

The prosecutor stood and said, "The Prosecution calls Raymond Davis."

Davis stepped forward, took the oath and sat in the witness stand. He looked to be about seventy-five, bald, in need of a shave and clothes recently pressed to wear.

"If the court please, Mister Davis is a handwriting expert. Mister Davis, please tell the court your qualifications."

"Yes, Sir. I have served as the handwriting expert for the Lexington, Massachusetts police department for twenty-five years."

"Thank you. Now, I want you to tell the court if you believe the signatures on these gambling IOUs belong to the defendant. He shuffled forward and gave two sets of Ed's signatures to the bailiff who in turn handed them to Davis. "I had the defendant sign, in front of his attorneys, the number one item earlier, and the number two item is a copy of a gambling IOU with the defendant's signature on it. Now, Mister Davis, would you please tell the court if you believe the signatures came from the same man. Take your time."

After a few moments of holding the two slips of paper side-by-side, the old man looked up and said, "No doubt in my mind. The same man signed both papers."

"Thank you, Sir. No other questions, Your Honor."

The judge turned to the Defense. "Mister Gruber?"

"Yes, Your Honor. Now, Mister Davis, I would like to know if you have had any formal forensics training for handwriting or forgery analysis. Please answer."

"Well, I think twenty-five years of on the job training qualifies, don't you?"

"No, Sir, I do not, but I am neither the judge nor a handwriting analyst. No further questions, Your honor."

Charlie spent the next ten minutes bombarding the judge with exactly the same accusations the NFL commissioner had employed while interviewing Ed. "There is no proof that Mister Conklin ever gave the General Manager or owner of the Harpoons any notice of being forced to comply with criminal elements to shave points. There is no proof of the defendant's alleged packet containing pictures of gambling slips. There is no evidence that the General Manager or the owner of the Harpoons football team were given pictures of Mister Conklin at a social event shaking hands with known criminal bookmakers. Both men rigorously deny such transactions. There is, by his own word, as attested to in the minutes of the recent NFL investigation, evidence that Mister Conklin deliberately and admittedly attempted to control the points scored by an opposing team. In other words, he has publicly conceded having attempted to throw a game in favor of organized crime. Mister Conklin is an admitted criminal. I yield the floor."

The judge's eyes rolled. "What was that all about? This is a tax evasion trial, Sir. Please stick to the subject at hand from now on. Now, Mister Gruber?"

"Yes, Your Honor. The Defense calls Gerome Skaliky."

After Skalicky was sworn and seated, Don asked what his qualifications were as a forensics handwriting and forgery expert.

"I have a Master's degree from Florida State University in forensics analysis, including handwriting, fingerprint and forgery evaluation. I am a retired FBI agent and have served on many occasions as a forensics expert for prosecution and defense at court."

"Thank you. Now, Sir, would you please give me your analysis about the validity of the defendant's signature on these IOU slips, as opposed to the signature he gave the court earlier today. Please." He retrieved the evidence from the prosecutor's table and carried them to Skalicky.

Skaliky took his time before looking up to say, "The signature on the IOU was not written by the same person who wrote the signature given by the defendant to this court today."

"No doubt in your mind?"

"None whatsoever. Do I need to explain the technicalities?"

"Not at this time. Thank you, Sir" He turned to the judge and said, "No further questions, Your Honor."

"Mister Prosecutor?"

"No questions, Your Honor."

The judge, longsuffering, sighed and said, "The witness is excused. Mister Gruber?"

"Yes, Your Honor. The Defense calls Anton Wyrick."

Anton's answers tracked, almost exactly, the previous witness. He held a Master's Degree from Albany Law, In Albany New York with a Masters in Forensic analysis. He also had served in the FBI as an analyst and functioned as an expert many times in court.

The judge turned to the prosecutor. "You are on, Sir."

"No questions, Your Honor."

The judge excused the witness and said, "Mister Gruber?"

"Your Honor, the Defense calls Jim Williams."

Williams had a Masters in Forensic analysis from Trinity College, Dublin Ireland. He also had retired from the FBI and served in courts as an expert for both defense and prosecutors. He also attested that Ed's signatures were forged.

The prosecutor had no questions.

"Mister Gruber?"

Yes, Your Honor. The defense calls Julia Skelton." After the swearing in, Don asked her title.

"I am an assistant federal prosecuting attorney for the Boston Attorney General's office."

"And your relationship with Mister Conklin?"

"He has functioned with me in an effort to help break the gambling organization linked, unfortunately, to both organized crime and parties associated with professional football."

"How long have you worked with Mister Conklin?"

"Since the fifth game of the past football season. I learned through an office contact that Mister Conklin was being pressured and threatened by members of organized crime in an attempt to shave points by using blackmail to control players and club officials."

"To what purpose was your relationship with Mister Conklin?"

"To obtain proof that the general manager and owner of

the Harpoons are both members of organized crime."

The courtroom audience erupted in a disorderly uproar. Some junior reporters ran from the courtroom to file a scoop. The judge tapped the gavel and ordered silence from the crowd.

Don continued. "Did you acquire the evidence you sought, Miss Skelton."

"We did. I have the evidence with me, both written and phone records, if the court pleases."

Don turned to the judge. "Your honor, if you please, we have recordings of the events Miss Skelton alluded to."

"By all means. Let me hear it. Will I need guidance?"

"Miss Skelton will provide, Your Honor."

After Julia finished presenting the recordings Ed had obtained from his secretly recorded conversations with the Harpoons general manager and from Benny Oldham, the judge turned to the prosecutor. "Questions, Charlie?"

"No questions, Your Honor."

The judge once again shook his head and sighed. "Proceed, Mister Gruber."

"As you now know, Your Honor, the general manager and owner of the Harpoons lied to Mister Conklin and to the National Football League commissioner. This trial should never have been ordered as the prosecution has no demonstrable or verifiable evidence that Mister Conklin ever gambled on any football game or cheated on any tax. Ever! There is no proof because Mister Conklin has *not* gambled on football, or, for that matter, anything else, ever in his life. Mister Conklin has never gambled so there can be no hard evidence in existence to prove that Mister Conklin cheated on non-existent gambling taxes. There is no evidence available that would lead anyone to believe he has ever cheated on any tax. None!

"The Defense has the past two years' phone calls from and to the suspected leader of the local Mafia, Alberto Romano, to and from the assumed owner of the Harpoons, Mister

Frederick C. Jensen. We also have corporate records, legally obtained, to prove that Mister Jensen is not the owner of the Harpoon and that Alberto Romano is the owner. The Defense yields. I place the physical evidence as exhibit A and B."

The crowd again erupted and a few additional reporters ran from the courtroom. The judge waited several moments before demanding order.

"Does the Prosecution need time to review?"

"No questions, Your Honor. The Prosecution rests."

The judge sat back and exhaled. "I see. Well then, I suppose, unless either of you have something else to enter, I suppose it's time for closing arguments."

The prosecutor once again struggled to his feet. "Your Honor, the Prosecution rests."

Judge Harmon spun his chair to face away from the court. He remained motionless for at least a minute before facing the court again. He appeared to be sad and disappointed. "Mister Gruber?"

"The Defense rests, Your Honor."

The judge looked even more perplexed, perhaps confused, but soon forced a disbelieving smile and said, "Unbelievable. The shortest trial I have ever attended. All right then, I am going to take a short break to gather my thoughts. I intend to be back here in thirty minutes. I shall, upon return, and this will be a very brief time out, attempt to keep the pattern of brevity in place."

"All Rise!"

After the judge departed, and over the buzzing hubbub of the amazed audience, Ed turned to the Gruber brothers and said, "Are you guys sure this is the way to go? I thought we had much more to say. Are we going to be okay?"

Don and Kirk both laughed and Don said, "Relax, Ed. Charlie had nothing and he knew it. He just went out with the tide. It's over, man, and we are the hell out of here. Now, all we need to think about next is working on the lawsuits. You are going to be one rich man, Ed."

Kirk added, "And this isn't going all that bad for the Gruber Group's bottom line, either. Take a day or two, Ed. Stay in contact, and then we need to put together claims against the Harpoons and the League. Smile for a change, Ed. It's over!

*****

"All Rise!"

The judge entered and took his chair as the courtroom settled into dead silence. He sat still, taking time to scan every face in the courtroom, procrastinating deliberately until everyone present became restless.

Don stood and said, "You Honor, a word with the bench please."

"Very well, come forward. And you need to come on up here, too, Mister Prosecutor. I expect you should be involved."

"Let me hear it, Mister Gruber."

Don leaned forward and in a low voice said, "Your honor, the Prosecution and Defense met before the trial at the Prosecution's request. We agreed that the Prosecution had no evidence available to convict my client. Charlie informed me at that time that he would not contest a demand for a mistrial. However, my client wanted a full trial so the world would know that he is innocent and has been acquitted of all charges rather than consent to a mistrial. He desires a verdict, Your Honor."

The judge exhaled and said, "Well I'll be damned. This has been nothing but a dog and pony show. You have handled me poorly, gentlemen. Well, okay, it's done. I had already reached a verdict anyway and that will not change. Take your places."

The judge sat quietly waiting for the courtroom noise to settle, and then, after slowly regarding every single person in the audience once again, he sighed and said, "I thank everyone here today for your attendance and patience. I must inform every news reporter present, and the audience you will report to, that this has been the strangest and hastiest trial I know of. I am not satisfied that the principals here today, me included, conducted ourselves in a satisfactory judicial manner. It pains me to know that the Prosecution came so scantily prepared. However, upon review, I recognize that there is also the possibility that the Prosecution should not have been here at all today, any more than I should have been here, or the Defense, or, for that matter, any of you present. But, and most regretfully of all, Mister Conklin certainly had no legitimate reason that I can determine to have his life placed on hold while we ran this circus.

"Now, what I say next is without reservation. Mister Conklin, to my great regret and embarrassment, has been subjected to nothing less than a legal travesty. He has been used dishonestly and ruthlessly by organized crime and by the Harpoons general manager and the purported team owner, and possibly by other team officials. Now, you can add to this to that: Mister Conklin has been exploited by the National Football League as a disposable shield for nothing less than their careless and substandard screening of a team owner. I can also assure you that there will be a Grand Jury appointed to look into the depth of possible Harpoon team criminal activities. Also, Mister Conklin has been used disgracefully by the National Football League leadership. There may also be a Grand Jury arranged for that offense. Now, last but certainly not least, he has been poorly used by this court and the American justice system."

He stepped down from the dais and walked to the Defense table where Ed and the two attorneys stood. "We have all failed you, Mister Conklin. A class of third grade kids could have seen the flaws in the charges against you. If you can find it in the goodness of your character to forgive me for my part, please accept my sincere and heartfelt apology. I am truly sorry, Sir."

The judge then walked back to a position behind his desk, pulled himself straight, a tired, dejected and disappointed old man. "First, you again, Mister Conklin." He directed his attention again to Ed. "You, Sir, stand acquitted of all charges. I find you innocent and apologize for the legal system that failed you so miserably by subjecting you to the charade we have all just witnessed. Once again, I am deeply sorry. You, Sir, are free to go."

He directed his next comments to the Defense team. "I am not certain that I should applaud what you two have achieved here today, but I will say that your technique, while successful, seems somewhat peculiar. Anyway, congratulations. You certainly saved all of us much time."

"Now, Mister Prosecutor–Charlie–I am sorry to see you go as I know this was your last go-around before retirement. You were placed in a dreadful situation here with no possibility of success, to what end I still do not know. However, in retrospect, I now believe the way you handled the situation will possibly be seen as laudable if anyone ever wants to dissect what happened here today. Goodbye, Old Friend.

"Now, I will now see the major newspaper and television reporters in my office. This court is adjourned."

*****

Julia met Ed as he left the courtroom and motioned him away from the Gruber brothers. "I need to say something that I know you will find comforting, Ed. I wanted to tell you sooner but thought it better to keep it secret. Please, don't you ever breathe a word of this to anyone, ever, except Amy."

"Wait. Amy? What about Amy?"

"Amy has been working secretly with me, Ed. She was instrumental in bringing the Boston Mafia to the surface and to justice. Amy got the information about their records from their meeting room at Olde Conceptions. She flipped on her family for you, Ed. She did it all for you. Amy took unbelievable chances to work with me. She did it to help you. If and when you get back with her, and I truly hope it's when, you may feel free to tell her that I told you and broke our agreement. But don't you ever mention it to anyone else. Alberto's bunch has no idea that she was the catalyst of their collapse. I want her involvement to remain a secret forever. Top-secret, Ed. Got it?"

"Thank you, Julia. Thank you so much. Yes, I got it. Thank you."

"One more thing. I tried every way I can think of to contact her after the raid, after Alberto and Carlo beat feet. I couldn't find her, Ed. The cops reported her car deserted near a little park in the western suburbs. They have it impounded. No sign of violence. The keys were under the front mat and the car was locked. I am worried for her, Ed."

*****

What Judge Harmon announced to the reporters appeared in every news outlet across America the next morning. He recommended that the Federal Attorney General appoint a special counsel to look into organized crime connections to the NFL. He recommended that the NFL Commissioner's office open an investigation into the procedures they employ to approve club ownership. He also recommended that the Boston Harpoons' schedule be suspended for a year until new ownership could be approved.

*****

The Grubers called Ed early the next morning to advise him that they wanted to get his lawsuit filed before Harpoons' finances were frozen. "The only question we have, Ed, is how much? We also believe you should sue both the team and the NFL. Don and I have discussed money and believe you should ask for what you would have asked from the team for in the upcoming contract, and what you would undoubtedly have been given. Sixty million dollars for three years, right? Wasn't that the preliminary agreement?"

"Yes. The team had already been notified of that number. I have the paperwork. As for the NFL? What do you think?"

"We believe you should go for one-hundred-million."

"Holy…. Really? They will fight that to the death."

"You bet they will. We also believe that they will settle out of court for somewhat less if you are so inclined. Shall we go ahead? We need to get it on the books."

"Do it, Kirk. I'm going to be around town for a couple of days, then probably to my hometown to take care of business there. Then, after that, I just don't know. Call if you need me. I'm going to sleep twelve hours a day for a week and eat everything I can find."

Chapter Nineteen

THE MIDDLE OF BRIDGE

E d called Celia after spending another sleepless night worrying that she might not want to speak with him, particularly not after the last time he tried. To his relief, she seemed pleased to hear from him. He breathed a sigh of relief and said. "I need to talk to you for a few moments. Face to face, Celia. About Amy. Don't hang up. Please listen to me."

"I have heard nothing from her since you and I spoke last, Ed. Nothing. Carlo took her phone away. When she did call, she called from work, but I have not heard from her in weeks. As I said, nothing."

"May I come over, Celia? I have some ideas worked out and I could use your opinion."

"Yes, and now would be a good time, Ed. The girls are in school."

After Ed stepped into her kitchen, Celia surprised him by hugging. She wanted to talk about his trial first, expressing relief that it was over and that he had been cleared.

"Thank you, Celia. The first thing I want to do is go over

to her place and see Amy. I need to see for myself that she is okay, and I want you to come with me. I know she will see you, Celia, but I'm not so sure about me. Will you come with me? Please?"

"Yes. I do want to go, but I need to be back here by three for the girls."

On the trip across town, she suddenly asked, "Why are you doing this? Are you still serious about her, Ed"

"Possibly more than ever, Celia. I am still desperately in love with her. Loving and being *in* love are different to me. I love playing football and I love my mother. I could probably love you as a friend, but being *in* love is different. I have never really been *in* love with anyone before Amy. I know that now. I have loved Amy from the moment she came to the stadium to thank me. Being in love with Amy hurts, Celia. My heart aches for her. The pain is real, Celia, and I know Amy also hurt. She told me that. I need her. I cry over her all the time. Every night, Celia. When I think about her during the day, I tear up. I have turned into a baby. Every time my thoughts drift to her, unless I find some diversion, I cry over her."

Celia's eyes glistened with tears as Ed spoke. She patted his shoulder and said, "You need to pull over and stop here, Ed. I have something to tell you that cannot be said while you are driving. What I am going to tell you will definitely come as a shock."

After Ed found a place to park, they faced each other nervously and Celia said, "I need to tell you something that I have sworn not to tell, Ed, and this is going to be tough for you." She cleared her throat and her unchecked tears began streaming. "Okay. Amy made me promise never to say anything to you or anyone about this." She looked away, cleared her throat again and turned to face him. "Ed, she married Carlo to keep you alive."

"What are you saying?"

"He threatened to have you killed if she didn't marry him.

That is what I'm saying. She loved you that much, Ed. She loved you enough to give you up and throw her life away to protect you. She detested Carlo."

Ed's jaws locked open. He couldn't close his mouth. And then his tears came. Celia held and rocked him.

*****

Ed left Celia in the car and rang Carlo's doorbell several times. He yelled loud enough to hurt his throat, waited, then rang and knocked again, yelling repeatedly. He walked around the house and rang the back doorbell. Nothing. He tried the door.

Open

Ed ran back to the front yard and signaled for Celia to come. He didn't think the neighbor could see that part of the house, so they crept in and began searching. Thirty minutes later they met to compare notes. They found no notes or phone numbers. Nothing was in disarray to indicate panic. Amy's suitcases and overnight bags were still there. Her clothes were hung and stored neatly. The house seemed to be waiting for her.

"Do you have enough time to run over to the Romano's, Celia?"

"Two more hours. Sure. We need to hurry, Ed."

*****

The maid came to the door and left them standing in the foyer. Mrs. Romano appeared, smiled agreeably and invited them in. They learned nothing.

"I have not heard from Anna for many days. I don't know where she is. Should I call the police?" She broke into tears upon learning that Celia had no recent contact with Amy.

Ed and Celia sat in the truck parked in her driveway while waiting for her girls.

"What are you going to do now, Ed?"

"About my life? For starters, I am never going to play football again. I'm through with that. So, I suppose this is where I start my life over, Celia. As of this moment, the only thing on my mind is Amy. If I have to, I am going to spend my life looking for her. That's the only plan I have or will have until I find her. When I find her, maybe then my life can begin again. Oh! I need a picture of her, Celia. I never did get a picture of her and I may need to show it."

Celia rummaged through her purse, took out a wallet and gave Ed the photo. "Here, I'll let you have this. I want it back, but only when you don't need it."

"I'll have a copy made. If you think of anything…. Well, you know the drill. Let me give you my numbers right now. Oh, and I took my old apartment back. You need to know I live there in case…well, you know."

"I am really worried about her, Ed. She must know about the raid by now, and what happened to Carlo and Alberto. She must also know about your trial."

"Maybe. No way to know. I just have to find her. I will keep you informed. These past weeks have been so…. Oh, dammit! Here I go again. The damned crying. Thank you, Celia. May I feel free to call you now?"

"Any time, Ed. I will always be here for you." She began sobbing and they parted.

*****

In the middle of the night two days later, after hours of pressing Leitha for answers, after hiring a private detective firm, and after driving the police crazy, Ed awakened from yet another nightmare. He suddenly sat bolt upright, eyes wide open, breathing hard. After a moment of confused thought, he threw the covers off and sprang from the bed, dressed without showering, packed a bag and ran to the truck. His excitement mounted on the road north from Boston. He drove too fast and recklessly, arriving at seven in the morning at the Elkhead lodge in Portsmouth, New Hampshire. He made a playful pact with Amy during their stay at Elkhead shortly after they met. Amy started it by saying, "We should always keep this place–this very room–to meet if we ever get lost from each other. Will you remember that?"

"Easy enough, but you are never going to lose me. Room 117."

Ed drove directly to 117 and knocked. No answer. He noticed three daily newspapers in front of the door. *No one is here.* He sprinted to the office and breathlessly asked, "I need to know who is in room 117."

The fiftyish man behind the counter backed away to separate from the tall, emaciated man he had never seen before, a dangerous looking animated man, excited and impatient. "Excuse me sir, but I am not permitted to give names of our residents."

"You don't understand, I...." Ed closed his eyes, took some slow deep breaths, then said, "Sorry. I'm not making a demand, but I need to find out if a woman named Amy Roman has taken that room. Or perhaps she could be here in another room. Maybe she registered under Anna Romano. Please, this is very important. I desperately need your help."

"I can tell you that there is no one presently in that room, Sir. That's about as much as I am allowed to say."

Ed covered his face with both hands, trying to think, trying not to provoke the clerk. He nodded and said, "Right. I know you're right and I'm sorry. I'm looking for my girlfriend. I am not here to harm her. I want to marry her."

The clerk's facial expression became less skeptical. "Is your name Ed?"

Ed stepped closer, sensing a breakthrough. "Yes! Yes! Here, I'll show you my ID." He fumbled until he could show it.

The clerk studied for a moment, handed the evidence back and said, "She said you would be very tall." After studying

Ed for a few moments, he said, "Okay, that is her room, but she isn't there. I called the ambulance for her about noon yesterday. She is at the hospital out on I-95."

"What...? Do you know...? Was she still...?"

"I think she was alive. The cleaning lady found her unconscious. We hadn't seen her in a while and the maid was worried. She kept the do not disturb sign up. Been here, let's see, about four days, I think, maybe five. She took the room for two weeks. That's really about all I know. I'm sorry."

*****

Ed arrived at the hospital in record time and went straight to emergency. While giving information about Amy to the front desk attendant, Ed was begging pitifully when a middle-aged nurse on the way by overheard and stopped.

"Are you Ed Conklin?"

"Yes! Yes. Do you know anything about–"

"Please, just come with me if you will. I am the head nurse in ER today." She reversed course and led the way into her ICU office. After closing the door, she said, "Now, who are you?"

"My name is Ed Conklin, I'm–"

"Who are you looking for, Mister Conklin?"

"Amy Roman. She sometimes goes by Anna Romano."

"What is your relationship with her?"

"We were planning to be married, but something terrible happened. I just need to see–"

"That's all I need. Just slow down, Mister Conklin and let me fill you in. Miss Roman had a note pinned to her gown that said you might come. She is in critical condition, severely dehydrated. That's the biggest problem at the moment. We are doing all we can about that and should know within a short time if she will recover."

"Wait! What? She's not dying, is she?"

"Unfortunately, she is in extremely dangerous condition. We are attempting to contain and reverse her deteriorating condition. We are doing everything possible."

"I want to see her. I need to see her."

"Sorry. We are not permitting visitors. If she shows signs of recovery, maybe sometime later."

"Nurse, I think if she could hear my voice, she might–"

She interrupted. "I am not authorized to change our rules. Wait here please and I'll ask the doctor."

Doctor Buchanan, thirtyish and already bald, stepped in and introduced himself. "I know who you are, Ed. I have followed you all the way from college. Congratulation on your verdict. Now, what can I do for you?"

"I need to see her, Doctor. Please."

"Very well. I am going to allow that for just a moment. If you talk to her, please do so in a soft voice. No theatrics, no touching, no excitement. Just for a minute, and then you will need to wait in the hall waiting room. Will that work for you?"

"Yes. Thank you. Thank you so much."

"Even when she is alert, she is not quite fully conscious. In and out. She mutters some when she is conscious. You might let her know you are here, Ed. Just a shot in the dark. Won't hurt to try. Please do not get carried away or emotional. Easy does it. You with me?"

"Of course. Yes. Let's do it."

She looked terrible. Ed hardly recognized her. *So thin*. Her face was sunken, her eyes recessed in dark sockets. Her hair was disheveled. He couldn't take his eyes from her face. He leaned close and spoke. "Amy. Amy, it's me, Ed. I came to take you home. Wake up, Amy."

She didn't move. Her eyes were open. He turned to the doctor for guidance just in time to see Buchanan's face light up.

"Look!" He directed Ed's eyes back to Amy.

Amy was smiling. She mumbled, "Hi, Ed. I'm so sleepy."

The doctor turned to the nurse. "Get him a chair and a mask. I think we may have our medicine."

She awoke momentarily several times during the morning—each time longer and each time more coherent. Ed held her hand as she slept and felt her squeeze occasionally, stronger as the morning advanced. Exhaustion finally took its toll and he dozed. Her voice, much stronger, woke him.

"I couldn't live without you, Ed. I'm sorry, but it was just too hard. I wanted to die." Her voice faltered and she dozed again.

During her next consciousness, Amy smiled and said, "You remembered. I hoped you would."

"You mean about the Lodge?"

"Yes. You remembered." She smiled and turned toward him for the first time.

"Took a couple of days too long, but I finally remembered the lodge and room one seventeen. "

By evening she could keep her eyes open for minutes, always on Ed. The doctor told him she was out of danger. "Her blood oxygen is near normal. That's a huge relief. You were a welcome sight to us, Ed. Perfect timing."

Amy asked to have her head elevated. Her voice was clear and strong when she said, "Do you know what happened to me, Ed?"

"Yes, I know everything. I know what you did, Amy."

"I never stopped loving you, Ed."

"I know that, and I know you gave your life up for me. I will never forget and I will never stop loving you."

She smiled and said, "You have been talking to Celia, haven't you?"

"Yes. She ratted you out. I know what you did for me, Amy."

"I knew she would. Almost counted on it."

"I will always love you, Amy."

"Oh, Ed. I have so desperately needed to hear that. Will you to promise me a couple of things before I drift off again?"

"I will promise anything."

"First, promise you will never leave me, Ed. I don't want to live without you. I cannot bear to think about living without you."

"I promise, Amy. I am going to be with you forever"

"And I want us to go away, Ed. Away from everything and everyone. Just the two of us. Maybe we could get a boat large enough to live on and just go away. At least a year, Ed. Will you promise that? "

"Yes. That also suits me perfectly. I promise."

"You look terrible, Ed. How did you get to be so thin? Are you sick?"

"No. We can talk about that later. I hate to tell you this, Amy, but you don't look so hot. I think we both need to spend some time eating and sleeping."

"We can talk about that later. Now, I would like one more promise. This is terribly important, Ed."

"Ask away. Anything, Amy."

"A glazed doughnut."

*...The link has always been there,
a cosmic bridge between our souls.
Meet me in the middle.*

...Author

About the Author

Larry Cunningham retired from the Marine Corps, a Lt. Colonel, fighter squadron commander. He wrote the USMC plans for the evacuation of Vietnam, Cambodia and Laos. He flew many combat missions and served as Air Officer during the siege of Khe Sanh. He is an ex-cattle rancher, high school science teacher, college fiction writing instructor and poet. He often speaks at writer's meetings and conferences.

*****

Cunningham has written four novels.

www.ingramcontent.com/pod-product-compliance
Lightning Source LLC
Chambersburg PA
CBHW061554170626
46811CB00001B/202